T0022072

Jonathan Stone has published nii
are currently optioned for film: .
feature at Lionsgate Entertainment, *Days of Night* has been
optioned by New Republic Pictures, and *Parting Shot* has
been optioned by Marc Platt Productions. Until his recent
retirement, Jon was also the creative director at a New York
advertising agency and did most of his fiction writing on
the commuter train between the Connecticut suburbs and
Manhattan. A graduate of Yale, he is married, with a son
and daughter.

Other titles by Jonathan Stone

The Cold Truth
The Heat of Lies
Breakthrough
Parting Shot
Moving Day
The Teller
Two For The Show
Days of Night
Die Next

THE
PRISON
MINYAN

JONATHAN STONE

Lightning
Books

Published in 2021
by Lightning Books
Imprint of Eye Books Ltd
29A Barrow Street
Much Wenlock
Shropshire
TF13 6EN

www.eye-books.com

The opening chapter of *The Prison Minyan*, 'Welcome to Otisville', was first published in JewishFiction.net, in its Spring 2021 issue.
New York Times article used with permission.

British Library Cataloguing in Publication Data
A catalogue record for this book is available from the British Library

ISBN 9781785632754

PART 1

New York Times, January 22, 2019

Michael Cohen's Prison of Choice:
Well-known to Jewish Offenders

by Corey Kilgannon

When Michael Cohen, President Trump's former lawyer, was sentenced last month to three years in federal prison on fraud charges, he had the right to request any number of prison camps favored by white-collar offenders for their relatively resort-like settings. But Mr Cohen chose a shabby, low-slung building 75 miles northwest of New York City, with an antiquated weight room, an uneven tennis court, and no swimming pool.

'For a Jewish person, there is no place like Otisville,' said Earl Seth David, 54, a former inmate who attended kosher meals, religious classes, and weekly Shabbat services...

Otisville's camp has long been the lockup of choice among Jewish white-collar offenders...

...Most inmates are Jewish – many of them orthodox and Hasidic – and many are doctors, lawyers, accountants, and businessmen who committed fraud. A few also have backgrounds as ordained rabbis and, once inside, some assume a spiritual leadership role...

There is never a problem reaching a minyan, or a quorum of at least 10 Jews needed to hold services, at the camp. Messages left for prison officials at Otisville were not returned, and Bureau of Prisons officials would not provide any specific information on Jewish services at the camp.

WELCOME TO
OTISVILLE

Yisgadahl, v'yisgadash, sh'mei raba...

That's his cue.

B'alma di-v'ra chirutei...

The Mourner's Kaddish. His signal to alert the other guards that the morning service is coming to an end. The prisoners will be shifting into the yard. A few hanging back to chat with the rabbi.

Ba'agala uvizman kariv, v'im'ru, amen.

This morning, fifteen of them, chanting it together. (A *minyan* – at least ten males – is required for worship, according to Jewish religious law. But no more than twenty at a time, according to State of New York policy and Federal Bureau of Prisons guidelines.)

Yisbarach v'yishtabach, v'yispa'ar v'yisromam...

At this point he can just about chant their prayer along

with them. He's had the morning shift six years now.

'Big Willie, you're like an honorary Jew!' Simon Nadler calls out to him with a big toothy smile. (Bank fraud, five years. Completely fictitious loan applications, fourteen million in loan approvals. The investigation turned up phoney applications all the way back to his Wharton School admission.) 'Join us anytime. You probably know the service as well as the rabbi at this point, eh Rebbe?!'

The rabbi smiles gently. (Rabbi Morton Meyerson. Five years. Embezzled 3.5 million from his New Jersey congregation. He's the minyan's spiritual leader. Their guide in worship and discussion.)

The fifteen of them are huddled together in their circle of metal chairs. Big Willie stands by the door all alone.

Their wild grey beards. Their round bellies. (Otisville Correctional, Otisville New York, is the only prison in the federal system with a kosher deli, and these guys take full advantage – pastrami, corned beef, tongue, gefilte fish, blintzes, rugelach.) In their loose-fitting light-green prison uniforms, they look more like a meeting of doctors and hospital staff than of inmates. Big Willie would never say it out loud – he knows how it would make him sound, and he knows it probably says more about him than about them, but he can't help thinking it: Prison is making them all look more Jewish. *Sound* more Jewish. More like one another. Their intonations going up at the end of their sentences, everything a mild question, like nothing is definite. Maybe yes, maybe no. Like they still don't believe in the definiteness of their verdicts. Most of them have this constant look of amusement. Or contentment. Cheshire-cat grins like they got away with something. Like they're sharing in some mild, continual little joke. Like they're a bunch of mischievous kids at some fancy Jewish day school or sleepaway camp.

Other prisoners, when they get here, commit themselves to weightlifting, exercise, working out, getting in the best shape of their lives. Not these guys.

V'yisnaseh, v'yis'hadar v'yis'aleh v'yis'halal sh'mei…

Big Willie watches them all praying, muttering, swaying forward and backward and side-to-side in their metal folding chairs. Trying to impress who? The rabbi? Each other? God?

And when they're not praying, they're laughing. Telling dirty jokes. Tilting back in their metal chairs and philosophizing. He has to sit here and listen to it. He tries to tune it out. He tries to be invisible.

He's been a guard here at Otisville twenty years. Married, two kids. Steady paycheck; raises are built in unless you have a violation. Even in a government shutdown, prisons need guards. They get by on his pay – barely. They shuffle their credit cards. The bank called their home loan last year on a couple of late payments, but he worked it out with them. Both his kids are at SUNY. He keeps to himself. And keeps an eye on this morning's minyan, in their circle of folding chairs, going left to right:

Matt Sorcher (Four years. Founded a chain of tax return centers in strip malls on Long Island; discovered a way to funnel a portion of his clients' electronic refunds to his own bank account.)

Abe Rosen (Eighteen months. Art dealer; forgery of old master paintings. Had archival photos of European nobles and Nazi officers holding the art. But the paintings were counterfeit, the photos were staged, the nobles and the Nazis were hired actors.)

Saul Solomon (Eight years. Solomon Automotive Auctions; hired bidders to inflate sale prices on his Ferrari and Lamborghini collection, declared the inflated value and then 'suffered' (staged) a warehouse fire to collect the insurance value. Some of the same Ferraris and Lambos showed up in the auction market years later with new serial numbers.)

Manny Levinson (Bribery, graft. Six years. Congressman from Queens. Jar of candies in his office. Literally a favor bank. When he invited you to take a candy, it signaled he'd do the favor you asked, and when you brought a candy back to his jar, it signaled you were ready to pay him. Someone finally told the authorities that taking candy wasn't just taking candy.)

The *cojones*. The balls.

Twenty-six million. Ten million. Eighty million. Fraud numbers so large Big Willie can't really get his head around them. Standing here watching the minyan one morning, with his cellphone's calculator, he figured that at his salary – $950 a week, $49,400 a year, call it fifty grand – it would take him sixty years to earn even the lowest amount that anyone here was convicted of stealing. And the higher amounts – say ten million – would take him around two hundred working lifetimes.

Oseh shalom bimromav, hu ya' aseh shalom aleinu…

Another time, watching them, he added up the total theft and fraud in the room. Two-hundred-eighty million. Give or take. *Definitely take. All take.*

Rabbi Moshe Samuelson (Tax evasion. Four years. Owned a chain of funeral homes. Had only one in ten bodies buried according to custom. Shipped the rest to a low-cost industrial oven facility for cremation, allowing him to re-use coffins, shuffle burial plots, save on corpse storage, and skim millions. Violated Jewish *and* federal *and* state law all at once. His sixteen children – sixteen! – come to visit him every Wednesday. The younger ones gather around his shoes and knees, as he tells them a Bible story, which they discuss afterward.)

Two rabbis here. Meyerson, who runs the service, is Reform. Has a degree in psychology. Samuelson is ultra-Orthodox. Looks down on Meyerson as not really a Jew at all. Two rabbis. Which originally stunned Big Willie almost as much as the $280-million fraud figure, but now doesn't surprise him at all.

Dr Phil Steinerman (Seven years. Chain of blood testing labs across Miami Dade County that weren't testing much blood. Another doctor eventually noticed how dozens of his patients were receiving precisely the same blood test results.)

Marty Adler (Nine years. President and COO of three successful family businesses. A parking garage empire. A Honda dealership. A Pepsi bottling plant. Marty managed to marry into all three of the families – no law against that, except if you do it at the same time. Three loving spouses, in three different cities. Finally discovered at a bar-mitzvah whose guest list included two of the wives.)

Gregg Lerner (Ten years. Stockbroker to the stars. Took thirty mil all told from his clients. Moved money out of their accounts, without their knowledge, into exotic investments pretty sure to lose money – air rights in western American cities, treasure diving expeditions – then harvested the tax losses and took the write-offs for himself, something Big

Willie doesn't even pretend to understand. Invested several clients in a new Caribbean island resort development that GPS revealed to be nothing but ocean. That part Big Willie can follow.)

V'al kol-yisrael, v'imru, amen.

Mourner's Kaddish. And sure, they're all mourning. But commemorating departed family members like you're supposed to? Come on. They're mourning their sentences. Mourning the one dumb little mistake they made to get caught.

To Big Willie, the dirty little secret is they're pretty happy here. Sure, they're caught, they're broke, their assets are pretty much gone. They're outcasts in their own communities. But here at Otisville, they're comfortable. They're with their peeps. For a lot of them, at this point in their broken lives, there's no place they'd rather be. Only a handful of people in the world really understand what they've been through; only a handful of people have been through it too – and at Otisville, they're literally surrounded by those people. People who get them, who can truly understand – every day, all day.

He's no shrink, but here's how he sees it: Each of them did what they did because in some way they didn't feel good enough. Not rich enough, not successful enough, not secure enough, not in control enough. And when they did what they did, they had to keep it a secret, right? The more people you tell, the more you risk being caught, so generally they were keeping it a secret, and it was lonely, anxious, nerve-racking. But once they're caught, once they're here, the truth is out, and the loneliness is gone; they're with their own, and they no longer feel like outcasts.

By the time their sentences end – five years, eight years, nine years (all Otisville sentences are ten years or less) – the world will have pretty much forgotten, they'll be long out of the news. Maybe even forgotten enough to scam the world again.

Meanwhile, plenty of bagels and brisket, plenty of good company, plenty of storytelling. They look all sorrowful and remorseful when visitors come. But behind closed prison doors, they're having a pretty good time.

The Mourner's Kaddish? Big Willie smirks – some of them are already mourning the day their sentence ends.

The Mourner's Kaddish? They're pretty damn happy as they chant it.

'Come on, have a seat, Big Willie,' says Simon Nadler again. 'Take a load off – you know we're not gonna bolt for the door.' They ask him to join them – and they know he won't. They know he can't. So they get to have it both ways. They get to look good for being friendly, inviting him, trying to include him – but they know he'll never be in the club. Even if he was to go over and sit with them and be part of the service, he's not in the club. They know it, and he knows it. He's kind of a loner anyway, and this guard duty, watching them, just reinforces it. With all their friendliness toward him, they get to look good to themselves, look good to each other.

It's like when they tease him about being a gentile – 'Big Willie, you're a Size XL goy!' – and about his measly pay check, and about his believing in heaven and hell, but they also ask him about his kids, and give him financial advice – so they get to be assholes, but they get to be good guys – they get to have it both ways.

Same thing with his nickname, in a way. You'd think it comes from him being six-foot-five, 260 pounds, so they can't help but imagine his big wiener, right? So maybe his nickname is their way of trying to get comfortable with that. Flattering him, buttering him up, to bring him down to size? But here's the thing. He's five-ten. A hundred and sixty pounds. Smaller and lighter than most of the other guards, but normal-sized. So OK, Big Willie is ironic. Then is the nickname supposed to be *only* about his wiener? Which they've never seen, and which is as normal-sized as he is? This is the kind of shit they've got him thinking about, as he stands there, watching them, listening to that prayer and keeping an eye on their morning service.

Lately, they've been tossing around ideas for a new nickname. Not for him. For a new inmate who's arriving shortly. The minyan is trying out nicknames aloud, to hear how they sound. Trying to one-up each other, to see which nickname will stick.

'The Cashmere Canary.'

'The Songbird Nerd.'

'The Songbird *Turd*.'

'The Mouth from the South.' (Meaning New York City, Big Willie knows, seventy-five miles downstate from here.)

'The Tasselled Tenor.'

'The Rat Man of Seventh Avenue.'

'Mighty Mouth.'

A pretty clear theme to them all. Someone who squealed. Who snitched. In normal prison culture, a snitch is the lowest of the low. A known snitch would be doomed already – about to be kicked, shivved, ready to meet his maker, if he were coming to any other prison. But Otisville isn't normal prison culture, and the guy who's coming is a *celebrity* snitch, and if you're a celebrity, it cancels out everything else. Like in the world beyond prison – if you're a celeb, nothing else much matters.

'The Unruly Stooly.'

'The Fink Who Got Ink.'

'Yellowbelly.'

'The Opera Star.'

'The Pisk.'

'What's a pisk?' he asks Nadler.

'Yiddish for mouth. A loudmouth. A blabbermouth.' Nadler smiles at Big Willie. *Perfect, isn't it?* Yiddish for Mouth. Couldn't be simpler. A nickname understood by only the minyan, a custom nickname that's theirs alone. Big Willie senses already that it's going to be the winner.

The Pisk.

The Pisk, who didn't make a quick perp walk with his face hidden under a raincoat like the rest of the minyan, but instead strutted around on national TV for weeks, climbing into and out of cabs in his loud sports coat, going in and out of that gleaming Fifth Avenue headquarters.

The Pisk, whose confession wasn't in front of an annoyed judge in an empty courtroom like the rest of them, but instead, in front of millions of viewers. To half the country, a devil in a dark suit. To the other half, a possible savior. Hah! How'd that turn out?

The Pisk asked for Otisville, the Jewish prison. Known for its Sabbath services and kosher menu by just a small circle of prosecutors and defense attorneys. But suddenly, Otisville is in the spotlight too.

And will he be beaten? Shivved? Get real. They've

already got a folding chair saved for him at morning prayers.

The Pisk.

Stepping right out of the national news, off the national stage, into a cell at Otisville.

Because he's one of them.

Big Willie had watched the minyan, all listening silently to his testimony.

Heads tilted up, as if to heaven, at the TVs mounted high on the dayroom wall.

Not caring *what* he said so much, it seemed – whatever the mix of truth, lies, shades of gray – as *who* was saying it, and *how* he said it.

Like a guy they knew.

A guy from down the street.

A guy at the next table in some overpriced New York steakhouse.

Squirming, blustering, bragging.

In the context of Otisville, a totally unremarkable guy.

Arriving from a totally remarkable situation.

Welcome to Otisville.

THE SEVEN QUESTIONS

(Rabbi Morton Meyerson: fraud, five years; embezzled $3.5 million from Agudeth Sholom, Parsippany, New Jersey)

'TODAY, I WANT TO DISCUSS the Seven Questions,' says Rabbi Meyerson, once the morning service ends and much of the minyan has wandered into the prison yard to take in the sunny, bright, irresistible June day. A half dozen of them have stayed for further religious discussion.

'The Seven Questions?' asks Simon Nadler (of the fake loan applications).

'I thought it was the Four Questions,' says Abe Rosen (of the forged old masters) 'you know, *Mah nishtana* – why is this night different? – all that *mishugas*…'

'Judaism is like Jeopardy,' observes Marty Adler (the

trigamist). 'Life's answers are always in the form of a question.'

'The Four Questions are from the Passover *haggadah* – the story of the Jews' flight from Egypt,' explains Rabbi Meyerson, in a tone of infinite patience that any first-grade teacher would recognize and admire. 'But the Seven Questions are from the Talmud.' Meyerson strokes his beard pensively. 'These are the Seven Questions you'll be asked at the Heavenly Tribunal, according to the Talmudic scholars.'

'You mean, to get through the heavenly gates?' asks Saul Solomon (warehouse fire insurance fraud).

'Now updated, I'm sure, with razor wire and surveillance cameras,' muses Abe Rosen, earning a couple of passing smiles.

'Well, Jewish tradition isn't explicit on whether there are physical gates,' says the rabbi.

'The Heavenly Tribunal…sort of like the Court of Appeals?' says Matt Sorcher (fraudulent tax return centers).

Laughs all around.

'State of One's Soul, Appellate Division,' Nadler adds on, smiling.

'Oooh, good one Nadler!'

'Yes, sort of. Sure,' allows the rabbi. 'Our tradition tells us that these are the seven questions each of us must answer sufficiently to enter the kingdom of the eternal.' He strokes his beard again, looks around at them. 'I want to ask about the first question first, not because it's first, but because it's pretty surprising that it's first. The first question is: Were you honest in business?'

Disbelief all around the half-circle.

'Come on – that's really first?'

'Ahead of questions about how you treated your wife or your kids?'

'Yes,' Meyerson affirms. 'And why would that be the first question?'

'No idea.' Head shakes. Looks of bafflement. Abstract strokes of beards, and tapping their chins, like rabbinical students from the thirteenth century.

'I'll tell you why,' says Rabbi Meyerson. 'Because the scholars felt that the way you treat those in business, where you are tempted and even expected to put yourself first, would be a good indicator of how you'd treat everyone else in your life.'

'Uh-oh,' says Nadler.

General laughter.

'Meaning a lot of us are in trouble right from the get-go,' says Adler.

Laughter again.

'Solly's not even getting in the door. Not even a foothold on the heavenly cloud,' Adler continues, nodding indicatively at Saul Solomon.

'No room at the In,' adds Sorcher.

Laughter.

'Where's my handbasket?' says Solomon. 'I'm going straight to hell. Hand me my handbasket, somebody.'

'Rabbi, what are the other questions?'

'We might score better on other questions,' Meyerson acknowledges.

'Nadler, doesn't matter what you score, you'll still fake your way into heaven.'

Laughter. 'Nadler, you gonna lie on this application too?'

'I'm gonna have to,' Simon Nadler shrugs.

More laughter.

'Question 2. Did you make time for your spiritual life?'

'Good news there!' exclaims Phil Steinerman (fraudulent blood-testing clinics). 'We're all sitting here with you, Rabbi, so we all qualify on that one!'

'Yeah baby,' says Saul Solomon, exuberantly. 'Check mark on that one. What's next?'

'You really think it means only your new spiritual life in prison?' asks the rabbi.

'Hey, it's a yes-no question, as I see it. Did you make time for your spiritual life? I'm here, so *a priori*, yes,' says Steinerman.

'*A priori*. Listen to Dr Steinerman. If you'd been a little more *a priori*, you wouldn't be here, would you?' says Nadler.

'Question 3. Did you busy yourself with procreation?' says the rabbi.

Uproarious laughter. The rabbi explains. 'Well, it really means did you occupy yourself with parenting. With continuity. With creating the next generation.'

'What you got to say about that, Abe?' Abe Rosen, the old masters forger, is gay. And immediately offended. Or pretends to be offended – he doesn't really give two shits what any of these felons think, and they know it. 'We adopted,' says Rosen. 'Parenting, continuity, next generation, I proudly check the box.'

'But it says *procreation*. Never mind what it means. It *says* procreation,' Nadler needles him. 'I go by the letter of the Talmudic law!' Nadler proclaims with a smile.

'Oy, listen to this,' says Rosen.

'Moving on,' says Rabbi Meyerson, 'Question Four: Were you hopeful?'

Silence, a pause, while they ponder the strangeness, confront the opacity of the question.

'Well yes, I was hopeful,' says Greg Lerner finally (stock brokerage accounting fraud). 'Hopeful about getting away with it.' He shrugs.

Nobody laughs. Nobody argues with his answer.

'It's true,' says Phil Steinerman. 'Our crimes show our optimism about getting away with them.' He tilts his head, squints his eyes. 'But also our pessimism about the nature of the world. That the world is cruel and tough so you have to cheat and steal your way through it.'

'But we were all hopeful that our crimes would work out, and that if our crimes worked out, then our lives would work out,' says Marty Adler. 'Pretty damn hopeful, if you ask me.'

'When it says *were you hopeful?*, I think it means did you live in an upbeat, positive, life-affirming way. Did you affirm life?' says Rabbi Meyerson.

'You mean, like that old song says, accentuate the positive?' says Sorcher.

'Exactly.'

'Well the fact that we're here says pretty strongly that we did not, like the song says next, eliminate the negative,' says Abe Rosen with a wry smile.

'Of course not, but did we try?' says Steinerman. 'That's the question. Not, did we succeed, but did we try? That's what they're judging at the gates of heaven.'

'See I think you're going all technical and lawyerly on us, Steinerman,' says Nadler. 'Trying to work the questions to get in the heavenly door. Falsifying one more blood test.'

The rabbi checks his watch, presses on. 'Question Five. Did you learn to discern what's true and false?'

A moment of quiet. They look at each other. 'Look, if I'm honest…' says Sorcher.

'You're not,' Nadler says. Scattered snickers.

Sorcher ignores the snickers. 'If I'm honest with myself, I always knew what was true and what was false. I could tell right off. I could look at my parents and my sisters and tell right off if they were leveling with me or not.'

'Sorch, that's not what they mean by telling the difference,' says Abe Rosen. 'Not like, as a weapon, or a point of advantage. They mean could you tell the difference *in yourself?* What was true, meaning what was *important* and real, versus what was false and fleeting. Like, did you try to learn, to grow, to understand people?'

'Yeah, yeah, I get it,' says Sorcher. 'I'm just saying, since I could always see the difference between true and false, maybe I didn't think it *was* a big difference. I don't know.'

A short silence again. While they ponder Matt Sorcher's answer: *Maybe I didn't think it WAS a big difference.* Maybe only judging Matt Sorcher by his response, or maybe relating it to themselves. Either way, they don't know exactly where to go from here. What else to say.

'Next question, Rabbi,' says Nadler, spinning one hand in quick tight circles to say, *let's move on, I've got places to be, things to do,* which of course, he doesn't. Nobody does.

'Question Six. Did you seek wisdom?'

'Depends on what you mean by wisdom.' Abe Rosen leans back. 'Did we seek knowledge? All of us, absolutely, each of us studied our business, our industry, studied the best way to pull off what we pulled off. So if knowledge is wisdom, yes, we all sought wisdom. Enough wisdom to do what we needed to do.'

Phil Steinerman smiles. 'But it wasn't all the wisdom we needed, "cause we ended up here, right?'

'Ah, one more bit of *a priori* from Steinerman,' Nadler teases.

Lerner jumps in, eagerly. 'Which means that we now all *do* have wisdom, because we've all learned what we did wrong.'

'Yeah,' smiles Nadler, almost laughing. 'We've all figured out exactly what we did wrong, so by definition, we're all wiser now.'

'But did you *seek* that wisdom you now have?' asks the rabbi. 'Did you look for it?'

'No,' admits Lerner, 'the wisdom I have now, it kind of had to seek *me* out. It had to clobber me over the head. I wasn't looking for it, so it had to look for me.'

Silence again.

'A lesson learned,' says Abe Rosen. 'A lesson learned would qualify as wisdom, right? So if, as they say, you've learned your lesson, then you have acquired wisdom.'

'But you can't be sure any of us has learned our lesson,' says Adler. 'You can't say we have while we're still in here. In here, it's just a lesson *heard*. You only know if you *learned* your lesson once you're out, and you don't do it again.'

'What's the last question, Rabbi? I gotta get outside and do my sit-ups.'

'I can see the difference it's making, Nadler. You're looking buff,' says Abe Rosen. All eyes in the Talmudic discussion turn now to the roll of fat around Simon Nadler's belly – which he grabs in both hands, in case anyone missed it.

'Yeah, what's the final question? Is this like Final Jeopardy, and the right answer could put us over the top, even if we fucked up the previous ones?' asks Adler.

'Enough already with Jeopardy, Adler.'

'Question 7,' the Rabbi reads. 'Were you true to yourself, by doing what you were meant to do, and doing your best with what you were given?'

'Oh, man, they overloaded that one, Rabbi. They shoved three questions into one. The Heavenly Tribunal is pulling a fast one on us!'

'Rabbi, read it again.'

Rabbi Meyerson does read it again, stopping on, accentuating, each of the three clauses: 'Were you: a) *true to yourself, by*, b) *doing what you were meant to do*, and c) *doing your best with what you were given?*'

'Yeah, well, I wasn't given much,' says Nadler, picking up on the last clause. 'So yeah, I did my best with it. Made the most of it. More than the most of it. I recognized who and what I was and went with it. A clever scammer. A hondler. A shyster. A schnorrer. A schlemiel. Does that get me in?'

Rabbi Meyerson smiles. Presumably they all know the answer to that.

'I'm wrestling with b,' says Phil Steinerman, '*doing what you were meant to do*'. I mean, the weird thing is, the feeling I always had growing up, was I think I *was* meant to be a thief. I think I was following my destiny. And destiny has to be something the Heavenly Tribunal understands. Hell, the heavenly tribunal is probably writing our destiny. So they knew what I was going to do before I did it.'

'Phil, I think you've just found an ingenious new way of letting yourself off the hook,' says Sorcher.

'The old written-in-the-stars defense,' says Rosen.

'I'm saying, maybe it was,' says Steinerman. 'And I can't

really know, until I get to the Heavenly Tribunal and ask them, right? We can't presume to judge from down here. From the position of mere mortals.'

'OK,' says Nadler, raising his new post-incarceration mass out of the folding chair. 'That's it for me. It just went too metaphysical for me. See you in the yard, Jewboys.'

'Yeah, OK.'

'Another day.'

A clattering of metal as they each fold their chairs, stack them in the corner.

'The Seven Questions of the Heavenly Tribunal. Interesting, Rabbi. Thanks.'

✡

Rabbi Morton Meyerson heads back to his cell.

He has to admit it. He loves these discussions. *Loves* them.

This is why he joined the Rabbinate in the first place.

This is the kind of discussion, the kind of gratification, he never got from his New Jersey congregation.

All those nice middle-class hardworking Jews had sat there mute, stiff, terrified at his attempts at Talmudic discussion.

But these guys – this is what he always wanted. Animated, hilarious, serious, accusatory, inquisitive, dismissive, raucous, genuinely curious, totally game. To some degree, they're all the same, his *minyanim*. They look alike. Sound alike. Transposable quick wits, interchangeable one-liners, you could easily lose track of who said what. In a medium or maximum security federal prison, they'd be called a wolf pack – and be feared. In here, though, the wolves slouch, joke, take a long nap. And when these wolves howl, it's with laughter.

He wonders, of course: If he he'd had a congregation like this all along – engaged, participatory, *alive* – would he have done what he'd done?

It's the Eighth Question, he muses. His own personal eighth question at the gates of heaven. If this had been the tenor of his congregation, would he have embezzled the money? Or would he have been satisfied enough with his spiritual life, and therefore not distracted by – and sucked into – the material world which so flagrantly consumed his congregation.

All those blank, well-scrubbed, expensively lifted and Botoxed faces staring back vacantly from the pews. Their pasted-on smiles clouding over in anxious discomfort, in censorious scowls, at the least bit of thinking or challenge from his pulpit. Anything that diverged from reassurance was unwelcome, and he would hear about it shortly, and sharply.

Had all the social climbing, the favor-currying, the ceaseless and senseless infighting among the members, finally just gotten to him? Had he wanted to get even financially because it was the only form of currency the congregation would understand? Was it, at some level, simply to wake them up – even if it took the theft of millions to do it? It might have been worth it, he reflects, to see their faces finally registering something authentic – variously shock, rage, disappointment, shame – but at least *something*.

He pulls abstractly but fondly on the beard he has grown at Otisville. He'd always been clean-shaven before, even as a rabbinical student. Clean-cut was what a suburban reform

Jewish congregation wanted, he knew. For their rabbi to look like any other lawyer or broker or financial type getting off the commuter train, to fit in, be a good neighbor, go with the communal flow. In here, he gets to be what he really is. Gets to look the part for the first time in his life.

His sentence will be up next year.

He's already decided. He'll volunteer to come up and continue leading the discussions. He hopes the warden and Federal Board of Corrections are open to that. He doesn't see why not.

He loves these felons. They're family. He'd go to the mat for them.

Otisville can weigh on a man.

But on Tuesday, Thursday and Saturday mornings, Otisville Correctional, for Rabbi Meyerson, is the best place on the planet.

JUJUBEES REDUX

(Matt Sorcher: fraud, four years. Operated a chain of tax return centers that skimmed government refunds)

BOTH PARENTS, PHARMACISTS. Two uncles, chiropractors. Another uncle, an acupuncturist and naturopath. His first cousin has a therapeutic massage practice and online supplements business. Matt Sorcher's whole family is dedicated to healing, but nobody is an actual doctor.

Nobody had the patience or the grades or the tolerance for debt, from what Matt can tell, but a lot of them put Doctor in front of their names anyway, to feel the prestige of the D and R. And they've all got some kind of professional licensing from the state, and some kind of diploma on the wall, and the autonomy of a small business. So everyone's operating within the system, but with their own businesses, they've got some wiggle room to work the system a little. That's the culture Matt Sorcher grew up in.

As pharmacists, his parents never earned a lot, but always earned enough. This is in the days, he remembers, when local pharmacists were mostly Jews or Italians, which was before they were Indians and Pakistanis, which was before they were Chinese, which was before they were Nigerians. His parents defined middle class – in income, values, clothes, haircuts: every way possible. His older and younger sister both turned out to be stars – a corporate lawyer, a private equity investor. He was the presence that everyone kind of…well…tolerated. He started as the golden boy, but quickly became the troublesome middle child.

A middle child in a middle-class household in the middle of Long Island – was there some unconscious yearning in him to escape the middle, no matter what? Yet even in here, he's ended up in the middle. His fraudulent tax centers conviction – compared to the elaborate felonies around him – is totally conventional and unremarkable. A low-end, low-interest, low-achieving crime. Middle of the pack, at best.

His straight-arrow pharmacist parents had locked up all the medications and ingredients every night, double-checked the locks and the security cameras like it was a jewelry business. Made a high art of responsibility. His father served as president of the temple, his mother chaired the Sisterhood. As if with every moment and measure of their lives, they were daring him…*daring him…tempting him*…to screw up. He eventually obliged.

We learn about work from our fathers, Matt thinks. Watching them shower, shave, grab their briefcase.

Internalizing their attitudes. Your whole adult working life is probably determined by whether your Dad smiled with adventure or frowned with grim pain as he headed off to work. Or was it just relief to get out of the house and away from the wife? Of course his own dad never got away from his wife. They worked together.

His parents' first pharmacy was in a strip mall in Syosset. Long Island was ground zero for consumer culture. A land mass developed entirely by the post-World War II economic boom. Cars, shopping, houses thrown up in Levittown to accommodate returning GI's and their young families. Driveways, highways, vistas of shimmering blacktop and neon invitation. His parents would try to escape it every so often in the dark-paneled dim sanctuary of the temple, but if they thought that would hold at bay the bright alluring flashing consumer culture surrounding them, they were sorely mistaken.

Their pharmacy, after all, was all *stuff*. Promises of health, happy photos on products and boxes; this is what he saw growing up, stocking shelves; this is all he knew. And the gleaming cars pulling into and out of the parking spaces in front, the boisterous families hopping in and out, mothers and daughters checking themselves in the car's rear-view mirrors, side mirrors, in the pharmacy's tall mirrors at the ends of the aisles; this is all he saw. From the time he was five years old, helping in the pharmacy.

They opened a second pharmacy when he was nine. He went along when they looked at space, overheard their negotiations for the rent, witnessed their excitement, their anxiety, saw the new store go in, saw them place the signs, arrange the aisles for maximal sales – all of which they explained to him.

His mother continued to manage the first store, his dad took over the second, they worked long hours, and got divorced a few years after that. Each took one of the stores, and then competed with each other. First subtly, then openly. Matt was soon part of that competition, like any other product on the shelves, each of his parents trying to win him over, to make the sale over the other.

There were no family picnics or nature hikes or outings to the beautiful, still bare, undeveloped beaches at the end of Long Island; there was no time. There was only time enough to work, to make money, to save it.

His parents must have felt guilty about that – no time for family, or leisure, or nature – and must have felt guilt about the divorce, because that's when they sent him off to Camp Wikiwandi in the New Hampshire woods.

His cabin was kids from Manhattan, Westchester, but mostly Long Island, including a kid they soon nicknamed Mighty Mouth. Which is why Matt suggested the name last week, but didn't push for it, didn't want to reveal their history together. So here at Otisville their new celebrity is known as the Pisk. But he'll always be Mighty Mouth to Matt.

His bunkmate for one summer, a lifetime ago.

Camp culture Matt remembers as basically, what could you get away with? What contraband could you bring from home and hide? Candy, playing cards, electronic handheld games, porno magazines. Your social stock went up, whatever you had. Matt Sorcher's social stock was consequently pretty low, but Mighty Mouth had lots of stuff. He was pretty slick for an eleven year old.

What animals could you torture without being discovered or disciplined? How many leaves could you set on fire with your magnifying glass? How dangerously could you wield your Swiss Army knife? The idea seemed to be to not respect the woods, but to carve out as much of a loud and bold presence as you could, as if they were Western explorers. Who would take on these New Hampshire woods and tame them?

He'll never know how much his own criminal bent was shaped by the acquisitive culture of Long Island, or by summer camp with Mighty Mouth at eleven. Both were presumably influences. Meeting Mighty Mouth that summer – observing his arrogance, his smarmy cockiness, and the resulting admiration and adulation of a bunch of eleven-year-olds – was it part of the reason Matt ultimately did what he did? Was it part of how he drank in, incorporated, a hardening attitude in himself? An increasingly cynical, furious, fierce view of the world? It's a question he's been brooding on, chewing on, forced to brood and chew on anew, since being informed about a new cellmate.

He was given no choice. No chance or right to say yes or no. Of the two hundred or so inmates in here, two hundred or so possibilities, why him? (Of course Rabbi Akiba's famously taut wisdom came to mind: when the question is *why me?*, the answer is: *why not me?*) It could have been a random assignment, but in such a high-profile situation, he doubted they'd leave that to chance. He was, apparently, the Chosen One.

Maybe they figured he'd leave the guy alone. The way you try to do when you see a celebrity in a restaurant. Some idiot pesters him or her for a picture, may ask politely or may demand and expect it. But generally, people just walk past, or at most, give a little smile and nod of acknowledgement.

Maybe it was their similar Long Island upbringings. A predictor for similar basic values, some prison psychologist might have suggested, and therefore a predictor for reducing stress and friction. And they happen to be the same age, of course.

But something tells him it's Camp Wikiwandi, on Lake Winnipesaukee, in Laconia, New Hampshire. They needed *some* reason to choose Mighty Mouth's cellmate, and this was as good as any. Or arguably better. Because Otisville is similar to summer camp. Hell: 'Camp' is sometimes an official designation for Otisville's minimum-security facility.

If it was entirely up to Warden Edwards and local prison staff, they would probably isolate the guy. Not risk any interaction. But it can't look like they're giving him unusual or preferential treatment. It needs to appear that they are handling him like any other prisoner. No better, no worse. And in Otisville, all prisoners have cellmates, so they had to choose someone. *A prisoner like any other.* That needs to be the mantra, Matt is sure.

But it's equally possible that they don't know anything about Mighty Mouth and Matt Sorcher and Camp Wikiwandi. Your criminal record does not include summer camp attendance. Camp Wikiwandi could easily be something that no one else knows about or realizes – including his new cellmate.

✡

'Hey.'

'Hey.'

From his new cellie, a dutiful head nod of greeting only. And clearly in the guy's nervous, darting eyes looking out from his famous hangdog punim: *Sorry to be bringing all this baggage in here. Sorry I'm bringing America to your quiet little jail cell.*

Matt can't tell if Mighty Mouth even recognizes him. Forty years or so, after all – both of them look pretty different. No flicker of recognition as Mighty Mouth heads for his bunk. But either way, their lives have come full circle. They are eleven-year-olds again, bunking together. They have learned nothing. They've gone nowhere. They're back where they began.

That first day, Matt never sees his new cellmate glance over at him even once. The Pisk is out of the cell most of the time, anyway – in the dayroom, in the yard, being introduced to the routines by Big Willie and the rest of the staff. Otherwise he keeps to himself. Seems to project strongly and bluntly into the space around him, *I'm done with talking.*

But at 10:30pm that night, as soon as the lights go out on the corridor, a voice comes out of the darkness next to Matt:

'Hey, Sorcher, want some Jujubees?'

Matt Sorcher can't help but smile into the dark.

CON, JOB

(Rabbi Moshe Samuelson: tax evasion, four years. Funeral-home director; outsourced illegal cremations and pocketed the unreported profit.)

EVERY WEEK, RABBI SAMUELSON'S family comes to visit him. Weekly family visits are routine at Otisville, but Rabbi Samuelson's family requires special permission from the Bureau of Prisons, because the rabbi has sixteen children. So the Bureau of Prisons insists that a guard be present in the visitors' room. Today, it's Big Willie.

This number of children, Big Willie has learned by now, is not particularly unusual for Lubavitcher rabbis. It's a tradition that, like many Lubavitcher customs – from their clothing to their hats to their dietary restrictions – dates directly and unchanged from the Middle Ages. 'The large family was seen as a natural right of the religious leader,' Nadler once explained to Big Willie. 'Procreation was a way to disseminate the rabbi's godly qualities. Send his wisdom rippling out into the gene pool,' said Nadler, adding, after a long beat, 'What a fucking crock.'

Each week the rabbi, all 260 pounds of him, takes a seat in the same unlucky, continuously moaning plastic chair in the visitors' room, and his sixteen children assemble in a circle around his ankles and prison slippers. A few of the very youngest perch on his lap and reach up to touch his gnarled, unkempt beard, while the older children sit close by, along with their mother, a small, mousy, silent human womb in a headscarf.

Every week, the rabbi tells them a Bible story. A smart option for spending an hour with sixteen kids, thinks Big Willie. And the guy is a rabbi after all. At least in name.

'Today, children,' Rabbi Samuelson intones, 'I shall tell you the story of Job.'

But with it, the story of Moshe. Who hates everyone. Who's always hated everyone. Who noticed it about himself fairly early in childhood, and assumed it was just a condition of humanity. Who thought everyone felt this way about everyone else, and only gradually discovered that it was only him.

'Job was a wealthy man. He had a thousand sheep, a hundred horses, countless children. In fact, he was the richest and most respected man in the kingdom.'

'Like you used to be!' says one of the children, beaming.

'Well…' Samuelson pauses, considering, but quickly beaming with pleasure back at the child. 'Yes…like me.'

'So what happened?' says one of the older kids, 'Did he get entrapped by the Feds too?'

'Entrapment! Entrapment!' two of the younger children start to chant – to a melody. A chant and a melody they've apparently heard before, Big Willie realizes. At some rally for their father? A judicial hearing? On TV? 'Entrapment is illegal, entrapment is illegal.' Clapping hands against one another, patty-cake style.

'Well, maybe something similar to entrapment,' says the rabbi. 'Because, in very much the same way, it was authorities operating behind the scenes. But in this case, the authorities were God and Satan.'

There was never any question in Moshe's mind. Everyone was an asshole – out to get him, so he had to get them first. Early on he saw the worst in people – a good skill to have, because there is a worst in everyone. Basic universal selfishness.

Rabbi Samuelson settles back in the plastic chair, which groans with fresh protest beneath his weight. (Big Willie hopes to be on duty the day it finally collapses.) 'See, Job became the subject of a bet,' says Rabbi Samuelson. 'A high stakes bet between God and Satan.' He holds up his two palms, presses them against one another forcefully. 'A bet between good and evil. What happens when there's a bet, *meine kinder?*'

'Somebody wins, somebody loses,' says one of the older kids.

'But a bet between good and evil, sometimes it's not so clear,' says the rabbi, his palms still pressing hard against one another, as if neither palm is able to move the other. The rabbi's face begins turning red with the effort – the older kids look a little alarmed.

Keeping things to oneself. Harboring secrets. Growing up, that's all young Moshe saw. Oh, a glimmer of joy here and there on a sibling's face, but he could see that glimmer lasted only a few seconds, as if the joy itself knew it would flicker out and die in the next few seconds, as if joy knew its fate. So joy – the joy he observed, anyway – was thus just a temporary delusion, and therefore just a version of stupidity.

Finally the rabbi releases his palms, settles them into his lap, and continues. 'Now even though Job was a wealthy man, he was also very just and worshipped God.'

'Like you!' says the same beaming kid.

What a suck-up, thinks Big Willie.

He remembers the anxious, nervous look that nursery school and kindergarten teachers gave him. They knew they were dealing with a criminal. It made them think about DNA, he's sure; nature versus nurture; predisposition. A kindergarten teacher can see, the way he himself can see, who's already irredeemable.

'God did not think that anything could shake Job's faith in Him. But Satan thought that if Job lost everything, Job would curse God and abandon him. God was so sure of Job's faith in Him, he allowed Satan to test him. So with God's assent, Satan killed all Job's livestock, his servants, his crops and even…' Samuelson leans forward, 'ten of his children.'

At this Samuelson points to the children nearest him, one by one, as if they are slated for death. Each child suddenly goes still, silent. One starts to cry. 'OK, not you,' says Samuelson, to shut him up.

'Poor Job! He's always been so faithful, so good, so upright, why is this *happening* to him?' the rabbi says, with such authentic and primal feeling, with such a sense of personal affront, the kids around him are stirred into response.

'Yeah, why?! It's not fair!'

'No fair! No fair!' – elevating into another faintly melodic chant, Big Willie notices.

'I agree,' says the rabbi. 'Very unfair.'

From deep within the gnarled, unruly beard, a satisfied little smile, Big Willie sees.

The only question was, how stealthy would he be? What kind of criminal? The kind of criminal who is totally transparent? Who transgresses, steals, robs, perverts, punches, accosts, strong-arms, threatens, lies, right in front of everyone? Can't stop, has no control over his impulses? The kind, for instance, who kills someone, inadvertently or purposefully, but either way almost casually, and it makes little difference to him? The kind who is so obvious, and spends his life, long or short, mostly in jail?

Or the kind, higher on the criminal food chain, who can control their impulses. Who can direct their criminality for maximum chaos, maximum damage to civilization. The kind that can be fairly stealthy about it. Hide in plain sight. That's the kind he managed to become.

'So Job gathers his three best friends around to discuss it. Eliphaz, Bildad, and Zophar.

To try to understand. Eliphaz says Job's misfortune must be because of some past sin Job committed, but nobody can come up with one. Bildad and Zophar suggest he pray for forgiveness. Forgiveness for what, Job wants to know. He's always been righteous and upright.'

For Moshe and his mother, it was a dance of rage right from the start. By all accounts, she was a terrible mother—incompetent, unreliable, unpredictable. She solidified all his defiance, she ramped up his fury with her own, with her increasing punishments, with her hateful words, but in fairness, he probably started it. Once started, though, she had no idea what to do except respond in kind. She was young – a kid herself. She did just fine with easier kids, his sisters and brothers. But she was ill-equipped for the slightest troublesomeness, so with a lot of trouble, she was completely out of her depth. His father had no better idea how to handle such trouble, but he at least had a solution. Head to the office. Avoid it. Hope it'll go away (knowing it won't) and if it won't go away, then he will.

'Indeed,' says Rabbi Samuelson, 'Job gets so impatient with the discussion and confused by his mistreatment, he wants to confront God directly about it, but God can't be physically found. It's as if he's hiding from Job. Playing hide-and-seek, just to get Job angrier and angrier.'

'Not fair, not fair.' The chant goes up again.

'That's how it can be with unseen forces,' says Samuelson. 'Like federal laws, and complex and nonsensical criminal codes. They're like an unseen god.'

Samuelson glances over at Big Willie, who won't give Samuelson the satisfaction of a reaction.

His mother mentioned something to him on her deathbed that she never had earlier. 'As a child, you never smiled,' she said. 'Not once.' A detail she found so disturbing that she chose to withhold it until then, until the last moment. 'Not even a smile of spite, of revenge, of satisfaction, when you did something mean to one of your sisters, twisted their arms, or burned a frog or quashed a bug,' she said. 'Not even then.' She was ready, apparently, to take a smile from anywhere.

If you grow up slowly realizing how hateful you are, and you are smart and aware enough to know you're going to have to hide that hate as shrewdly as you can in order to survive with it, then it's understandable, and arguably ingenious, to gravitate to the Rabbinate, where all the talk was of doing good.

'All their talk is inconclusive, because they can't know the mind of God,' says Rabbi Samuelson. 'Job is annoyed with God. He's frustrated. But eventually, he teaches the others that there is no understanding of God. That mere humans can't understand His ways. That sometimes the forces which are greater than you, more powerful than you, are simply incomprehensible, and you have to accept that.'

'So what happened, Poppa?'

His universal hatred conferred on him a competitive advantage over the other Lubavitchers of his community – confused, questioning themselves – but he was so clearly who he was, he had so little question, that his lack of confusion came across as moral authority, as certainty, as a direct line from God, so it was understandable how he rose in the Lubavitcher community, rose to the position of rabbi.

As it was also understandable how he gravitated to the business of death. It is, as they always say, recession-proof, and people are naturally vulnerable in their time of grief, so the funeral and crematorium business was just sitting there, practically asking to be skimmed, revamped, to be hustled in as big a way as he saw fit. And he was obviously in the perfect position to do so.

'Well, eventually, after a few years, no one knows how many exactly, but I bet it was three to five or so, a sixty-month maximum with good behavior,' looking again over at Big Willie, a thin little smile beneath the wild beard, 'Job's wealth and respect were restored, because his faith had remained true, and he was never tested like that again.'

'So maybe you'll get it all back too? If we believe in God?'

'Why not?' says the rabbi.

'But he didn't get those children back.'

'Nah, they were gone,' shrugs the rabbi. 'But he had

others. That's one advantage of a big family like ours, right?'

They all nod unsurely. 'Right.'

To be a Lubavitcher rabbi keeps him separate from people. It keeps him elevated, insulated. Which is perfect for him. And once he's done at Otisville, it'll be perfect for him again.

Is he an imposter as their spiritual leader? Not at all. He is steeped in the necessary Biblical knowledge. He is well versed in the faith. He is only a moral imposter. And is that really an imposter at all? Who are any of us to say anything about morality? There's only one authority on morality, and he keeps his opinions to Himself. Like he tells his kids, we can't know the mind of God. As they grow older, they'll discover what a huge convenience that is. What a gift from the Eternal, blessed be He.

'So what's the moral of the story, Poppa?'

The rabbi gestures to the older kids: What's the moral?

The older kids start taking stabs at it:

'All that matters is a faith in God?'

'The richest and most respected will end up that way, even if something bad happens in the middle?'

'You should have lots of children?'

Rabbi Moshe Samuelson rises slowly. 'What good listeners. But we can't really know the moral, because as the story tells us, we can't know the mind of God. So all your morals are right. And none of them are right. Right?'

Rabbi Moshe Samuelson stretches his arms wide as if awakening from a satisfying nap.

Pats a few heads.

Not even a glance to his headscarved wife. Not another glance to Big Willie.

Turns, and shuffles back toward the cells.

THE RULE
OF THREE

(Marty Adler: matrimonial fraud, nine years; married to three women simultaneously, CEO of three family businesses concurrently)

Take a close look as he stands naked in the mirror. Not especially hung, as you can see. Not particularly sexy. Kind of, well, bland. Kind of compact and tidy-looking – constructed for no drama, for not even a second glance one way or the other, but outwardly healthy, built for the long run. To a woman, he looks, well, reliable. Manageable. To a woman he looks, above all, safe.

The question he gets most often: Was it tough to pull off? Not particularly. Takes some skilful scheduling, which you need to keep in your head because you can't have a wife leafing through your appointment book. But it's like anything: the more you practice, the better you get, so getting experienced in one marriage only makes you better in the other two. These are lessons many men take into second or third marriages, but of course, he deployed the lessons simultaneously, which was not that different. It's like learning a language – the language of marriage. As you get 'fluent', learn to speak in one, it makes learning other languages – getting fluent in even a handful of them – that much easier.

Just for example, the Sunday-morning-waffles-for-the-family thing. You learn it, fumble around with it, your timing the batter and the eggs and your kitchen moves are way off at first, but you get much better at it in marriage number one; you're really good with it, impressive, *wow, honey, thanks*, in marriage number two; you're a wizard in marriage number three, like a TV chef, totally intuitive, and yet you're making use of the same Sunday-morning-waffle skill in all three, not having to learn something new.

Same with sex. The constant rotation, the constant extra interest and conscious attention and involvement required – you just get good. On the one hand you're a gigolo, but on the other, your wives have the security and relaxation and comfort of being *in* a marriage, with their trusted partner. What can he tell you? It just works really well for marriage-bed satisfaction.

Did he love them? Did he love them all equally? Did he actually love them at all? He gets asked these questions here in Otisville, and the answer is yes, yes, and yes. The answer for him may lie in the fact that he loved *being* married. Loved everything about it – the routines, the sound of children's voices, the rambunctious activity underfoot, the laundry and shopping routines, the responsibilities of house care and repair and upkeep, the plumbing and electrical and HVAC problems and solutions, the lawn care, the obligatory social occasions with neighbors and with families; for whatever reason, he liked all that. Enjoyed it so much, he was even happier reproducing it. Compounding his happiness by repeating it. Happiness squared, then cubed. And fortunately, his jobs were viewed as demanding by his spouses, and they had each grown up with absent, ambitious, workaholic fathers, so his absences explained themselves. When people ask, did he ever have a free minute, a minute to himself, the answer is obviously no – and yet, because he had to keep the truth of his life such a secret, he always had *every* minute to himself, in a way. He was always alone, at peace, in his head.

Fortunately, there were enough out of town Pepsi bottlers' conventions, regional Honda dealer meetings and such that it gave him a good way to explain his absences.

And three weddings? In one year? He gets asked about that a lot. Not as tricky as you'd think. The marriages were simultaneous, but obviously the weddings were sequential. May 30, August 14, October 16. A spring wedding, a summer wedding, a fall wedding. Each with its own seasonal charms. The dates ingrained in him so he never missed an anniversary. He just invited different friends to each – he had enough friends and acquaintances to cover it. As for his own family – he actually had them to wedding number one *and* wedding number three. He told them that marriage one hadn't worked out and he'd had it annulled – and they certainly weren't crass enough to mention his failed, mercifully short first marriage at wedding three's celebration.

For wedding number two, he simply planted and cultivated the idea that he wasn't on speaking terms with his own family – to the point where wife number two and her family never even brought it up for fear of upsetting him.

He was the right guy, with the right personality, for this. He thrived on the routines. The odd thing is, the marriages were good – all three. He was happy, his families were happy.

Really, the only problem with it was the lies. Mountains of lies. Compounding piles of lies, like a hill of trash in the backyard, at some point visible to the neighbors. The sins of omission. And, of course, the fact that it was illegal.

These were family businesses, small, lean operational staffs, so it's not such a surprise that he eventually become CEO or COO at all three. And again, the same dynamic applied in the C-suite as applied in his marriages. You get good at one business, and you can immediately apply those same skills to the next one. There's no learning curve. Which partly explains his meteoric rise as well. (Plus, of course, being married to the boss's daughter.)

As CEO, eventually running each of these businesses, it was his responsibility to make certain ethical decisions along the way. There were unethical temptations all along. Stuff they could probably get away with in their corporate taxes, in their bookkeeping. But interestingly, considering where he is now, he always made the ethical choice. He always resisted the temptations. He was cautious in business, played it safe, never put the businesses at any legal risk or jeopardy. Everything totally above board. Some of the founding family members teased him a little about that – for being such a straight arrow – but they appreciated it. He supposes – he knows – it made it all the more surprising to all of them when the news of the three marriages came out. His unassailable business ethics were, he supposes, part of his disguise.

Part of what made the marriages work so seamlessly, and helped him succeed in all three family businesses, are two personality traits of his that he's noticed are kind of rare in combination, and, well, contradictory. He's blessed (or cursed?) with an enormous amount of energy (as Rosen and Nadler have said to him, 'Jesus, Adler, who the fuck's got the energy for all that?') combined, though, with a natural passivity – which lets strong, independent women and their strong family-patriarch business-founder fathers all feel that *they* are in charge, that he is cooperative and collaborative, that he recognizes their intelligence and good decisions, and that he therefore must be extremely bright and capable, and a great partner. Enormous inborn energy, masked by outward passivity. No wonder no one ever suspected the three marriages.

The Hebrew Bible, of course, is filled with bigamy. The greater the leader, the more wives, it seems. Some of those old patriarchs in the Old Testament had hundreds. When they discuss these sections of the Bible in the minyan, when these passages come up, a lot of eyes turn to him. Some of the guys seemed to have some pretty decent, loving, conventional marriages and families that they were actually trying to preserve with their financial shenanigans. Some of them had miserable marriages. A number of the guys had mistresses of long standing. That's who they miss the most. They don't understand why he didn't just go that way. *Jesus, Adler, a mistress is so much easier.* But his genuine response is that he actually loved all three. And wanted to commit to and spend his life with each of them.

And when he says that he did love them, loved all three of them, he knows the reaction from many women and plenty of men is: you don't know what love is. You don't begin to understand the meaning, the idea of love. But he asks that you step out of your perspective for a moment, your preconceptions about romance and love and marriage shaped by our culture. He asks you to consider the idea, just for a minute, that spending all your time and effort and energy eagerly and actively immersed in love and marriage, you actually come to *understand* love and marriage a lot better than the next guy. Better than just about any other guy. You bring a level of experience and commitment that no one else does. If a marital problem arises, you work that much harder for a resolution, because the risks of failure – exposure, prosecution, prison – are so much higher. You bring all your energy to solving it, to smoothing things out, to making everyone around you happy. Just think about all that for a moment.

There are a lot of interesting scams in here. Scams Marty Adler would never have been able to dream up in his wildest, darkest four-in-the-morning swirls of imagination. He's a much simpler guy than that, than most of these guys. But one thing he's noticed. Of all the fascinating scams in here, the one that seems to be the most fascinating to the most guys is Marty's.

THE TWO-TV
SOLUTION

OF THE ROUGHLY TWO HUNDRED inmates at Otisville, ten to twenty or so are usually in the dayroom, craning their necks up at the television screens (two screens, on opposite sides of the room), watching the national news – silent, spellbound, mesmerized as always.

Silent, spellbound, mesmerized, because one of their own – a white-collar criminal from New York, whom several of them know personally, whom several of them have had business and social dealings with – is currently President of the United States.

✡

Originally the dayroom (or TV room, or break room, or lounge – Big Willie has heard it referred to in all four ways over the years) was arranged like any other minimum-security prison dayroom: a single TV set up high against one wall, all necks raised like mammals stuck in a hole, to get a daily sense, a taste, a whiff of the outside world.

The problem, of course, was agreeing on the channel. CNN, MSNBC, or FOX (the comedy channel, as some of the inmates called FOX. But others referred to MSNBC as the comedy channel, which made things confusing in the dayroom). The prisoners initially negotiated among themselves to come up with a complex system of rotating hours, but that just meant equal low-grade frustration among them all.

A better solution: two TVs. One set tuned to MSNBC, the other to Fox. (They agreed that if MSNBC and Fox were both available, CNN could be abandoned.) A group of chairs is now permanently clustered around each screen, occupied by each channel's regulars. But a lot more prisoners than one might think go back and forth between the two. Get tired of the news, wander over to hear the comedy station across the room. Laugh out loud. Good for everyone's health to move around. Physical health of course. But mental health too.

They called it the Two-TV Solution. They had pitched it to Warden Edwards that way, without cracking a smile, hoping it would carry for the Warden echoes of the Israeli-Palestinian peace proposal. Big Willie didn't get all their inside jokes. But he got that one.

'You don't think two TVs is just going to divide you all even more into two camps? Two tribes?' Warden Edwards had asked in his typical tone – that of a gently inquisitive therapist rather than a prison warden. The prisoners could never get over this placid, contented man's career choice.

Neither could Big Willie.

'On the contrary…it will bring peace,' said Nadler, grandly. 'All people deserve a degree of autonomy. Of self-determination. To feel a sense of belonging.' Hitting the Israeli-Palestinian angle hard.

Warden Edwards shrugged, relented, and two days later, there was an identical TV mounted on the opposite wall.

The Otisville prisoners find it understandably fascinating to have a white-collar criminal running the country. Some of them are genuinely proud, Big Willie can see. Others are embarrassed. Many seem mystified. To some, it obviously feels unfair that while he's there, they're in here. He should be letting them all out, for doing exactly the kinds of things he did.

They all recognize the tactics – tactics many of them employed in the years preceding their Otisville arrival. Tactics employed to *stave off* their arrival here, justice delayed and hopefully denied. Falsification of loans and other documents. Inflating and deflating asset values. Keeping it in the family, playing it close to the vest. Distraction tactics. Lawsuits and countersuits. Double talk and slippery obfuscation. Elaborate legal maneuvers. And now, one more tactic: getting a lead tactician – a tactician of long tenure and high visibility – to take the fall, and join them here at Otisville.

Was he out there, on Pennsylvania Avenue, while they're in here, because he proved better at it? A cagier criminal? A criminal mastermind? Hardly. And he'd been totally exposed in the press. Long, detailed, carefully researched articles and exposés. The FBI, law enforcement, every prosecutor in the country was onto him. All of which made it even more outrageous and incomprehensible – and therefore, even more fascinating – that he was unbowed. That his criminal enterprise was proceeding intact.

In other prisons across the federal system – medium- and maximum-security facilities – the dayroom TV screens brought NFL and NBA games, which in turn brought cheering, camaraderie and raucous but good-natured rivalry, contests in which the prisoners saw heroic versions of themselves. Here, the field of play was, instead, the national news. They watch the current president with the same arrogant, egoistic, primal private thought that the inmates in the other prisons harbor about a talented halfback or wide receiver: *That could be me.* But this is a contest of constantly moving goalposts, of Democrat and Republican teams doing end runs, executing punts, moving the ball incrementally up and down the field, and sometimes there are shouts of victory, unencumbered glee or pure fury from the dayroom fans, but mostly there is silence, fascination and disbelief at the game they're watching, unable to look away.

The president is on. Another rally in Florida. Big Willie watches some of the inmates gather around the screens more closely. They always watch when he's on. Yet it's always a little surreal for them, Big Willie can tell, to see him, to listen to him, because it could be any of them. They can see how it could happen. Luck, circumstance, a traceable series of events. Each of them got caught, and he hasn't been caught yet. Simple as that.

For some of them, the president's electoral victory was their victory. A vindication, a quiet affirmation of their life choices.

For others, it was an object lesson. The unfortunate end result, the logical conclusion of a path of criminality. A cautionary tale staring them in the face. The best possible rehabilitative tool. *Look what could happen unless you change your ways. You could end up in charge of a country. You could end up personally and irrevocably destroying the greatest nation on earth.* It was a frightening lesson. A clarion call to mend your ways, to make amends, to finally go straight.

Those two camps, those two points of view, had nothing to do with Democrat or Republican, Liberal or conservative. Nothing to do with which screen you were gathered beneath.

That could have been me! A realization bathed in either starry-eyed wonder and awe, or stunned, abject terror, depending on your point of view.

It sometimes led – naturally, unsurprisingly – to a vigorous minyan discussion.

Sitting forward, leaning back, comparatively young Marty Adler even sitting cross-legged, on the metal folding chairs.

Abe Rosen hangs the fact out there like a bar mitzvah piñata, ready to be batted around. 'Rabbi, what are we to make of the fact that our president is a white-collar criminal like us?'

Rabbi Meyerson smiles obliquely. 'What do *you* make of it?'

'I mean, to me it just makes a mockery of all 613 commandments in the Talmud and the countless directives in the Midrash. A mockery of laws in general. I mean, what's the point of obeying them if disobeying them sets you on a path to be the leader of the free world?'

'Well, I think we can agree that whatever our political leanings, it surprised most people when he became president,' says Rabbi Meyerson.

'And he's not Jewish, Abe,' Nadler chimes in. 'So he doesn't have to follow all those laws.'

'Yeah, but a lot of them are laws of basic decency to your fellow man. He *does*, or *should*, have to follow those, right? And he doesn't,' observes Phil Steinerman.

'He's always had a lot of Jews around him, though,' says Saul Solomon. 'Serious ones. His son-in-law, his accountants, his lawyers, his CFO…'

'He said Jews are the only ones he trusts for financial and legal stuff.'

'Then they should be telling him the rules.'

'Hah! They're the ones telling how to get away with stuff!'

'He's a friend of Israel, don't forget. Of Netanyahu and the Likud. For a lot of Jews, that forgives everything,' Abe Rosen points out.

'He's practically Jewish. Honorary Jew. Like Big Willie!' says Nadler, ebulliently.

'I know his treasury secretary's parents. They were members of my third wife's temple,' says Marty Adler.

'So what, Marty? What's your point?' says Rosen.

'Are we supposed to be impressed?' says Nadler.

Marty shrugs. No point, really.

'Let's face it,' says Rabbi Meyerson, 'it's obvious why we're all so fascinated with him, like we've never been with any other president. Because like it or not, he's a lot like one of us.'

'Sounds like us.'

'Some of us. Speak for yourself, Rosen.'

'Golfs like us,' says Adler with a smile.

'Same slice.'

'Same *adjustments* on his score, I'm sure.'

'A couple of my buddies have played with him,' says Phil Steinerman, the Floridian, 'and yes on the score adjustments, FYI.'

'He eats like us.'

Smiling. 'Like *all* of us.'

'Point is, to some degree, he's a guy like me,' says Nadler. 'And truth is, I don't know how I feel about that.'

'Well…how *do* you feel about that?' asks Rabbi Meyerson.

'You already asked us that, Rabbi.'

'I'm asking again, because I'm hearing that you don't really know how you feel about it. That it's not at all clear to you. You've got mixed feelings.'

'Very mixed,' Nadler admits. He pauses. Ponders. 'I'm kind of resentful, I guess, being stuck in here while he's out there changing the world.'

'Changing it for the worse, though, Simon. Putting the country at war with itself. Stopping immigrants like most of our parents were from coming here and finding freedom,' says Steinerman.

'Yeah, but that's not the point. The point is, he *could* change it for the better. He's put himself in a position to,' says Nadler.

'But you really think he's trying to? And not just trying to make things better for himself and his friends? I mean, what would you do, Nadler? Think about that. If you were forced to choose, let's say, either-or, would you act for your fellow man, or for yourself?'

A reflective silence descends on the minyan.

Into which Abe Rosen says quietly, 'It's not just that he sounds like us and eats like us and golfs like us; that's not really the problem. The problem is that we all know at some level, to some degree, he *is* one of us. When we watch that dayroom TV, we're looking into a mirror too. Wondering about ourselves. Isn't the issue that we don't really know who he is, because we don't really know who *we* are? And that's why he's so familiar to us… We know him – his type – so well…and yet he still seems so strange to us.'

Another reflective silence.

'Truth is,' says Nadler, 'he's the one thing that makes me feel anxious in here.' Sitting up, realizing, lighting up with the crazy realization. 'Everything else, I'm OK with. Bed's fine. Food's fine. My sentence is reasonable. You guys are great,' says Nadler. 'Only thing that makes me really uncomfortable…is him.'

Silence, as they ponder the truth of that. For Nadler. For each of them.

AUSCHWITZ

(Simon Nadler: bank fraud, five years. Fictitious loan applications, $14 million in approved loans.)

SIMON NADLER ARRIVED AT Otisville, like most of his fellow prisoners, escorted by several U.S. marshals in their sharp grey uniforms.

Herman Nadler arrived at Auschwitz, like most of his fellow prisoners, escorted by men in sharp grey uniforms too.

Herman Nadler – Simon's father.

Simon had looked out the black Suburban's big second-row window at the Hudson River glistening in the sun, the city and dense suburbs gradually giving way to rolling hills and thick woods, as the SUV made its way up the West Side Highway, up the Taconic, up Route 87.

Herman, of course, did not look out. The car he rode in

had only a couple of small, high vent windows, providing minimal air circulation for the livestock that was normally the cargo, but it was not very effective air circulation, as those around Herman were frantically attesting. His view was of the Hieronymus Bosch and Edvard Munch faces pressed close to his in the hot airless dark.

Simon Nadler had been arrested in the morning at his place of business, his suite on West 45th, after the authorities had not found him at home.

Herman Nadler, too, was arrested at his place of business – a well-known, successful Viennese fur store – arrested at his desk, after he, too, was not found at home. He quickly discovered that his family had been rounded up just hours before him – his wife, his daughter, his three sons. He was the last. The full set.

So Simon was not the first in his family to be imprisoned.

Of course, Simon's own arrest had everything to do with his own decisions, with his behavior, with how he had conducted his finances over the previous decade.

His father did nothing to bring on or deserve his arrest, except to simply be himself.

Simon Nadler got five years.

His father got death.

Simon thinks about that death sentence. He's thought his whole life about that sentence, and in here, not surprisingly, he's been thinking about it anew. A sentence of no deliberation, no due process, a sentence deliberated only by a madman's perverse vision of an Aryan future.

It was a death sentence that, truly miraculously, his father escaped. Herman Nadler had the necessary animal instincts, or the odd skills to navigate the camp hierarchy, or the random good luck, to be one of those who survived, who was still breathing, still somehow standing when the camp was liberated.

And he is heading up here now, frail, old, stubborn, determined, on the Hudson line train, to visit his son Simon.

'Pop, please, let me hire you an Uber, they can pick you up right at your door, bring you straight here, nice and easy; you don't even have to talk to the driver.'

'No,' he said to Simon, 'If I'm going to a prison, it'll feel more familiar if I take a train.'

And true to his father, and to their relationship, Simon couldn't tell if it was a little joke or not.

His father hasn't been here before. Simon has been here eighteen months, with a lot more to go. The convenient lie that they've been telling each other up until now, is that Herman is too frail to make the trip. It's too risky. It'll take too much out of him. But the fact that he now *is* suddenly feeling more frail, suddenly *not* feeling as well, is why he apparently feels he'd better get on a train and come up. Because now there might *not* be another chance. Which of course proves that he could have come up before, anytime, and chose not to.

The truth that they have not discussed is arguably fairly straightforward: They are both too embarrassed to see the other under these circumstances. His father survived Auschwitz, made his way to America, struggled and saved and worked and slaved, only to have his son end up in an American jail.

As if to say, what was the point of his surviving? Simon feels tremendous guilt that this is what he's delivered. A heavy, potentially lethal dose of his father's embarrassment and disappointment over his son in jail. As if Herman Nadler's own life has come full circle, back to imprisonment. The Nadlers who escaped – only to be recaptured a generation later, put back where they obviously belong. Like father, like son: they're embarrassed for the same reason. At least they're in sync on that.

Of course Simon offered to pay for a car service. He had no access to credit cards or bank accounts, but he has friends who would gladly forward the money for this worthy visit. But his father dismissed such an extravagance, insisted on taking the train. Simon doesn't know whether it was to worry him further – to make him picture Herman stumbling around Grand Central Station with his knobbed cane, making his way down the busy train platform, people rushing around him, the risk of being inadvertently pushed or shoved, the risk of falling – or to show him that see, Simon, you don't need to spend heedlessly, you don't need to cheat the system, you can get by like everyone else, take the train like everyone else, or did he not even think in those terms, and was it simply his own frugal practical self without reference to Simon or anyone else?

And when Herman doesn't show up here as scheduled, does not arrive when he said he would, is that to worry Simon more, to terrify him, to make him picture Herman staring confused at the vast departure board in Grand Central, unable to make sense of it? Or to make Simon picture him fallen on a platform? Or incommunicado, on a respirator in a New York hospital, his stripped-down eldercare cellphone lost, stolen or fallen from his coat pocket? Or did he simply take a different train, because he was running behind? Simon, what's the big deal? I survived the Nazis, unimaginable horrors, impossible odds; how can you think that I can't get a comfortable, clearly marked train to a destination eighty minutes away? That's pretty insulting to me and my intelligence and my good sense, Simon, don't you think?

'Pop,' Simon says, seated across from him in the day room.

Herman looks around the day room slowly, observant. 'So this is it.' He seems more fascinated by the surroundings than interested in his son in front of him after a year and a half. 'Not much security,' he observes.

'Well, *minimum* security. That's the official category.'

'They hardly even checked me. I could be handing you a gun.'

'Pop, they hardly checked you because you're a ninety-four-year-old man.'

'A perfect disguise, if you ask me.' He squints out the windows to the lawn and woods beyond. 'Is there even barbed wire? Anyone who wants to could escape anytime.'

'Well here's the thing, Pop. No one wants to escape here, because they'll be caught pretty fast, and in more trouble, and just add to their sentence. You're much better cooperating, serving your time, and getting out. Everyone knows it.'

His father looks around the dayroom some more. 'Candy machine. Soda. Sandwiches. Two TVs?' He sees the newspaper rack. '*Times, Journal*, and *Post*.' A small nod of modest approval.

He can't help but compare that experience to this one, Simon supposes. Place them side by side. And with his self-guided visual tour finally done, apparently, he looks back at Simon. As if awakening from the darkest reverie, from the darkness required to obliquely relive it, in order to compare.

He leans forward conspiratorially toward Simon. 'We would all have run for it,' he says quietly, firmly. 'If we had this, we'd all have just run for it.'

But Simon hears his deeper meaning: *You have it so easy, you've had it all so easy, and yet this is where you end up.* The deeper meaning, the sting, of anything and everything he'll say to Simon today. Or at least it's the way Simon hears it. The way he's always heard it.

There is of course another, much simpler reason why perhaps he has not visited Simon before.

Because he did not want to ever be inside a place like this again. A place that reverberates even slightly with or reflects at all the place he survived for three years. The place that made him, the place that broke him, the place that defined him – he does not want to re-experience it, in any way, for even a moment.

But he is seeing, Simon thinks, how different this place is from that.

As different as his son is from him.

'I've never told you many stories about it, have I?' his father says.

Understatement of the century, and he knows it. Simon's mother always warned, *Don't ask him about it. It's not to be discussed. It will only bring back your dad's pain and suffering to be asked anything about it.*

'Maybe I should have,' his father says now. 'Maybe I should have terrified you with it, maybe it would have kept you out of here.'

'Pops,' Simon says, too loudly, forcefully, hurt. 'Please. My being here has nothing to do with you. It was not your job to prevent it. It was *my* job to prevent it. This in no way traces back to you.'

Herman Nadler simply shrugs. To deny what Simon just said? To grudgingly accept it? To pretend he didn't hear it? To start the visit over? Simon Nadler hasn't the slightest idea. Has never understood his father at all.

'So.'

'So.'

'I'm here,' his father says. 'Although,' and he looks harshly at Simon, 'I'm not sure exactly why.'

So it's clearly not as simple as *I came to see you*.

Obviously it was a more fraught and complex decision.

I gave you everything.

Why did you do this to yourself? To your lovely wife? To your sweet children? Why, Simon-boy, why? And of course, worst of all, beneath it all, *Why did you do this to me?*

But these are, in point of fact, the thoughts in Simon's head. The thoughts he's assigning to his father.

Because these are all the avenues of accusation and exchange and intercourse that his father typically will *not* go down. He is a survivor. He, his survivorship, his provisional and nearly mystical and magical continuing presence in the world, is too big for that. Transcends all that. That's how it's always been with him. Simon doesn't know if it's made Herman Nadler a good father, or the world's most difficult father.

But his father will steer the conversation somewhere, Simon knows. Somewhere unexpected. Unanticipated. That's what he does. That's what he's always done. So Simon is just sitting here waiting. As always. As he has for his whole life.

'So there are religious services here?'

'Yes. You've heard.'

'I've read. Run by rabbis who have also committed crimes, yes?'

'Yes.'

He raises his eyebrows a little now. 'Do you go?'

Simon shrugs. 'It's something to do, Pop. A chance to connect with others.'

His father never practiced Judaism. Thought it was parochial, backward-looking, superstitious, foolish. He was rounded up with the other Jews and didn't even believe in the practice of the faith. 'Golden rule, that's plenty,' he would say.

'The golden rule…' he says now – predictably, automatically – but then stops and looks at Simon, and doesn't say anything more for a moment. He's thinking about something else.

It seems like a good moment for Simon to ask him the obvious question. The question that hangs in the air.

'Why today, Pop?' *Mah nishtana*. 'Why is this day different from all other days?'

Herman Nadler looks at his Simon, smiles. 'You know why.' Because time is running out. 'You've got three years to go, Simon. But who knows if *I* do.'

'Come on, Pop.'

He frowns, waves off Simon's pat dutiful protestation and

any cheerleading. 'My kidneys, liver, lungs…' he looks down at his torso, 'they're whispering to each other, shouting at each other in there, plotting their rebellion, planning their big prison break.'

He smiles a little. 'So the clock is ticking for both of us. For your freedom, release.' He shrugs. 'Maybe the same for me.'

There's nothing Simon can say to that. He won't expend another empty *C'mon Pop*. He sits quietly.

'And in here, you're still the cut-up, Simon? The class clown?' his father asks. The meaning of his question jumping out at Simon Nadler: *Have you changed at all, Simon? Have you learned anything? Or are you destined to be the same?* It's true, he's always been that overly verbal cut-up kid. Even as an adult. He's always wondered whether his fast talking, his jokes, his quick retorts, are at some level to differentiate himself from his father – from Herman's own halting, deliberate English, or from his earnestness. Is it self-protective wit to protect Simon from the burden of him?

Simon shrugs. 'Pop, it's a lot of Jews. The quick wit is right at home here.'

But his father doesn't want to hear any more about that apparently. He sits up, suddenly straight in the plastic chair. 'We're allowed to walk around?'

'Sure, we can stroll anywhere within the fencing.' Simon stops himself short. They look at each other. That's what it must have been for the survivors in Auschwitz. Wandering aimlessly. Utterly free, utterly not.

✡

Nevertheless. They go for a short, very slow stroll in the sunshine – the man is ninety-four, after all. He squints into the slanting autumn sun, adjusts his black fedora to shield his eyes.

The last walk of father and son? Very possibly. And they both know it. So Simon pays close attention to everything his father says.

'You know I don't like to talk about that time,' his father says, shuffling along, 'but there is something I want to tell you today, a story that I never told anyone – not even your mother.'

Simon's heart jumps a little. His father and mother had a marriage that anyone would envy. Close, warm, loving – a miracle of connection and sweetness. He could tell that his mother in many ways had saved her husband. So what could this be?

'You remember I told you that your grandfather and his brother had a farm at the base of the Carpathians, yes? And that your grandfather had a degree in botany?'

They've made their slow way by now to the perimeter fencing. There is meadow on the other side, and woods beyond, whose dramatic change of seasons Simon has witnessed several times now. 'Auschwitz was very large,' his father continues. 'Thirty hectares. People don't realize that. Scrubby, weedy. And against the western fencing, along the bottom, there was a weed...*Lillialusus Nomus*.' He looks at Simon, smiles. *You see, Simon-boy? I still remember the botanical Latin name*. 'It was edible.' He smiles. 'You cut off the bitter top,' he explains, 'score the blade below it with your thumbnail, and there's a sweet white paste inside. Tastes almost like coconut meat. A vegetable. Has nutrients. Your great-uncle showed me how to get to the paste inside when I was a boy.' He lowers his look. 'All these Warsaw ghetto Jews – no one knew about plants.' He stares at the ground. 'No one knew they were edible but me.' He keeps his gaze down – averted, Simon realizes. 'Simon, it was just a little patch of this stuff. This weed. Not enough for others. Just enough for me.'

Unsaid. Clear. Screaming out at Simon:

It's how I lived. How I lived and others didn't. How I ate and survived. And the guilt I carry about it, but there was not enough to share. Simple, but painful. Painful, but simple. There was not enough to share.

'I've never told anyone that story,' his father says again. As in: *don't repeat it.* As in: *I'm not proud. I have a hard enough time living with it myself. I tell it for its meaning, for its use, to you. But please, do not tell it again.*

Herman Nadler reaches a hand out shakily in front of him, places it gently on his son's shoulder for a moment. *We do what we must to get by. To live. To survive. Please understand. Please forgive it.*

And Simon, unconsciously, does exactly the same. Places his hand on his father's shoulder too. *Of course I understand. Of course I forgive it. How could anyone not?*

'So now I've seen it,' Herman Nadler says abruptly after a few minutes of their sitting quietly on a bench in the yard, and he rises. 'And now I've seen you.' And accompanying that sentence, his smile of disappointment. Disappointment that is a constant. Disappointment that hangs under his eyes. Disappointment that emanates from every pore of him. Disappointment with the human race, or disappointment with Simon? Simon could never be sure which, and he's still not.

'You take care, my boy,' his father says, looking up at Simon with that disappointed smile. *There is still time to make me proud.*

But that thought, too – that interpretation of his smile – is only in Simon's head.

It's only weeks later that he realizes it. He's been thinking, remembering, bits of family history and lore coming back to him, as if released, emancipated by his father's visit.

And there *was* no botanist great-uncle brother of his grandfather. His grandfather had only two sisters. His father would probably never imagine that Simon would remember that. This is the advantage of whole families exterminated in the camps. You can recreate them. Shuffle the ancestral, familial chess pieces around. *I've never told anyone that story.* Because it *is* a story, Simon is realizing. Totally made up, but he wanted Simon to believe it, to say to Simon, we do what we must do. *Sometimes, we must put ourselves first. Sometimes we must be selfish.* A story powerful enough, outrageous enough, bizarre enough, to *have* to be true. But it's not.

A story he told his son to help Simon live with himself? A story he told because he loves his son, and will do anything for him? He gets the point: We must be able to tell the story of our lives to ourselves. We tell ourselves a good story. That allows us to live with ourselves. *I never told your mother.*

Someone his father confided everything to. Why wouldn't he tell her? Because he wouldn't dare lie to her with a story like that. Why didn't he tell her? Simple. Because it wasn't true.

The Auschwitz survivor's lesson to his imprisoned son is clear.

Not: *don't do it again.*

Instead: *Do it again if you have to. But this time, don't get caught.*

And if you do get caught, for god's sake, come up with a good story.

CAMP WIKIWANDI

Camp Wikiwandi, on Lake Winipesaukee, summer of '77.

Matt Sorcher is lying on his cell bunk, vividly remembering.

It's long before the rise of political correctness, and of the term *Native American*, so the cabins all have Indian names in bright hand-painted signs over each cabin door. Navajo, Chippewa, Cheyenne, Apache, Comanche, Sioux, Iroquois, Shawnee, Pawnee. But don't be fooled by the evident tribal commitment – the raucous, gleeful, exuberant loyalty of campers to their respective summer clans. Because really there are only two tribes, opposites in every way.

Tribe One is Midwestern Counselors – big, blond, rosy-cheeked, healthy, tanned, muscular, cheerful and outgoing young men and women recruited for the summer from college campuses across the Midwest – Ohio State, Indiana

U, University of Nebraska.

Tribe Two is Tri-State Jewish Campers – pale, spindly arms and legs emerging like twigs from the sleeves and shorts of their baggy blue uniforms, coke-bottle glasses, curly black hair, fast-talking, all hovering uncomfortably to one side of puberty or another, neurotic, anxious, obsessive, obnoxious, annoying, unnecessarily loud, most of the campers hardly looking twice at the serene woods around them, marking the eight weeks till they can head back to Park Avenue, Chappaqua, Westport, or Bergen County.

Between the tribes, an uneasy summer-long truce. An eight-week assessment and informal study of the Other. And of course, as in any uneasy co-existence, occasionally hostilities erupt.

Tribe One is paid in weekly wages.

Tribe Two – via their parents – are paying those wages to Tribe 1.

This is the unstated economics that undergirds the tribal interaction. All war may on the surface seem ideological, Matt remembers a history teacher saying, but underneath, it's all economic.

The Midwestern outdoorsy counselors each came with some specialty, from waterfront to archery, baseball to horseback riding, riflery to pottery and arts and crafts.

The Tri-State Jewish Campers turned out to have specialists, too. Card sharps who carried a deck everywhere in their baggy blue shorts and could beat anyone at poker; joke machines who could rattle off a couple of thousand, one after the other; procurers – of candy, record albums, contraband – anything prohibited from camp, they somehow had it. Its prohibition and banning seemed to be the *reason* they had it. They were all expert too. They were becoming what they would be.

Matt's gauze of memory quickly sharpens focus to the Navajo.

Because he and Mighty Mouth were Navajos.

Eleven-year-old Matt is awakened by someone pushing on his shoulder in the middle of the night. He opens his eyes. Mighty Mouth is standing there – '*shshshsh*' – his index finger against his lips to keep Matt quiet, high excitement written across Mighty Mouth's face. He whispers. 'You gotta come with me, Sorcher. I need a witness.'

A witness.

Today Matt Sorcher would hear all the legal implications of that word – testimony, verification, a confirmatory recitation of events. But his just-awakened eleven-year-old self understood *witness* as only, *you gotta see this*. He was sure that's all Mighty Mouth meant by it, so he silently pulls on his shirt and shorts, and he's ready to go.

They can't risk using a flashlight, so they make their way carefully in the dark, opening and closing the cabin's wooden door slowly enough to outfox its usual squeaking; tiptoeing down the black path they know by heart. Once they're past the dense canopy of trees that shades the cabin area, they can see well enough in the pale, shadowy light of the night's half moon. Halfway to the waterfront, Mighty Mouth stops him, makes him stand quietly, and listen. Carrying on the lake's breeze, Matt can barely hear it: urgent whispering, and then a low moaning, keening sound, that he first takes to be some unfamiliar wildlife on the lake. But it soon enough proves to be…well, exactly that: unfamiliar wildlife.

They follow the sounds, make their way to the boathouse.

Inside are two representative specimens of the tanned, muscular Midwestern tribe.

Specifically, Don from Waterfront, and Dawn from Arts and Crafts.

Specifically, both naked.

Specifically, Don on top of Dawn, on a picnic table in the boathouse. Don's butt pumping. Dawn moaning, keening. Moonlight pouring in.

For an eleven-year-old, this is a lot to take in. This is a lot of excitement. In a lifetime since then, sex has never been as exciting for Matt Sorcher as it was at that moment.

Through the big screen window, they watch, transfixed.

'Pretty good, huh?' Mighty Mouth whispers. 'They come down here every night.'

'Best thing I've ever seen,' he whispers to Mighty Mouth. Because it inarguably is. His heart is pounding. His forearms are tingling. His whole body is alive.

'I come down to watch them. But I wanted you to come with me, 'cause I need a witness.'

That word again. Matt's heart, pounding already, thumps into a new gear of alertness and fear. He smells trouble. 'Witness to what?'

'Witness to this…' says Mighty Mouth.

And he steps to the boathouse's screen window. 'Hey!'

Don and Dawn stop their sound and movement immediately, look our way.

'Whatcha doin' in there?' says Mighty Mouth – pretending it's an innocent question from an innocent eleven-year-old.

'Get back to your bunk!' hisses Don.

'And miss this?' says Mighty Mouth.

'Get out of here!' says Don. The anger gathering in his muscles, every one of which Matt can see in the moonlight.

Matt takes a step back in response, terrified.

But Mighty Mouth takes a defiant step toward them. 'No way.'

Don gets up off Dawn and Dawn sits up – revealing to Matt in one vision, in a snapshot that has never faded, Don's hard-on, Dawn's breasts, Dawn's bush – a lot *more*, a second wave of stimuli, for his eleven-year-old brain. He guesses their clothes aren't within reach, because they just stay there, naked. They are both beautiful. Blond, tan, sleek, perfect.

'I'm *telling*,' says Mighty Mouth – the prototypical eleven-year-old's threat – vague, unfocused, kneejerk. But then he adds to it, amplifies it, in a uniquely Mighty Mouth way. 'I'm telling *Bruce*.' The camp director. 'He's a friend of my dad's. My dad helped him get this job.'

Whoa. Laying on the politics, the power play, right there. All the insolence, the snottiness, the arrogance, of an overprivileged eleven-year-old kid. Everything that would cause a guy like Don to finally deck one of these campers. And be fired immediately.

So instead:

'Please don't tell Bruce,' says Don flatly.

Even Matt's eleven-year-old self senses this is a critical error on Don's part.

'Why not?' The insolent eleven-year-old again. ''Cause you'll both be in trouble? 'Cause you'll both be fired? Having sex in front of campers?'

By now Dawn and Don have reached for their clothes. Tee shirts, shorts, flip flops, which don't do much to cover up or disguise or blur or cancel what Matt has seen.

Don takes a breath. Stares at Mighty Mouth. 'I'll pay you not to tell.'

Some part of Matt's eleven-year-old self senses this is a second mistake.

Mighty Mouth doesn't miss a beat. 'How much?'

Don pauses for a moment, considering. 'Ten bucks.'

Mighty Mouth looks at Don evenly, unblinking, assessing. Calculating, as it turns out. 'Ten bucks every week.'

'What?!' Don does some calculating of his own. 'That's eighty bucks by the end of summer! Listen, you little shit, we only make two bucks an hour! I'm paying for college expenses with this stupid job! It's my summer savings!'

Once again, exactly the wrong thing to say to Mighty Mouth. Once again, even Matt's eleven-year-old self can sense that. It only empowers Mighty Mouth, emboldens him. It only shows him even more how tightly he has Don in his pudgy grip.

'Eighty bucks. Because, face it, the cost is a lot higher if I tell.' Mighty Mouth shrugs again, and adds, as if with sympathy, 'At ten bucks a week, I'm making it easier for you to pay.'

And then Mighty Mouth, god bless him, throws an interesting wrinkle in. Or tries to, at least.

'Of course, every time you let us watch you two, I refund you five dollars.'

'You little…' Even in the moonlight, even through the screen window, Matt can see Don's face turn from waterfront suntan to the color of rage. But Don says nothing more.

'The offer stands,' Mighty Mouth shrugs again. And Matt realized just then that Mighty Mouth didn't expect them to say yes to any of it. He was only proposing it to annoy them. To solidify his position lording it over them. Matt started to wonder whether Mighty Mouth's father even knew Bruce, the camp director.

Here's the thing. Ten bucks a week wasn't all they got out of it. They got out of stupid cafeteria duties whenever Mighty Mouth asked Don. They got out of art class. They got out of swim tests. All summer, Don was always available to make an excuse for them.

So Mighty Mouth got the eighty bucks, sure, *and* everything else he wanted. The deal he negotiated got him way more than just the deal itself. Just the fact that there *was* a deal let him take further advantage of it. Boy, that was a lesson.

'Don's already giving you the eighty,' Matt pointed out to Mighty Mouth a few weeks later, feeling some remorse about Don, who now turned away from Matt when he saw him at the waterfront.

'That's the beauty of it, Matt. I've got the eighty, but we're getting more out of it.'

'So can I have some of that money, since I'm in on it with you?'

'No friggin' way.'

'Just a little? For being part of it? Just whatever you want. Something. A couple of bucks to buy candy from Ari.'

Mighty Mouth looks at Matt like there's something wrong with him. 'No friggin' way.'

'Why not? We're friends.'

'It was *my* deal.' And then, 'Matt, you should never let

money get in the way of friendship.'

Which sounds so reasonable and adult to Matt, he lets it drop without his eleven-year-old brain thinking much more about it.

But there was one more thing he did need to ask Mighty Mouth about. Something he couldn't understand and couldn't get out of his mind. One more question into the dark, once everyone else in the bunk was asleep.

'But why did Don let it happen?' Matt whispered to Mighty Mouth. 'Why was he so scared of you?' *He's so much bigger, stronger. Why didn't he come out and grab you by the back of your neck and pin your arms behind your back and march you straight to Bruce? Why didn't he get in our faces and threaten us back, when you threatened him? Why didn't he come at us, make us run away? Why did he cave in so fast?*

Matt can practically feel Mighty Mouth's satisfied smile into the cabin's darkness. 'I knew he'd be scared.'

'But I mean…*how'd* you know?'

He can almost see Mighty Mouth's nonchalant shrug. ''Cause most people are. Scared about breaking the rules and getting caught. Scared of their bosses and getting fired. I just figured Don would be too.'

That summer was of course Matt's first exposure to sex. So he learned that sex is apparently not warm, sweet, and safe, but illicit, desperate, and secretive. And tied up with money.

Is any of that really wrong?

It was a summer of memories. Like camp is supposed to be.

✡

And something he's been forced to wonder about ever since: can the course of a life really be determined by a single event? Well, of course it can, in the case of a parent's suicide or a sibling's murder, but that's not what he means. That kind of life event is represented much more heavily at other federal prisons. Prisons where an inmate has seen, say, the stabbing death of his mother by his father, or the accidental murder of his sister by a stray bullet as he stands next to her in the street. No, what he means is, can the course of a life be determined by what you witness one night at summer camp? What you witness, as it happens, with one other witness, who is at the moment the most famous and notorious of witnesses.

Matt only knows that he has never since seen sex that exciting, and that any adult sexual experiences he's had have always paled next to that one. And that the sudden intermingling of sex and power and illicitness, stewing and stirring together, has never left him. That startling example of power suddenly reversed, suddenly transferred to an eleven-year-old kid, is part of the weird potency of that night. And the image of Dawn, the arts and crafts counselor, haunts him, stays with him, never leaves him, and all his own pale sordid sexual experience has been judged against it – and found wanting.

Can the course of a life really be determined by a single event? Matt Sorcher has followed Dawn for years, once he was a little older, and had the means, the money to do so. Not stalking, exactly. But curious. Drawn to her. He couldn't help himself. He couldn't stop. He observed her from afar, carefully, respectfully, never intruding. He kept tabs on her series of dolt midwestern boyfriends. He watched her marriage, and watched it dissolve. Her first child – a daughter – its adoption, her boyfriends, her drug addiction. He never swooped in to rescue, he never interfered.

And with the same care and caution and discretion, he was all the while building his tax center business – building it with an illicit little corner to it.

Constructing it so carefully that law enforcement never would have caught it.

What they caught was his interest in Dawn. His 'spying' on her, his 'stalking' her, across decades. That's what Dawn had noticed, on social media (where Matt's so-called 'stalking' had migrated), and she had been so unnerved by it, she had reported it, so they had tracked it for several years. And when he was busted and questioned about it, when his computer was searched – that's when local law enforcement literally stumbled across the separate books and files and receipts and bank transfers of his tax centers.

They would never have discovered them. They would never have known.

It was Dawn that brought him down.

Dawn that put him in here.

With Mighty Mouth again, as it turns out.

So yes, the course of a life can be determined by a single event.

An event you can't un-see.

A course you can't undo.

That's his story of summer camp.

And Mighty Mouth is, once again, in the bunk next to his.

JACOB, ESAU
AND PHIL

'RABBI, I WANT TO ASK YOU about Jacob and Esau,' says Phil Steinerman *(fraudulent blood testing clinics, nine years)*, as they arrange the folding chairs into a semicircle after the service. 'I've got an issue. A big issue,' warns Steinerman.

'OK,' says Rabbi Meyerson slowly. 'Let me catch the group up so we're all on the same page here,' and then, once they're all seated, 'Everyone remembers that Jacob and Esau were the twin sons of Isaac and Rebekka, and grandsons of Abraham, yes?'

A few tentative nods. Several blank stares.

'In fact,' Meyerson continues, 'we know, very significantly, that Esau was the first-born and Jacob the second-born. Jacob's name in Hebrew actually means *he grasps the heel*, because Jacob emerged from Rebekka's womb clinging to the heel of Esau. He was that eager to get into the world, I suppose, and not be left behind.'

'Schmuck,' says Abe Rosen. 'He didn't know how good he had it.'

'Or right from the get-go he was trying to get out ahead of Esau,' says Marty Adler. 'Relevant for what comes next, right, Rabbi?'

The rabbi nods.

'So here's my issue,' says Steinerman. 'Esau's the big hairy alpha male, right, and Jacob's the smooth hairless pipsqueak weakling, comparatively speaking?'

'I don't know exactly where you're getting that, Phil, but OK, we'll go with that, comparatively, for now,' says the rabbi.

'Well, that's why Jacob got a furry bear arm or some damn arm from somewhere – to fool his blind father Isaac into thinking he's Esau,' says Steinerman. 'To deceive his rich dad into granting him his brother Esau's birthright. 'Cause the first-born inherits all the cattle and lands, right?'

'That's right.' But the rabbi regards Steinerman suspiciously. Not sure where this is going.

'My point is, Jacob deceived his father, and that's how he got rich. That part I get. But more than that, Rabbi, it's that Jacob took Esau's place as one of the patriarchs of Judaism. A patriarch who prospered, whom we admire, sing about; we praise and recount his story, while Esau is kind of shunned and forgotten. Jacob's a scam artist. And that's who the Jews are descended from. That's our role model! No wonder we're in here, Rabbi. We're just dutiful Jews following the religion's example, as far as I can see. Don't you agree? Don't you have a little ethical issue with Jacob being a patriarch?'

'Now wait a second,' says the rabbi. 'It's a little more

complicated than that. Esau *sold* his birthright to Jacob beforehand. Esau bartered it away in exchange for a bowl of lentil stew. They had a deal.'

'Come on, Rabbi. Esau, strong as a mule, was coming in from the fields, where he'd been working. He was famished, right? Totally beat. Jacob, who was too small to work the fields, could stay inside, sheltered by his doting over-protective mother, Rebekka. He was well rested, and proposed the deal to Esau when Esau was hungry and vulnerable. That's not a fair deal, Rabbi,' says Steinerman.

'Hey, that's the kind of deal *I'd* be trying to cut,' says Nadler with an urchin smile.

'Jacob pulled one over on him,' Steinerman continues. 'Let's admit it, OK? Jacob's a crafty, lazy bum, and for that he becomes a patriarch?'

'Yes,' says the rabbi.

Stunning them all.

'What? You agree?'

'Yes,' says the rabbi, again. 'Jacob, as you see him, Phil, is guilty as charged.' Meyerson smiles suddenly. 'But, this being a discussion group, guilty with an explanation.'

'Of course,' says Nadler.

Rabbi Meyerson adjusts his yarmulke. 'Look, for better or worse, Judaism admires wits, cleverness, brains, and creative solutions. All of which Jacob is demonstrating in spades. Judaism shuns and devalues and dismisses stupidity and brute dumb animal strength.'

'Didn't Isaac actually love Esau more?' says Abe Rosen, the story coming back to him from long ago. 'A fellow hunter: robust, strong outdoors guy, right? But Jacob was his mother Rebekka's favorite. Inside guy. Momma's boy.' Abe Rosen now wonders aloud, his discomfort and distaste for the idea evident in his pinched mouth and reluctant expression. 'Jew versus Gentile, Rabbi? Is that, in a way, what you're saying?'

'I don't know if I'd put it like that,' says Rabbi Meyerson. 'But if you read all those Old Testament stories closely, it is a tradition of complex relationships between right and wrong – between good and evil – and while we're at it, fraught relationships between competing brothers – Esau and Jacob, Moses and Aaron, Cain and Abel; the list goes on. So it's good versus evil, but notice that always, literally, even genetically, the two are closely related to each other. Good and evil, right and wrong – they're all in the family. Inseparable. Two sides of the same coin.'

'Presumably the idea is that we all have the capacity for both?' posits Matt Sorcher.

'Exactly,' says Meyerson.

'But that's what we all are,' says Steinerman, gesturing around the semicircle of folding chairs. 'Clever deceivers – all of us. Jacob's children. Go crime by crime, if you want. Therefore, all good Jewish boys, dutiful to our tradition. So why are we in here?'

'Well, we all broke the law,' says Rabbi Meyerson, 'and Judaism is a religion of laws, so our being here is not inconsistent with our faith. Commandment Number 4, Thou Shalt Not Steal.'

'Either the system is fucked up, or the religion is. They can't both be right,' says Steinerman.

'Yes, clever deceivers. But we weren't clever enough,' says Abe Rosen. 'So maybe if we *hadn't* been caught, we would still qualify as clever deceivers. We would still be biblical. We would still be admired.'

'It's true,' says Greg Lerner, shrugging. 'If I wasn't caught, I'd still be admired. It's true for all of us.'

'So our only sin, as far as the Bible and Judaism and our faith goes, is in getting caught,' says Nadler.

'Jacob is the original grasper,' says Rosen. 'Trying to get ahead, right from the womb.'

'Trying to get in *front* of his rightful place,' adds Nadler.

'But he thinks it *is* his rightful place, in front of Esau. That's the thing,' says Lerner.

'So the Bible is teaching that it's OK to take advantage of dumb fucks,' says Steinerman authoritatively. 'And the world is full of them.'

The rabbi looks horrified. 'That's the lesson here?'

Steinerman nods, crosses his arms conclusively. 'That's the lesson.'

'Oy,' says Rabbi Meyerson.

'Oy is right,' says Steinerman.

THE HEART OF
SATURDAY NIGHT

KICKING BACK. SATURDAY NIGHT. Big Willie and his pals. The prisoners' Sabbath ends at sundown Saturday night, and that's when his shift ends too. Off until Tuesday, and the local Genesee Ale flows, a stack of twelve-packs, plus a few Olde English 40s, chips and pretzels and cheese. Then it's burgers out or pizza in, and guys he grew up with: Tommy, Andy, Other Billy (because Big Willie's real name is Bill Richardson, and he's a year older than 'Other Billy', Bill Simpson), Gene, Gordo – guys he went through high school with. They know each other inside out.

These woods were theirs, hunting, fishing, trapping – no licenses needed for any of it back then. No city folk coming up here back then. But toward the end of high school – this is maybe thirty years ago – that's when some of the New York City folks started buying houses up here, because the

Hamptons were too expensive. At first they were a pretty good source for odd jobs – lawns and snow-plowing and gutters and gut renovations – and the money flowed even for high school kids, especially for high school kids like them, who could do basically any kind of labor. For them it was a sudden boom economy in what had been a pretty depressed area. At just about the same time, the Hasidic community set up just north of them in Otis, paid cash for about nine hundred acres from a couple of farmers – and they heard the Hasids negotiated hard – and eventually, over the next ten years, they basically took over the town of Otis. Their long black coats, wide-brimmed black hats, long wild beards, their women all covered-up head-to-toe even in summer, him and his pals hadn't seen all that much in their lives to begin with, had never really spent much time away from here, so they definitely hadn't seen or imagined anything like that.

Plus the dialect – English, supposedly, but you couldn't understand what these people were saying, and they couldn't understand you. It was pretty much like an alien invasion. Tommy and Andy said there should be a video game of it. They actually got it pretty worked out one night over Genesees. Advancing armies of bearded black hats, and targets and scoring, and even some of the game's cheats. They all laughed a lot. Big Willie would not be telling Rabbi Meyerson or any of the minyan about *that*.

Anyway, tonight they're in their regular circle in Big Willie's little living room, the wooden chairs from his grandparents arranged around his three-milk-carton coffee table so his pals can all reach the Genesee Ale easy and put their feet up easy, and it's occurred to him before, and it occurs to him again now, that this is a circle of guys pretty much like the minyan circle at Otisville, and some of the conversations are closer than you'd think, but he doesn't say that to his friends. He senses how it would just bother a couple of them, get under their skin for no real reason. That's why he's never told them the minyan's nickname for him either.

'So how's the Jews this week, Billy? Eatin' good? Sleepin' in?' That's how Andy always starts, but then again, it's what he always wants to know. To be fair, he's curious. Curious about prison life, curious what the prisoners are like. And of course he knows you're not supposed to say shit like that – 'so how's the Jews?' – but he likes that this is about the one place he can say shit like that and get away with it. In this little living room surrounded by their high school pals.

He's explained to these guys plenty of times, every way he can think of, that these are a different kind of Jew that he's guarding. 'These aren't the black hats; you know that, right? These are white-collar criminals, stockbrokers and financial wheeler-dealers and bigwigs. Believe me, they hate those black-hat Jews as much as you do.'

'Yeah, well, do they hate 'em because down deep, they know they're really just like 'em?'

'What do you mean, Andy?'

'I mean, the same religion, the same beliefs, the same god, but your Jews are just a lot richer.'

'Yeah,' says Gino. 'Maybe they don't like 'em 'cause they remind them of themselves.'

'Yeah, like that's what they'd be if they didn't have their money,' says Tommy.

'The Otisville Jews,' Big Willie explains to them, 'you

gotta understand. Lot of them, they got practically nothing to do with being Jewish. Most of 'em don't know anything about it. Hell, they're taking classes in it! Learning about their religion for the first time now. Just for something to do.'

Hell, a lot of them are married to beautiful non-Jewish women, he's thinking, but something in him knows not to say that. He knows it will distract from what he's trying to say by just pissing his friends off, and he'll hear some bitter shit about the Jews are taking away the best-looking women with their money. He knows his friends don't really believe that. But he knows that...well...they partly do.

This is just the usual pre-pizza or pre-burger bullshit. Shooting the breeze a little before they head into town or pop on ESPN. They'll shift soon enough to Tommy's stories of his illegal no-permit construction projects, and Andy's cushy stop/go sign-turning gig with the highway department.

But tonight becomes a little different. Because tonight, Andy tilts his head and looks at his old friend Billy and says something he hasn't said before, but something he's clearly been thinking about. 'How can you do it, Billy? How can you be with those people?' And behind it is something else, pretty clear to Big Willie because he knows Andy so well, because he's known him forever. *I think you like those people.*

Big Willie puts his Genesee Ale down carefully.

'OK, what are you saying, Andy?'

'You're kind of, like, defending them,' Andy says.

'I'm not defending them. I'm explaining them, is all.'

'Trying to explain them to us, OK, but why? Because you think we're too stupid to understand?'

Big Willie is not taking the bait on that. He ignores it.

'Hey,' he tells Andy, and he's feeling suddenly annoyed, a little pissed off himself, at the direction of this conversation. 'These guys are fucking criminals, OK? They're bad. They deserve their jail time. But come on, you spend time with anyone, you get to know them, right?'

'And what…get friendly with them?' says Andy.

'That ain't what I'm saying.'

'But what, you start to see things from their point of view?'

'No, but…you get to know their world a little, that's all.'

He's thought about the contrasts in the two groups before. How he and his pals were hunters, grew up physical, did everything with their hands. They could set traps – deer, turkey, beaver; you name it. They could all of them plumb-set toilets, do electrical wiring, sheetrock, could nail-gun studs. Some of them were better at it than others, but they could all do it. Practically from childhood, learning it from their fathers and uncles and older brothers, and even though most of their fathers and uncles and older brothers rarely said a word of instruction about any of it, the knowledge was simply somehow in their hands.

The minyan Jews, Big Willie could tell, had done pretty much nothing with their hands. Everything was in their heads. Their fathers and uncles and brothers had taught them that was their world, that using your head was how the world worked and how you got along in the world, that was the expectation of them. From what Big Willie could tell, they never changed a light bulb, never used a screwdriver or held a hammer, but more than that: they weren't supposed to. That was for the gentiles to do for you. Let the gentiles do it. They were so good at it. They were meant for it. They were made for it. Look at their hands, Moshe, and look at yours!

So adding, multiplying, dividing in your head until it's second nature, having, what would you call it, *head-instinct* like Big Willie and his friends have hand-instinct; that's their culture.

For the Jews it was all about the mind, from what he could tell.

For his pals, it's always been all about the hands.

What he doesn't know yet for sure, what he's still not clear on – for the Otisville Jews *or* for his friends – is about the heart. Where and how the heart figures in.

And he's not about to bring any of this up with his high school pals after a shitload of Genesees. And sure as hell isn't going to talk about 'heart' with these guys, drunk or sober.

He definitely knows the coldness of his own upbringing. How the hand knowledge seems to cut off the heart knowledge, how the heart is cut off for most of his friends. How a pal of his can still surprise him by being such a cold bastard – but then again, how it's no real surprise at all.

Whereas listening to the Jews, to certain ones of them – Nadler, Rosen, Adler, a few of the others – he hears how they relate to each other. It's this – what would you call it – this built-in warmth, this shared, in-on-the-joke feeling, this all-in-this-together-from-birth-to-death *agreement*, almost – and hearing it at the minyan is how he could first hear, in contrast, the natural, built-in coldness of his friends.

But then again, listening to the Jews (he pretends not to; he pretends to give them their privacy, their space, but how can he not hear what he hears?), he notices the same coldness in plenty of them too. Plenty of them with no more heart than many of his pals. For all their education, no education or knowledge about the heart. The minyan and his friends. Very different, and very much the same.

Back at the prison Tuesday, he looks at them. Thinking about what Andy said – that confusing little moment of conflict, a weird little instant of heat and spark, coming suddenly out of nowhere.

He does not like being in the position of defending these people. Of being seen by Andy and Tommy as being on their side. And the thing is, he can tell it's making him angry at them. He can feel it. Like *they've* put him in this position. Like it's their fault. Which of course it kind of is. If he wasn't guarding them – if this was just typical low-life prisoners at a typical American prison – none of this stuff would have come up for Andy and Tommy and his friends. It all makes him feel a little pissed off and irritable. More than a little.

'Hey, Sorcher, pick up those plates.'

'I didn't put them there.'

'Did I say you did? Pick them up!'

Sorcher looks at him. Doesn't know what this is about.

Big Willie doesn't exactly know what it's about either.

But he and Sorcher both know it's about something.

THE TEN
COMMANDMENTS:
A REVIEW

'HEY, SINCE THOU SHALT NOT STEAL came up last time with Jacob and Esau, I thought today let's talk the Ten Commandments,' says Rabbi Meyerson.

'I still got big problems with Jacob,' Steinerman grumbles, reminding them. Not letting it go.

Rabbi Meyerson ignores him. 'The Big Ten. The original laws. As much as it's a religion, Judaism is a system of laws, and the Big Ten are at the summit of that system – literally the summit – brought down from a mountaintop, after all. And since we all seem to have some trouble with the idea of laws, I thought we'd go back to the basics.'

In preparation for today, the rabbi has taken the trouble to handprint the ten commandments on two sheets of paper. Five commandments on each sheet, the two sheets of paper standing in for the twin tablets, the rabbi standing in for

Moses – delivering the laws to the encircled heathen.

Nadler reaches out to see the two sheets more closely, and without thinking about it, the rabbi hands them to him.

As Nadler looks over the commandments, a slow smile crosses his face.

'Ten commandments,' he says, looking around at the rest of the minyan. 'Let's have a test. See how we all do.'

'You mean like how many can we remember?' says Sorcher.

'No,' says Nadler, dismissively. 'I mean, who's broken the most.'

Their eyes light up. Their competitive juices start to flow.

'I'll read each one; you raise your hand if you've broken it,' Nadler says. 'Lerner, you keep count.' Lerner, who can do algorithms in his head. The human abacus. He'll keep the running total on everyone in the minyan.

'You OK with this, Rabbi?' asks Nadler.

Meyerson shrugs. 'One way to refamiliarize yourselves with them, I suppose.'

'Thou Shalt Not Steal is the price of admission, I guess,' says Nadler, consulting the second sheet. 'Every one of us gets a black mark on that one.'

'Plus Thou Shalt Not Covet,' says Phil Steinerman. 'If you're here, you coveted. *Ipso facto.* Case closed.'

'OK, so on to the other eight,' says Nadler. 'That'll start to separate the men from the boys.' He consults the sheets again, and soon frowns with annoyance. 'The first three are about God. Which is pretty narcissistic of the Commandments' author, if you ask me.' Rattling them off quickly; irritated. 'Number one is I'm the Lord your God, two is you'll have no God beside me, three is you won't take my name in vain. Which most of us are fucked on with just a single *goddamn*, technically speaking.'

'But Jesus fucking Christ is OK, right Rabbi?' asks Lerner. 'He's not our god, so his name in vain is a good substitute, right?'

They don't even give the rabbi time to formulate an answer. They want to get back to the game, to the final tally, see who's the broken-commandment champ. 'Four is remember the Sabbath and keep it holy,' says Nadler.

'Hey, on that one, we're all doin' great! We're getting together, we're keeping it holy,' says Rosen, sounding quite pleased and proud.

'Yeah, but it took prison to get us to obey number four,' points out Sorcher.

'So what? Still counts,' says Rosen. 'We're all even on that one. No one goes ahead or behind on number four.'

'So far it's neck-and-neck!' says Steinerman with excitement. 'A close race coming out of the gate, rounding the first turn.'

'Five. Honor thy father and mother,' reads Nadler.

'Oy. Tricky one. Might have to get a prison shrink in on that one – go case by case,' says Adler.

'Although you could argue that if you're in here, *a priori*, you haven't honored your father and mother,' says Phil Steinerman.

'Again with the Latin, huh Steinerman,' mutters Adler.

'But I don't agree,' says Matt Sorcher. 'My mother and father wanted me to be a big success. A *macher*. So I'm here because I *was* trying to honor their wishes.'

'But is that the only reason you're here? 'Cause you were trying to honor them?' says Nadler.

'Maybe. Maybe not. I agree, we need the shrink. Maybe

we have to come back to that one,' says Sorcher.

'Six. Thou Shalt Not Murder,' intones Nadler ominously, now reading from the top of the second sheet. The second tablet.

'We're even on that one too. Because if we committed murder, we'd be in a different prison. We've committed all kinds of crimes, but not murder,' says Rosen.

'Well, now, wait a second,' says Phil Steinerman. 'We're not here for murder – but that might only be that they didn't *get* us on murder.'

'Come on, Phil, nobody here's a murderer.'

'I'm not saying anyone is. I'm saying one of us *could* be. Any one of us could be here because this is what they got us on. We've proven ourselves criminals. The question is how far we'd go.'

'Phil, look at us,' says Sorcher. 'We're a lot of things, but we're not murderers.'

'Most of us, of course not. But maybe one? Maybe just one?'

And then they all begin to look around at one another.

And then they start laughing.

'Phil…look at us! Really?'

Phil looks. Smiles. 'OK. I guess not.'

Nadler presses on. 'Seven. Thou Shalt Not Commit Adultery.'

'All, right, now we're talkin'!!'

'Now things get good!'

All eyes turn to Marty Adler. The trigamist.

'Don't look at me!' he says. 'I didn't commit adultery. I was married the whole time.'

'To three women, Marty.'

'So? Adultery means going *outside* marriage,' Marty Adler points out. 'Which I never did. And besides, these biblical figures, these patriarchs we've been talking about? Four wives. Five wives. Eight wives. A hundred twenty wives. A lot more than me.'

'You're in the Biblical tradition,' admits Saul Solomon.

'What about the rest of us?'

'OK, number seven, adultery. First predictions, then show of hands,' says Nadler.

'OK, I'm gonna say fifty percent of us slept outside our marriages at one point or another,' says Steinerman.

'I'm going just twenty percent.'

'I'm going seventy-five percent.'

'OK, adultery. Hands?'

Half shoot up.

'I win! I called it!' says Nadler, triumphantly.

'What about Rosen being gay? Is he not subject to the commandment?' asks Steinerman.

'Yeah, is Rosen exempt on that? Or does he need to start counting from when the Supreme Court made gay marriage legal?'

'This is not where I saw today's discussion going,' Rabbi Meyerson says ruefully.

Nadler presses on. 'Eight, stealing, which we already covered. All guilty.'

'Still a close race,' says Steinerman, excitedly. 'Rounding the final turn, a lot of competitors still neck-and-neck!'

'Nine. Thou Shalt Not Bear False Witness.'

'Basically, lie.'

'We can take care of this one quick. Anyone here who *hasn't* lied?'

No hands.

'And Ten is covet,' says Nadler, finally setting down the two sheets of Commandments.

'Which we all have, like I said,' Steinerman reminds them. '*Ipso facto.* Your neighbor's house, his Ferrari, his hot wife, his new grill, his pool table, his infinity pool – anything.'

'That's all of us.'

'Maybe not the rabbi. What do you say, Rabbi Meyerson, have you coveted?'

The rabbi squints, angles his head in a contemplative pause, trying to decide.

'OK, we'll give it to you, Rabbi. If you're on the fence like that, then you haven't really coveted,' says Nadler.

'So who wins? Who broke the most commandments?' asks Steinerman eagerly.

Lerner, keeping count, doesn't hesitate.

'Three-way tie. Nadler, Steinerman, and Solomon, assuming they didn't honor father and mother – which I personally feel is a generally safe assumption – broke nine out of ten.'

'Way to go, minyan!'

Exuberant hi-fives from Nadler, Steinerman and Solomon, slapping their palms together in the center of the minyan circle.

'You're only missing murder,' says Lerner.

'There's still time,' says Nadler. 'Who wants to make it a perfect ten? Anyone?'

'Or maybe one of us *is* ten for ten?' says Rosen. 'And is pulling a number nine about it?'

'Number nine?'

'Bearing false witness. Jesus, Steinerman, you forgot nine already?'

'And at the other end,' says Lerner, 'Rabbi Meyerson has broken only two.'

'Whoa, Rabbi, impressive.'

'The holiest among us. The holy of holies, blessed be He.'

'Yeah, big surprise,' says Rosen.

'And for next time, an assignment for all of us, including me,' says Rabbi Meyerson.

'Which is?'

'What's a good eleventh commandment? What did Moses miss?' A smile, as he adjusts his yarmulke. 'Until next time.'

They rise, fold the chairs, head into the sunlight of the yard.

Simon Nadler strutting proudly. Nine for ten. Although it's an achievement he won't be sharing with his dad Herman.

Saul Solomon. Ten for ten. And definitely keeping it to himself.

DISCO BALL

IT's ALWAYS JUST A FEW MINUTES after 10:30 lights out. And it lasts only a few minutes at best. A brief exchange – just a safe, careful joke or two – to make them both comfortable enough to fall asleep. Matt Sorcher understands – Mighty Mouth is guarded now; careful, measuring every utterance, hyper-conscious of his words being high-value targets. Matt knows that's why Mighty Mouth said no to joining the minyan – to everyone's disappointment and dismay. But to Matt it's obvious: he can't risk being quoted. He needs to lie low. Stay out of the news cycle. Sink back unobtrusively into the fabric of prison life, avoid notice, provide no excuse for attention – or risk a longer sentence. The folding chair of welcome to the Pisk has been removed from the minyan circle.

For many of them Otisville provides, oddly, a temporary

safety and cover, a time-out from the world. But Mighty Mouth seems only to experience the moment of safety and cover and time-out in these few minutes of darkness before sleep.

'Tonight, I've got Good & Plenty,' Mighty Mouth whispers quietly.

'Mmmmm,' Matt replies. They both know he doesn't. It's just an imaginary moment of return to Camp Wikiwandi.

'Obviously, you remember,' Matt says into the dark.

'Sure do,' says Mighty Mouth.

That same accent. Older, deeper, familiar from TV of course, but the same kid in the bunk near Matt. Wearier of course, world-worn, a lifetime passed, but still him.

'Don't worry, I'm not gonna wake you to go see Don and Dawn down at the boathouse,' says Mighty Mouth.

Don and Dawn. Matt Sorcher's snort of recognition carries into the dark. Mighty Mouth acknowledges it with his own mild snort in response.

'Think they know we went to camp together a hundred years ago?' Matt whispers.

'I've been wondering that since I heard you'd be my cellie,' comes the disembodied reply. 'Maybe they did their homework, maybe it's a total accident. But I didn't want to ask and open a can of worms. So I kept my mouth shut. That's why I pretended not to know you when they brought me in here.' That round-sounding, slow, deliberate way of talking. A little dumb-sounding, even when delivering legalese, or a threat. A little like Eeyore, the cartoon donkey, Matt thinks.

'You mind bunking with one of the most hated men in America?' More words coming at Matt in the dark.

'Hey, to me, I'm bunking with eleven-year-old Mighty Mouth.'

'Who was hated even then,' he says.

Matt feels himself smile into the cell's blackness. 'I'm taking the fifth on that,' he says.

Another snort of laughter.

They listen to the dark together. Someone snoring down the hall. 'Sounds like a counselor,' Mighty Mouth whispers, and again Matt can't help but smile.

'I bet your sentencing deal's a pretty thick document,' Matt says.

'Lots of conditions and negotiations,' comes the reply. 'Can't profit in any way from my notoriety for thirty-six months.' *Notoriety* – the five syllables seem to bounce around in his mouth. 'The judge warned me not to discuss anything with fellow inmates, since prosecutions and investigations are ongoing. But I'm starting to make notes for a memoir.'

Of course, thinks Matt. Post-incarceration income stream. Book and movie. Goes without saying.

'For now, I can pretty much only talk to you.'

Matt presumes that he means like this – whispering here in the dark, after curfew. Not shooting the breeze in the dayroom.

'Say whatever you want,' Matt tells him. 'It stays right here. Like I'm a priest. You can't see me, and I can't see you.'

A pause. And then:

'I still picture Dawn,' Matt says suddenly into the dark. The nighttime confessional goes both ways.

'Hey, who doesn't?'

'I still don't know how I feel about you bringing me to the waterfront with you.'

'Hey, I chose you. You should be flattered.'

'You chose me because you knew I'd do whatever you said. You knew I'd go along. You were preying on my weakness.'

A pause. 'I guess,' says Mighty Mouth. 'But I was eleven. I didn't really understand what I was doing.'

Which sounds honest enough. Or is Matt just falling into his trap again?

'But you understand more now?' Matt says.

A pause.

'Not really,' says Mighty Mouth.

Matching snorts into the dark. Both of them. A duet of sarcastic connection.

'Get some sleep,' Matt tells him. 'You don't want to confess all your sins at once.'

'No danger of that.' One more snort into the dark. And then: 'Good night, Sorcher. I'm glad it's you.'

'Good night, Mighty.'

I'm not so glad it's you.

A disco ball spins above them, slashing five hundred kids into prisms of color and motion. The bass and drums pound against their temples, burrow into their chests, vibrate against the gym walls around them. Tenth graders from all Five Towns are gathered here at Lawrence High. They'll attend many more events like this in the course of their awakening social lives – proms, parties, after-hours clubs, places designed to welcome them but also pleasurably disorient them, to lift them out of their circumscribed existence of homework and organized sports and obedience, but for many of them, this is their first such experience.

Boys in sport coats and slacks and expensive wild-colored sneakers, girls in slinky tight dresses, glitter sprinkled fashionably on their faces and shoulders, it is what Matt Sorcher now recognizes as a surging sea of hormones, the Five Towns like five hormone-stocked rivers flowing into a roiling churning gymnasium sea, a hormone festival, an adrenal summit, but in tenth grade, he had no understanding of that; he was shy, overwhelmed, and he tried to hang out with the one kid he knew from summer camp, Mighty Mouth.

They'd both grown almost a foot in the five years since Wikiwandi. Matt was lean as a pole, while Mighty Mouth had filled in and muscled up, and at first they didn't recognize each other.

'Whoa. Mighty Mouth? Is that you?'

'Sorcher? Whoa, look at you! You're a friggin' stick!'

In their blue blazers, they shook hands, in a quick little mimicry of adulthood. Then stood looking around.

They'd been camp bunkmates five summers ago, and shared some adventures, but the truth was, they'd never been very close. The problem being, no matter how hard Matt tried, he just didn't like the guy, and no matter how hard Mighty Mouth tried, he couldn't really get himself to like Matt. The good thing was, they both seemed to know it and accept it.

But they did remember each other. So, for a few minutes, here in this disorienting space, they could pretend to be friends. So at first Mighty Mouth accepted Matt into his shadow.

'Lot of talent here,' Mighty Mouth points out, his voice

now changed, deepened into a menacing growl, looking around at girls from all five towns. '*Fresh* talent.' Girls neither of them had ever seen. Hundreds of them. All dressed to impress. And it was working.

A tight group of five girls strutted by them, and the one in the middle was, well, to Matt's mind at that moment – the best and most succinctly he could put it for a boy's tenth grade brain – *otherworldly hot*. Beautiful in an absurdly perfect, picture-book way, seemingly pore-less skin, just the right amount of Long Island tan, a chest that invited exploration, naturally sexy way beyond the situation.

Without a word to Matt, without any hesitation or even thought, it seemed, Mighty Mouth left his side and headed straight for her.

Matt Sorcher never saw Mighty Mouth again – until he saw him on TV, and then he showed up in the same prison cell, thirty years later.

Matt did however see that same girl, later that night.

She was alone. At some point abandoned by her friends, apparently. Sitting on the curb, sobbing. Curled into herself self-protectively. In the parking lot light, Matt could see that the hem of her dress was muddy. Sobbing like that, she no longer looked so otherworldly hot. That's what his tenth-grade brain was telling him, he's embarrassed to recall now: that she no longer looked quite so hot.

He'd wanted to go over, ask why she was crying, see if he could do anything for her. But even though she was not quite as hot-looking, she was still way too intimidatingly hot for him to talk to.

Matt doesn't know what happened, if anything, between that girl and Mighty Mouth that night.

But he knows that something must have. And whatever it was, that night wasn't the end of it.

Because that hot girl eventually became Mighty Mouth's mistress.

Still to this day, according to Nadler, and Adler, and Rosen.

'The mistress thing. Still common practice in that crowd.'

'The mistress – that's what these guys do.'

'Practically expected for executives in that business. Lots of nice apartments to keep a woman.'

'No one knows if his wife knows or not – if that's just part of the arrangement. Just part of the lifestyle.'

It had been surprising to Matt. For a moment or two. And then, not surprising at all.

THE SIXTH COMMANDMENT: FURTHER READING

WHEN THEY ALL LOOKED AROUND at each other at the Sixth Commandment – *Thou Shalt Not Murder* – all of them eyeing each other before dissolving into laughter, Saul Solomon laughed right along, and didn't say anything, of course.

He's in for tax evasion, for fudging on the Solomon Automotive tax returns. He's in here for the warehouse fire and the insurance scam. That's what the world knows. That's what his fellow *minyanim* know. That's the big, lovable, short-legged, barrel-chested Saul they know.

And nobody knows – nobody – that in the course of running Solomon Automotive, he had to murder three people.

He presumes they'd see murder – even one murder, much less three – as a big dividing line between him and everyone else here. But he doesn't think of it that way. He just sees it as a somewhat more extreme version of criminality – of what they're all here for. Hey, they're all criminals, to varying degrees. He knows there might be something fundamentally wrong with his seeing it that way. He recognizes that. But hey, what can he tell you?

One thing he's noticed about himself that he finds kind of interesting: he's never given the three murders much thought. Not before, and not afterward. They were just three people who happened to get in the way, that he had to get rid of. Push to the side. He would have avoided it if he could – no sane person *wants* to murder people – but he had no other good options. A junior accountant who asked too many questions, who was getting ready to be a backroom hero; an immigrant cleaning woman who saw what she shouldn't have one night; a waiter who overheard what he shouldn't have. The murders were spaced out, in time and place – different locations, different contexts – so no one would necessarily connect them. In fact, Saul is their only connection at all, and it's unlikely that anyone will ever figure that out. Possible, he supposes, but they haven't done it yet.

Three murders. He always thinks of the three murders when they talk about Marty Adler's three marriages. 'Not all at once, Marty, you can't have three all at once!' 'One at a time, Marty,' the other guys have said to Marty. If you ask Saul, Marty Adler kind of murdered all three marriages by getting greedy. Any one of the marriages might have survived. But he's getting off track.

Right now, ironically, he's got one of the shorter sentences here. The least left to go. Two years. The other *minyanim* have even started teasing him about it. Two years to go: 'A cakewalk, Saul.' 'Like law school, or junior college.' 'Or the National Guard, or the Peace Corps, or Teach America.' Picturing Saul in all those roles, apparently.

They don't understand of course, that while it's now just two years left, which seems easy to them, it's kind of a tense two years. All three murder cases are still open and active. State police could crack any of those cases anytime. If he can just make the two years, he can walk out of here, grab about two million bucks he's stashed, go under the knife for a new face, disappear, set up somewhere overseas, start over.

Point is, he knows he doesn't really belong here. He doesn't really fit in. He's supposed to be in some other, tougher prison, in with the spree killers, drug kingpins, neo-Nazis – the kind of prison that, let's face it, he might not survive: his paunch, his bad back and knees, his shiny bald head, would make him a target. Here, though, all that makes him fit in. Or look like he fits in.

So he's doing his time here. All his time, he hopes. Paying his debt to society. Just two more years of minimum security for three murders, if it works out. A lenient sentence, ok, but a sentence nonetheless, jail time, incarceration.

Maybe he'll even change a little while he's here. Get rehabilitated. But he knows he can't really. How can you really rehabilitate yourself from committing three murders? Say to the world and yourself you'll do better, act better, be kinder, be a better person from now on? Come on. That ship has sailed.

He can barely picture any of the three of them, which he finds interesting too. He knows that could be just some human protective mechanism, like when the pain of childbirth or the agony of a kidney stone kind of retreats, so you can handle another kidney stone or stick it into your wife to have another kid. He can barely picture any of them, but in fairness he didn't know any of them too well to begin with, so that might explain it right there.

He doesn't feel any remorse, he doesn't think. Sure, if there was a way to avoid killing any of them he would have. So not wanting to have to kill them – is that what they mean by remorse?

In a sense, he's hiding out here in Otisville. Hiding from the police, in prison. Hiding from both state and local authorities. Hiding in plain sight. Wearing the disguise of lesser charges. Camouflaged in financial fraud, in false insurance claims. Crimes which were interesting enough to the authorities that it qualifies as a pretty effective, distracting disguise.

He participates fully in the minyan. Throws himself into all the discussions as much as he can. It's the best disguise of all.

He's staying hidden from everyone. The detectives still investigating the three cases. The guards here. His fellow prisoners. Just stay hidden. That's Saul Solomon's morning and evening prayer. *Two more years. Just two more years.* Should be easy.

POETRY 101

THE WRITING WORKSHOP.

Like yoga classes, group therapy, and lending libraries, a staple of federal prison.

Originally provided to teach basic and remedial writing skills, to encourage self-expression and reflection, to foster an appetite for further education and self-improvement.

One of the few federal facilities which did *not* offer writing workshops was Otisville Correctional. Ironic, since many Otisville inmates would eventually be penning tell-alls (some that were dangerously close to how-tos), making publishing deals, and selling the movie rights to their life stories.

But in the past, such highly profitable Otisville literary output had unleashed considerable cynical commentary from the tabloid media and outrage from the public at large, which embarrassed and annoyed DA offices to no end, so after a couple of fresh million-dollar advances to high-profile inmates, prosecutors learned their lesson, and began to write into subsequent sentencing agreements strict rules governing memoirs and prison writing in general, holding out placement at Otisville itself as a bargaining chip – *if you want Otisville, then you agree to no publication of memoirs or thinly veiled 'fiction' or any prose for profit for the duration of your prison term.* Otisville was enough of a lure that prospective prisoners readily agreed. The ACLU promptly challenged those agreements on the grounds of freedom of speech, but so far the Justice Department and the Bureau of Prison had prevailed, holding any prospective court proceedings at bay in a blizzard of legal motions. It was, after all, only a tactic to forestall the inevitability of prisoners profiting from their story. In any case, they were not about to encourage those pursuits and hone the prisoners' literary skills with writing workshops.

All of this arcane history – of writing workshops, Otisville, the ACLU, all of it—was well known to Deborah Liston, a faculty member of the SUNY Buffalo Department of English, which had repeatedly proposed writing workshops for Otisville, and were disappointed by such sentencing agreements, but understood the rationale.

Until Professor Liston offered an ingenious counter-proposal.

A variant that, her fellow professors argued earnestly, had the same rehabilitative elements, but no commercial endgame such as the Justice Department feared.

A variant that was purer, less commercially viable, and would self-select in its appeal to only the most self-reflective, contemplative, spiritually focused prison audience.

She proposed a weekly poetry workshop.

In their monthly operations meeting, Otisville's warden, chaplain, and other prison officials discussed it, unable to suppress laughter and derision, imagining the poems from certain inmates and, thus loosened and amused, voted to allow it.

'Poetry!' said Simon Nadler, when informed that the first workshop would be offered this coming Monday.

'You gotta be kidding me,' said Marty Adler.

'Class will be taught by Professor Liston from SUNY,' Rabbi Meyerson informed them. Adding, after a pause, 'Professor Liston is a well-recognized and highly regarded young poet. Has published several volumes of poetry, been runner-up for the Bollingen Prize and on the short list once already for a Pulitzer.' And then, after a dramatic pause, 'And, by the way, a woman.'

'Rabbi, is she hot?' asks Nadler, point-blank.

'I have no idea. I only know her by her literary reputation.'

'A woman,' says Marty Adler, ruminatively. There was only a smattering of token female guards, and some female kitchen staff – Eastern European *meiskeit*, as the inmates said. Apart from those exceptions, Otisville was an all-male world.

'A *young* woman,' says Nadler. 'Bet that was part of the discussion at the warden's monthly meeting.'

✡

Fifteen prisoners' names are selected at random. Fifteen men file into the workshop classroom Monday morning.

One look at Professor Liston, and Sam Roth (illegal arms sales to Kazahkstan, eight years), and Greg Lerner (illegal tax shelters, fraudulent Caribbean land investments) though lucky enough to be selected – file right out. No pretense. 'I'm not voluntarily spending any time with *that*,' says Roth.

Professor Liston is five feet tall, with thick glasses – a scholar who has clearly spent her career so far deep in the research stacks.

'No, no , no, no…' Greg Lerner mutters on his way out.

Thirteen students are left.

'So. I'm Professor Liston. Welcome to Poetry 101. It's taken our staff at SUNY a lot of work to get to this stage, to convince all the parties involved, to get all the approvals needed to have this course finally accepted, so I'm very excited to be here, and I hope you are too.'

'Normally on the first day of a workshop, I'd go around the room and learn a little about each of my students – your names, a little something about yourself.' She smiles. 'But here, I feel that's a little too nosy.'

'And besides,' says Abe Rosen, 'you've been briefed on each of us already, right? They wouldn't let a woman in here without thoroughly briefing her.' Calling her bluff.

'Even a woman who looks like you,' says Nadler.

Professor Liston ignores all this. Pretends to ignore it. Makes a show of ignoring it. *See how I'm ignoring it? How I barely notice?*

'What are they paying you?' says Adler. Cutting to the chase.

Professor Liston smiles. 'I'm not doing it for the money.'

'Yeah, yeah, sure,' says Adler, 'but still – what are they paying you?'

She ignores this too and continues. 'I know that for many of you, a condition of your incarceration is no memoir writing or op-eds or profiting in prose form in any way for the duration of your sentence. So I made the case for poetry. And while we will begin, as you might expect, with some poetry reading of some of the American greats – Wallace Stevens, Elizabeth Bishop, Walt Whitman, Emily Dickinson – before turning to the composition of your own poetry, we need to first have an understanding, up front, about what constitutes prose and what constitutes poetry. Any thoughts about some guardrails for us? This isn't abstract. I need to demonstrate to Warden Edwards and other Bureau of Prison authorities that as a class you have some understanding of the difference. That we've together created some literary rules that we'll abide by. So…any thoughts on the differences between poetry and prose?'

There is silence at first.

'Sentences versus phrases?' offers Saul Solomon unsurely.

'No punctuation?' says Abe Rosen.

She smiles. 'Those are a good start. But they are only about the appearance on the page, aren't they? The superficials.'

'What about facts versus feelings?' says Matt Sorcher.

She purses her lips. 'OK. Interesting.'

'But wait. I'm confused by this,' says Adler. 'I mean, if the Pisk over there writes a book of poems in here, publishers will clamor for it as soon as he's out, no matter how bad it is, so it doesn't matter that it's poetry, not prose, he'll be profiting, and defeating the terms of his plea agreement.'

The Pisk (Professor Liston quickly realizes it's their nickname for the celebrity prisoner) is seated in the back row, next to a small, shy, heavily bearded and studious-looking inmate named Jonathan Levy. (Antiquities scholar. Stole antique maps and atlases from university collections across the world. Five years) The Pisk, as they call him, made the lottery cut for inclusion in the class and is going ahead with it, surprising everyone. Minyan no, but poetry yes. 'So maybe I have to write *bad* poems,' he says from the back row. 'So bad nobody wants them, and then I'm not violating the terms.' Professor Liston can tell that Levy chose the back row to remain as invisible as possible. She fears that the Pisk is there for the exact opposite reason – as a vantage of maximal disruption.

'But the worse his poems are, the more everyone will want them. If they're good poems, they're not gonna be as interested,' says Abe Rosen. 'If they're really bad, that's when they'll be bidding on them, running them on front pages.'

'I think *anything* the Pisk writes, they're gonna want,' says Nadler, crossing his arms firmly, as if there's no real argument.

'Well, anything *any* of you write, I will be collecting at the end of class, so as not to risk violating any prior agreements,' says Professor Liston.

'So our poems are kinda like sand sculpture,' says Rosen. 'Just disappearing with the tide.'

'Poetic already, Rosen. Trying to get in good with her. Teacher's pet,' says Nadler.

'Like writing with sidewalk chalk,' adds Adler, 'washing away with the rain,' throwing in his own metaphor to one-up Rosen.

'Yes,' acknowledges Professor Liston, 'but I think you'll find this guaranteed impermanence very freeing. You can say anything. No one sees it but your classmates and me. It's confidential. It goes no further than this classroom.'

'Maybe *you'll* try to sell it,' Mel Salzman accuses, suspiciously. (Rock festivals, 1.5 million in advance ticket sales, no signed acts, no venue). 'An Otisville Omnibus. Even more valuable and desirable 'cause it's been smuggled out!'

Professor Liston shakes her head. 'That's not happening.'

'But if we can't eventually sell it, then what's the point?' moans Adler.

In answer, Professor Liston looks out the window, silently. As if simply waiting for the objections to cease. For their fevered brains to simply calm. To reset. The strategy works.

'I'm going to pass out a section of this poem from Walt Whitman. Song of Myself.'

'Song of Myself. I like the guy's focus,' says Nadler.

And so Poetry 101 begins.

Ninety minutes later, at the end of class:

'Here's your first exercise. I know this will surprise you a little. But I want you to each write a poem about your crime.'

'What?' says Abe Rosen.

'About your crime, specifically.'

'A poem about fraudulent bank applications?' asks Nadler.

'Yes,' she says. 'Because this way, it's a poem that is uniquely yours. Uniquely *you*. One that, when read aloud, your classmates can say, 'Oh that's Simon Nadler. Or, oh, that's Abe Rosen.'

She confronts their puzzled expressions head-on. 'Because you know your crime. Because no one knows it as well as you. No prosecutor's file, no court reporter, no judge or jury can lay out the truth of it like you can. Because no one's thought about it more than you,' she says. 'You can write about how you did it. But I'd prefer you to touch more on *why* – what were your thoughts and feelings about it, as you committed it, before, afterward.'

'What's the point of this exercise?' asks Saul Solomon.

'It will start getting to your unique voice.'

'I would think you'd want us to get past our crimes, leave them behind,' says Adler.

'Yes, but the best way past them, is to understand them deeply. I believe that's a crucial step in letting them go.'

'White collar crime poems,' says Nadler.

'New genre,' says Adler.

'Everyone's got a pad of paper and a pen, right? Let's take the next fifteen minutes and see how you do.'

The room goes quiet. Suddenly, like obedient schoolboys, they stop their banter, bend to the task. Silently staring at the blank pad, eyes searching aimlessly around the room – and then, after a few minutes, each of them begins to write something.

✡

While Poetry 101 was a new wrinkle in prison life for a handful of the inmates, it was, paradoxically, a demonstration of life at Otisville continuing much as always. The class's introduction showed, by contrast, how little change there ever was.

The same meals. The same discussions. Moment by moment. Decade after decade.

Each inmate serving out his sentence in a serene predictability of minutes and hours and days and weeks and months, previously discrete and noticeable segments of time now melting into one another. Time, which is an enemy, an antagonist when a prisoner first arrives, becoming a familiar, trusted companion, a fellow cellmate, soon enough.

Reading, rest, food, talk, a modicum of exercise, a dearth of genuine contemplation. An unvarying pattern whose unvarying nature was thought by many to be the most therapeutic aspect of an Otisville stay. The shift of seasons outside the windows. The breezes. The stillness. The gentle gears of the cosmos. The monk-like calm. The pared-down existence – something new, something alluring in its own way, for each of the felons. The routine providing a naturally meditative state, even for those who could never focus or be still long enough to meditate otherwise.

Slowly, inexplicably, and faintly at first, these measured, quiet, predictable patterns began to change.

Faintly at first – then markedly, profoundly – and irreversibly.

No one understood why at first.

But soon enough they did.

As soon as they understood that it was not a matter of why, but who.

PART 2

A prison is a world unto itself, with its own rules and culture, which can be neither ascertained nor understood except by experience
– Alfred Dreyfus, *Devil's Island*, 1896

NO RUGELACH

THE BEGINNING IS BARELY noticeable.

Unless, like Nadler, you really love rugelach.

'No rugelach,' says Ezra Kleinman at lunch, passing their table, sharing the mournful news. (Ezra Kleinman. Mail fraud, seven years. Founder of the Silver Star Charities, providing health care and education funding for the children of our veterans. Enticing brochures. Powerful testimonials. A patriotic way to say thank you to our selfless, deserving vets. An impressive board of advisors, from government, academia and entertainment. Silver Star Charities, however, was a PO box across from Kleinman's apartment. And conveniently close to Kleinman's bank. Which first reported the charity's banking irregularities.)

'What do you mean, no rugelach,' says Nadler, indignantly.

As if Kleinman is to blame.

'Read my lips,' says Kleinman. 'No new rugelach.'

No rugelach? No way.

'Svetlana, Magda, Trisha, what happened to the rugelach?' Nadler asks, bursting into the cafeteria kitchen, polling the Slavic kitchen staff. They shrug indifferently, as Nadler fully expected, so he waits to ask the chef, Dmitri, the rotund heavy-bearded Slav who is an undiscovered culinary genius, as far as the prisoners are concerned. 'Where's the rugelach, Dmitri? There's always rugelach.'

Dmitri smiles, shrugs too. 'No ingredients. I cannot make rugelach without ingredients.'

'But…did you not order the ingredients?'

'Oh, I order them, just like as always. But,' he shrugs, 'no delivery.'

'No delivery?'

He struggles to correct Nadler. 'Yes, delivery come like always no problem. But no honey, no cinnamon, no walnuts, no chocolate. Everything else there. Except ingredients for my rugelach.' He furrows his brow. 'Someone don't to like rugelach, I guess.'

'Who?'

Dmitri shrugs.

'Did you complain?'

'To who? I don't know who. I write weekly order, and I am always getting order. But this time, no.' And he shrugs again. 'Rugelach ingredients, they is just…not there.'

Nadler returns to the table.

'So?'

'No ingredients.'

'Why?'

'Doesn't know.'

'Small thing, Simon. Don't worry. We know you love it. We know you count on it. Maybe next week.'

No rugelach.

And no real explanation.

WHO AM I REALLY?
BY SIMON NADLER

I am Stanley Aronoski, wealthy real estate investor
I am Chris Allen, from third grade with Miss Lester
I am Paul Whittaker, a name from the obits
I am Marvin Albertson, my cousin with zits
I am Lars Ohlgotaaseonnu, a name too crazy to steal.
I am all of them; I am none of them.
I am fake; but I am real.
As real as the paper I am written on, that can be crumpled into the trash.
As real as the same paper that can instead be stamped, approved, and loaned the cash.
I am all.
I am none.
But ONE is in NONE, don't you see?
A man rich in identity?

Or devoid of personality?
I am a loan.
I am alone.
I am them.
I am me.
But ME is in THEM, don't you see?
A man of proven
Identity.
Yet merely a legal
Entity.
Who am I really?
I am who I say.
Depending on
The time of day.
Who am I really?
I am who I am.
Depending on
The kind of scam.

NADLER FINISHES READING HIS POEM aloud, looks up at Professor Liston.

Professor Liston smiles. 'So…a poem about your multiple identities that landed you here. Leading to the larger question, who am I really. Very good.'

'Thanks.'

'Very good at framing the question, Simon. But I don't feel like you've really tried to answer it. Who am I really, you ask, but you don't even try to say.'

'Well, I'm just trying to be poetic here,' he shrugs.

'But *who am I really* – that's an existential question. A question for each of us to contemplate as we hear your poem.'

Nadler tilts his head, looks at Professor Liston. 'Yeah, but that's not what I meant.'

'It's not?'

'No, I just meant like, look how good I am at fooling people with all these identities. Like being a master of disguise. That's all.'

'So, you didn't mean this to ask questions about identity?'

He looks at her, uncomprehending. 'Identity? Who am I really? The answer is, I'm Nadler. Five years for fraud. Trying to get along in a poetry seminar.'

Professor Liston is silent. Impassive. She senses that he's only pretending not to understand. Playing dumb in order to needle her, to annoy her.

'I'm Nadler,' he reiterates. 'Prisoner 289544, State of NY. But I was pretty good at fooling bankers into thinking I was someone else, wasn't I? Until I wasn't.' He looks around the room. 'Sorry it doesn't mean more.'

'So…the poem is about your…pride?' She pauses on the word, hearing it, trying to comprehend it for herself, 'Your pride in your multiple identities?'

Nadler shrugs. 'Well, yeah, I guess.'

Professor Liston nods. Trying to understand. Needing to shift in her understanding. 'Simon, is there some other way to explore your feelings about your crime? Can you explore some other approach to the poem?'

'She's giving you another chance,' Abe Rosen calls out from across the room. 'Nadler fucks up. Take two.'

'Sure,' Nadler shrugs. Then, an impish, mischievous smile. 'Sure, I can try it again.'

NO BLINTZES

THE NEXT WEEK, THERE IS still no rugelach.

And no blintzes.

'Dmitri, what is going on?'

Dmitri shrugs. 'I try to find someone talk to. Order sheets is picked up like always.' Dmitri shrugs and smiles again. Clearly this inexplicable alteration in the routine doesn't trouble him. It seems perfectly natural and acceptable to a son of the Soviet bloc.

'This kind of Soviet shit – disappearing ingredients – it doesn't really bother you, does it?' says Nadler.

Dmitri shrugs.

'Sudden shortage, no explanation. Makes you feel at home, huh?'

'Thou Shalt Have No Rugelach,' mutters Marty Adler, when Nadler gets back to the table.

'That Shalt Have No Blintzes,' adds Phil Steinerman.

'Hope we don't keep learning these new commandments,' says Rosen.

They spin their forks idly over their trays. They know that this deprivation would warrant no sympathy in any broader context, in the wider world. In fact, it would have the reverse effect. *Otisville Inmates No Longer Have Rugelach or Blintzes.* The outcry would be over the fact that they had them in the first place. Otisville inmates don't have their rugelach or their blintzes. Big fuckin' deal.

FAMILY MAN,
BY MARTY ADLER

I love my families. Love them all.
Molly, Minnie, Sarah, Paul.
Little Julie, little Saul.
The Jane Adlers who are short.
The Marcia Adlers who are tall.
The Sarah Adler girls who love the mall.
The Marcia Adler boys who love softball.
But then of course, I took a fall.
I hit the wall. My engine stalled.
And soon I heard, 'What chutzpah, what gall!'
'What cohones, some set of balls!'
But I love my family, love them all.
A family man, for once and for all.

ADLER FINISHES READING AND LOOKS UP.

'It's a love poem, I guess,' says Adler, shrugging. 'A simple little love poem.'

'That's it?' says Abe Rosen. 'That's all you've got to say about being married to three women at once?'

Adler shrugs. 'I love them all.'

'Professor Liston, make Adler think more deeply. Make Adler be more reflective,' says Rosen, annoyed.

Knowing, as they all do, that she can't do that. That that is a task beyond the classroom and the parameters of Poetry 101.

The next week – no rugelach, no blintzes, and no Dmitri.

'What do you mean, no Dmitri?'

'Gone,' says Seth Levinson (Fake foreclosure notices. Issued months before the mortgage-holding bank does it. Did it to retirees in Missouri and Arkansas. Repossessed the house and flipped it to real estate investors before any bank knew about it. Did it on twenty properties, until he was caught. Five years.)

'Wait. To another job? Dmitri was so happy here,' says Abe Rosen.

'Transferred to another prison. No explanation given,' says Levinson.

'Thou Shalt Have No Dmitri,' says Phil Steinerman.

The rugelach, the blintzes. Then the chef creating them.

A cruelly logical progression. As if to show there is an awareness behind it.

The quiet disappearance of rugelach, and blintzes, and the chef who created them. Mere precursors, obvious signals, to what comes next.

'You guys hear the latest?' Ezra Kleinman asks them cheerfully.

What now, Ezra, upbeat prophet of doom?

'The kosher deli is about to be eliminated.'

'What?!'

'Budget cuts. Just a small part of a massive Bureau of Prisons re-org, according to Macy's and Porno,' Kleinman tells them. Macy's and Porno. Nicknames for two of the prison guards – both ironic, as is the minyan's custom for guard nicknames, like the utterly average-sized Big Willie. Macy's is rail-thin, so they named him in honor of the fat Thanksgiving Day Parade blimps. Porno is, in fact, a completely straightlaced evangelical Christian.

'The disappearance of rugelach. Blintzes. Then Dmitri. Then his deli. It's all a little Kafkaesque,' says Abe Rosen gloomily.

'More than a little,' says Marty Adler.

'Chef Dmitri had it down to a science,' says Rosen – almost mournful, eulogizing. 'Great taste, no waste.'

Greg Lerner's math brain weighs in. 'In incremental expenses, that kosher deli costs this prison nothing. I bet no one's even looked at that.'

'But it's symbolic,' says Abe Rosen. 'It smacks of privilege. It's optics. It's politics.'

'Who's doing this? It's starting to feel like someone has it in for us,' Nadler says, and they all stop, and are silent, and look at one another, because they all realize at once. Because it's suddenly so obvious.

'The Pisk.'

'The fuckin' Pisk.'

'The Pisk is doing it?'

'No, the Pisk *being* here. It's being done 'cause he's here.'

'If X is the Pisk's arrival date, and Y is changes at Otisville, it's pretty easy to solve for X,' says Lerner, the math guy.

And Abe Rosen's eyes go wide, and he looks around at the rest of them. 'Do you think this so-called re-org, these so-called budget cuts that Macy's and Porno were told about, are only to disguise the changes going on here? To make everyone just accept these changes?'

'Disguising it with bureaucracy, with policy – but getting even with The Pisk,' says Nadler.

'Yeah, getting even with the Pisk,' says Marty Adler.

'Revenge,' says Matt Sorcher, more to himself than aloud. But he feels a shock of sudden comprehension course through him, an understanding so deep, so sudden and thorough, he experiences it physically.

'What do you mean, revenge? Revenge on someone who's already in prison? That makes no sense. Who would?...'

They go silent again. Look at each other. All realizing, again in the same moment, what is happening. All realizing in the next instant, what Sorcher had only a moment ago.

'Revenge,' says Sorcher again. This time more definitively, fully comprehending, the comprehension washing over him now.

'Before the guy leaves office. Before he loses his power to do any of this,' says Rosen.

'And if people see him, suspect him of getting rid of

privileges for prisoners – all the better in the eyes of his base,' says Nadler.

'Is that possible?'

'Sure. And we're caught in the crossfire.'

They are all silent for a moment. Absorbing it.

'The word has to get out,' says Abe Rosen, 'what's going on here.' They're prohibited from communicating with reporters without prior clearance – which would never be provided if the purpose is to criticize their prison treatment – and their family visit conversations are closely monitored. But certainly there would be ways to leak the information – passing notes to family members, a whisper while hugging a spouse, etc.

'Oh, you mean alert the world, no rugelach? No blintzes?' says Marty Adler, smiling wearily.

'You don't think it's newsworthy that they're closing our kosher deli?' says Rosen.

'Kosher Cuts,' says Nadler, smiling. 'Huge type on the front page of the *Post*.'

'A Way Of Life Goes Under the Knife.'

'Say Kaddish for This Kitchen.'

'Hold the Tongue.'

'Last of the Latkes.'

'Deli De-Lighted.'

'Prisoners Get Their Last (Kosher) Meal.'

They joked, but many of them knew what the joking was. What it didn't really mask. Their discomfort, their anxiety, with what they were starting to imagine. To see clearly in front of them. Clear as night. The rules changing. More and more privileges taken away. Steadily. Systematically. With no direct explanation.

All their lives, they had never followed the rules. They were always rule-breakers, but rule-breaking always meant knowing, thoroughly understanding, the rules you were breaking. So, paradoxically, they liked rules. They liked knowing the rules in order to break them. And here the rules, the rules they hated and loved to hate, were suddenly disappearing…suspended…unclear…

SECOND THOUGHTS, BY SIMON NADLER

PRESUMABLY THE TITLE OF HIS POEM, thinks Professor Liston.

But beneath *Second Thoughts, by Simon Nadler*, Nadler has written nothing else.

Professor Liston frowns, looking at the sheet of paper. She turns it toward Nadler, and the class, so everyone can see that it's blank.

'So I guess you didn't get very far, Simon, in thinking about a second poem?'

He looks confused. 'Sure, I did. That's it. You're holding it.'

'That's the title, *Second Thoughts?*' asks Professor Liston, to confirm.

Nadler nods.

'But there's no poem below it. The sheet is blank.'

'But there *is* a poem below it, because the blankness *is* the poem.'

Professor Liston looks at the blank sheet again. 'I must be missing something,' she admits.

'No, that's the thing, you're missing nothing!' says Nadler. 'The title is *Second Thoughts*. And it's blank below it because I *have* no second thoughts. That's the point. As far as my fraud conviction goes, I have no second thoughts. As you can plainly see.'

Professor Liston looks again at the blank page, as if expecting something to appear.

'I have no second thoughts, no regrets, no shame about having committed it. I had to. I needed the money. I was cornered. I had no choice. Would I do it again, if given the chance to go back in time? Absolutely. The only difference is, I would be more careful to do a better job.'

'But Simon,' says Professor Liston, 'wanting to do a better job – that *is* a second thought, isn't it?'

He shrugs. 'OK, maybe. But you get the point of my poem, right? And if you get the point, if it's clear, then why make it longer? Why belabor it? It's the simplest way possible, an attention-getting way to say, I have no second thoughts. Why try to make it more? Why try to fill it in with needless wordiness? The absence of words is the presence of meaning.' He smiles a little at the sudden felicity of that.

Professor Liston looks at him. 'OK, you did the assignment, and you did it very cleverly, and I'm not going to quibble or argue with that. You've made your point. But the point you've made is not the point of writing this poetry, and not the point of this class. The point of our poetry is to reflect, to understand ourselves a little more deeply and fully. So I would just ask that, during the rest of today's class, you try to flesh out the poem a little. It's voluntary in here. Obviously you don't have to do anything at all. But I would just ask that over the next hour or so, you try to go a little further, see what happens.'

✡

At the end of class – reading and discussing William Carlos Williams' 'The Red Wheelbarrow' and some e.e.cummings – Professor Liston hasn't forgotten what she asked at the beginning. 'Simon, have you got anything?'

Much to her surprise, Nadler hands her a new sheet of paper.

A poem that, she can see, is arguably the exact reverse of what he'd done previously. No title. But this time, at least, a poem.

Not One Small Morsel of Remorseful.
Not One Small Spot of Maybe Not.
Not One Iota of Oughta, Or Shoulda,
No shameful nod to God or Buddha.
No genuflection, or reflection, or Zen.
Remorse?
How coarse.
I'd do it again.

'Multiple interior rhymes,' says Nadler proudly.

'So I see.' Professor Liston reads the poem over, looks up. 'So the same idea…'

'But expressed differently. Expressed more…like you asked,' says Nadler.

'But as far as the meaning… You've just basically doubled down,' she says.

'Pretty much,' says Nadler. 'But it's more of a poem, right? It's more of a poem, it's expressed there on the page, so that's good, right?'

'Right,' says Professor Liston, ambivalently. 'And when you say, *Remorse, How coarse!* That's a surprising line to me. Can you explain that a little?'

'Well, I mean it to be surprising. Remorse, like guilt, is generally seen as a kind of higher-up, more evolved emotion. But that's not how I see it. I see it as an emotion for ninnies, for children, for the frightened, for the mentally and emotionally impaired. I see it as an immature, unevolved emotion. So to me it's a coarse emotion. Low and basic on the emotional scale. Instead of *How coarse*, I also considered *off-course*. Like, *Remorse? Off course.* But I didn't know which was better. What do you think?'

'Simon, you're so witty, you have such command of the language…and yet you used your cleverness to simply double-down, to dig in to your point of view.' says Professor Liston. 'Finding a witty way to not explore your crime at all.'

Nadler shrugs. 'Pretty much.'

Regardless of literary quality or ability, Professor Liston is indeed getting to know them each through their poetry. This guy Nadler, for instance: He's one of those people who thrives on being adversarial. Who rises to a challenge. For now, she keeps her most acute observation to herself: that Simon Nadler, over the course of a handful of workshops, is actually becoming a better poet. Tighter, craftier, more focused, more mature. Go figure.

✡

'You guys heard the latest?' Ezra Kleinman stops at their table again. 'About the transfer?'

'Dmitri?'

Kleinman smirks. 'Not Dmitri.' He pauses. 'Ready for this?'

Kleinman looks at them. Overtly relishing the power of the moment. Waiting for the annoyance to cross their faces.

'You sure you're ready?'

'Christ, Ezra. Out with it.'

'Johnny Two Screens.'

'What?!'

'No!'

'You're kidding.'

A small, disconnected, confused chorus of shock and disbelief.

Johnny Two Screens.

The nickname bestowed in admiration on the day Warden Edwards made his Solomonic decision to allow two TVs in the day room, one for MSNBC and one for Fox.

Johnny Two Screens. A.K.A. John Edwards. The prison warden forever. *Their* warden.

In a reversal of conventional prison culture, the Otisville minyan does not assign nicknames to its members (there are explicit proscriptions against using nicknames in the Torah and Talmud) but they bestow them freely – and with consistent, though sometimes arcane, irony – on the gentile guards and staff. Beyond Big Willie, Macy's, and Porno, there are Shaky Jake (Jack Ventresca, a power lifter, a solid citizen, nothing even faintly shaky about him) Chatty

Chas (Charles DeBenedetto, who rarely utters a word), and Lightning Larry (Lawrence Robbins, a slow-moving, sweet-natured Filipino who is always a few steps behind – both literally and, they surmise, mentally.) But their naming convention is gladly broken to commemorate a deserving moment or memorable event.

Johnny Two Screens. Thirty-five years in criminal justice. A sweet-natured family man, quick with a bad joke, impossible to dislike. His office is filled with photos of his children and grandchildren, and shots of him grinning, holding the winning fish in various fishing contests. A mensch. St. John. What the hell?

'Where's he going?'

'No one seems to know. Elsewhere. The Land of Else.'

'You can be sure he didn't request it. The guy's whole life is around here.'

'So somebody's pushing him.'

'Maybe it's a forced retirement?'

'Same thing. Doesn't matter. Somebody's still pushing him out.'

'Johnny Two Screens. I can't believe it.'

'So there's a new warden,' says Ezra. Still standing there. Still obviously eager to dangle more news in front of the minyan. To hold center stage.

'What's his name?'

'Well, it's a secret.'

Oy. Fucking Ezra. Mister Drama. 'Come on. What are you talking about, Ezra?'

'I'm *telling* you. They're keeping it a secret! They're not saying his name. And get this: he might not even have an office on the premises, is what Macy's told me. He might oversee the prison remotely. No way to even get in touch with him. That's all apparently to ensure the safety of him and his family.'

'From us? We're *prisoners*, for Christsake. What are we gonna do? It's bullshit,' says Nadler.

'No name? No office? Maybe there is no warden,' says Rosen. 'If it's really about cost-cutting, maybe they're just saying this about cutting off our access, because maybe there is no actual warden.'

But clearly there is a new warden – phoning it in remotely from some featureless corporate park – because further edicts continue to come down.

Rabbi Meyerson dolefully informs them the next morning: 'Big Willie passed me this earlier.' He holds up the sheet of paper. 'New directive.'

'Oy. What now, Rabbi?'

Meyerson shakes his head, narrows his eyes. As if trying to squint into the universe. A rabbi puzzling with the ceaseless dilemmas of existence. 'It says the minyan must now be limited to eight.'

'What!' says Nadler.

'That's ridiculous!' says Adler.

'I tried to ask him about it, but Big Willie says he doesn't make the laws,' says Meyerson. 'He added that the administrative guy who handed him the directive doesn't make them either.'

'He's got that right, Rabbi,' says Abe Rosen, indignantly. 'He doesn't make the laws for the minyan, nobody makes them. God makes the law. And God says ten.'

'God may say ten, but the Federal Bureau of Prisons now says eight,' says Meyerson, looking at the printed sheet again.

'Totally arbitrary, isn't it? This doesn't cost the government a thing. It's not even a safety issue, although that's how they'll try to justify it. This is just a power thing. To show that, hey, we can.'

'It's all about the Pisk, isn't it? Making us all suffer because of the Pisk.'

'Maybe hoping we'll turn on him,' observes Rosen.

'Hey, maybe we will,' says Nadler, bitterly.

Rabbi Meyerson looks around at them mournfully: 'Big Willie told me to expect the minyan to go to six, then four, then two.'

'Oh, come on!'

'Two!' Saul Solomon pictures it, shaking his head.

'They're playing with us. They're trying to prove they have more power than God. Than our god. Probably just to annoy us.'

'A minyan is ten,' says Phil Steinerman. 'It has been for ten thousand years. Since the Second temple, right, Rabbi? Since time immemorial?'

'They're saying it's not,' says Nadler. 'They get a kick out of saying it's not.'

'So it's not enough for this administration to rewrite the federal rules protecting our natural resources and our national parkland and our immigrants,' says Abe Rosen. 'They're rewriting religious rules too.'

'Wait a second,' says Adler, noticing. 'Limiting minyan. Eliminating kosher food. Even the specific little treats – rugelach, blintzes. It's not just random privileges.

It's *Jewish* privileges.'

'Wait a second is right,' says Steinerman, who hadn't explicitly noticed it either. 'Could this really be about…' he wrinkles his face in mild distaste, confusion, seems genuinely puzzled by the thought: '…our being Jewish?'

For most of them, their Jewish heritage was either so distant, or so ingrained, they hadn't actually noticed the directives' common thread. To them, it was *prison* privileges being systematically removed, not *Jewish* ones.

'I've got to admit,' says Matt Sorcher, 'it never even occurred to me. Even this minyan limitation just seemed like some dumb bureaucratic adjustment.' Rugelach, blintzes, kosher deli – he's amazed that he never even noticed the theme.

'The senseless edicts,' says Abe Rosen, quietly.

'Like the Nuremberg laws,' says Steinerman, quietly.

'Little by little,' says Nadler ominously, 'decree by decree.'

They were dutifully serving their federal sentences, paying their debt to society, taking their lumps, when suddenly their Jewish past had reared up. In prison, no less.

The minyan services, the incantatory prayers, the Talmudic discussion – for most of them it's all just been something to do, a place to hang out. The ethos of survival for six thousand years in a cruel surrounding world, the inchoate vision of a fragile existence – it doesn't have much to do with their own individual experiences. After all, they brought on their own miseries themselves; they have only themselves to blame. As far as a cruel world goes, *they're* the ones who brought cruelty to the world – financial cruelty, most of them – and now they're paying the price. The services were just a place to pass the time, to remember some prayers and traditions that had been forced on them in their youth. A place to mildly and genially and even thoughtlessly connect a little with their heritage and culture, but now their Judaism was looming up; rearing up front and center. Not just summoning up the past, but recreating it wholesale.

'Just like my ninety-four-year-old dad Herman always said,' says Nadler, now quieter, reflective. 'It starts with small things, hardly noticeable' – *no rugelach, no blintzes* – 'and accelerates so slowly that you're never even aware… until it's too late.'

'All that stuff we'd hear from our grandparents. Suddenly it's back. Like a bad joke.'

'Yeah, but it's no joke.'

'It's like someone's spoofing Jewish history.'

'Then where's the line between spoofing and actually happening?'

'We're Jewish. We take it for granted,' says Phil Steinerman. 'But it's like someone is now going to actually *make* us Jewish. Make us actually *be* Jewish. Make us suffer. Make us actually face, inhabit, our Jewishness.'

'Punish us with it.'

'Make us re-live it.'

Rabbi Meyerson is listening to all of it. 'It's true, this loss of privileges, this siphoning of rights, these summary, nonsensical decisions – they have dark echoes,' he says.

'What do we do?' says Sorcher.

'We do *something*,' says Nadler firmly, angrily. 'I don't know what, I don't know how. I only know that, this time, we do *something*.'

This time, we do something. They all hear, understand, the implication. The echoes with a horrifying, powerless past.

'Protest?'

'A hunger strike?'

They look at each other's bellies. Their untucked tops. Nadler, Sorcher, start laughing out loud at the very idea.

'Jews don't do hunger strikes,' says Adler. Redundantly.

'What about Masada?' says Rabbi Meyerson.

'OK, let me rephrase,' says Adler. 'A bunch of Jews in minimum security for financial malfeasance do not do hunger strikes. Look at us. We are not equipped to go on a hunger strike.'

'So what *are* we equipped to do?' asks Lerner.

It's as if a light bulb dangling above them blinks on suddenly, a light bulb they all see at once. Sly smiles. Sudden delight fills the minyan.

What are we equipped to do?

They look at one another; silent, smiling.

They know exactly what they are equipped to do.

WATCHING MY FERRARI BURN, BY SAUL SOLOMON

It scorched me too, to see it burn.
Those beautiful lines, that sexy shape, tits and ass in
     aluminum and steel
And never talking back, just going where you want, at
     any speed you want, curling felinely around you,
The perfect mistress, purring, reacting as little or as
     much as you want on your command.
And red, so red, pure red to match my red heart pumping
     with the excitement of seeing it, loving it, driving it
That lustrous red paint – going grey and black before me,
     flaring up in a sudden finale.
To see that burned-out shell and know
That my Ferrari would never go.
Would never cruise Mulholland, or the Champs-Elysées,
As it had in its former day.

With former owners – a prince, a sheikh,
A famous Hollywood sports-car freak.
Up in smoke. A burnt-out husk.
Its day of red glory turned to dusk.
My pumping red heart turning black.
To match the color of the fire's attack.
Blackness and grief is all I really earn.
Watching my Ferrari burn.

HE LOOKS UP AT THE CLASS. They are silent.

'It was a horrible day,' says Saul Solomon.

'I noticed,' says Professor Liston, 'that you chose to focus on just one car.'

'Yeah, I did that on purpose, to make the poem more meaningful and more personal. See, I had to sacrifice several cars in the fire to collect the full insurance value, but the red Ferrari 308 was the one I felt the most emotional about. It had the most history. Like I say in the poem, what with princes and sheikhs and such.' He looks around a little sheepishly. 'Frankly, it was also the most valuable. And I'd gotten the best deal on it initially, so it would pay out the most in insurance.'

Nadler eyes him. 'No wonder you loved it the most,' he says. Managing not to smile or laugh.

But Professor Liston nods somberly. 'I also can't help but notice that there are no other people involved in this very emotional moment. It is just you and your cars.'

Saul looks quizzically at Professor Liston. 'What are you saying?'

'I just wonder if in your thoughts about the poem, it occurred to you that this love was purely between man and machine, and no other people were involved.'

'Are you saying I should have mentioned the guys who did the actual torching? They were just hired pros, I didn't even know them.'

'No, I just…just curious…'

'Professor Liston,' says Nadler, 'Saul is expressing the love between man and machine. That's a pretty strong love, with a long history. That's a form of male love and male bonding that perhaps as a woman you don't fully understand.'

Clearly meant to provoke. To see how she responds, how she handles it. Professor Liston is quiet for moment. 'You might be right, Simon. OK.'

Saul Solomon asks, 'What did everyone think of the poem?'

'I really felt your sense of loss,' says Adler. 'We're talking what, 2.5 mil, something like that?'

'2.75 mil,' says Solomon. And he tears up a little. And the class is silent.

Adler, Nadler, Steinerman, Rosen, Lerner, Sorcher and Solomon, sitting together at lunch.

'A new warden,' says Nadler. 'Who's never even set foot in the place, but he's already making changes.'

'Apparently so,' says Sorcher, gloomily.

'So if it's a new warden who's already making changes, wouldn't it make sense to the guards and administrators that this new warden will be bringing, you know, his own way of doing things?' asks Nadler.

'Sure,' shrugs Adler. But they're all looking at Nadler.

They know Nadler. They can feel he's going somewhere with this.

'Like, you know, a whole new set of rules and procedures,' says Nadler.

They all go quiet. Waiting for him to continue.

'Like if some new change from the previous system suddenly appeared, it would make sense that it's coming from him, right?' Nadler says.

Steinerman smiles slowly. 'Probably no one would question it.'

'A new, more law-and-order type of warden, shaking things up a little, tightening up the place; it would make perfect sense that he'd insist on, for instance, new stricter requisition forms,' says Nadler.

'Sure. Totally new forms,' says Adler, smiling now too. 'A fresh start.'

Otisville inmates' use of gmail and other online communication is strictly limited and closely monitored, but they are allowed access to a single library computer for online research under their constrained, but marginally protected, First Amendment rights. It's the only computer the prisoners have access to, available to them for a few hours each day, with a sign-up sheet to reserve a time slot.

Abe Rosen is picturing that bulky desktop computer and its ancient, balky printer. The printer's poor print-quality and tortoise speed discourage any use of it at all.

He's also keenly aware – as they all are – that Nadler's sentence for fraud – counterfeit loan applications, fake paperwork right back to business school – indicates a significant adeptness with documents, generating and manipulating them. Still, he can't imagine where Nadler is going with this.

'Sure,' says Steinerman, his excitement growing. 'Issuing new forms. And just so everything's clear from the get-go, the new forms might even say something like, *This is the new requisition form, Form 182. It replaces ALL previous forms. This MUST be used for all requisitions going forward.*'

'But you've never even seen the old requisition forms, have you?' says Abe Rosen, leaning in, whispering nervously, irritably. 'Do we even know what the old ones look like?'

'Doesn't matter,' shrugs Nadler. 'The new forms will completely replace them.'

'It's a new day. It's a new system,' announces Adler – quietly, but confidently.

A POEM FROM
THE PISK

'So you have a poem for us?' Professor Liston asks him, with a kind smile of encouragement.

The Pisk is in his usual seat in the back of the room. He fusses with a sheet of paper in front of him. 'Nah,' he says. 'Not really.'

'It's your turn,' says Professor Liston gently. 'It's your day today.' Professor Liston gestures to the piece of paper he's holding. 'You say, not really. But you've got something there in your hands, yes?'

'I know, but I don't like what I have,' the Pisk says. Scrunching together the features of his famous hangdog face. Slouching back in his chair.

'We try to be very non-judgmental here,' Professor Liston says.

'You're withholding evidence,' says Nadler.

'Listen,' the Pisk says, 'Let's get real. It's just gonna be criticized by everyone here.' He looks around. 'And it's gonna somehow make its way out of here, and find its way to the tabloids, and there'll be some offer of payment to run it, which will put my plea agreement in jeopardy.'

He looks around sheepishly at the class. 'I hate to say it, but this poem here is the only poem in here that has financial value.'

'Gimme a break,' says Nadler.

'Not literary value. It's a piece of shit, believe me. But potential financial value.'

Adler looks at him. 'We're not going to let it out of here. Look around. Don't you trust us?'

Con artists, fast-buck experts. The answer is clear: when it comes to a quick, simple chance for financial gain, there couldn't be a less trustworthy group anywhere.

'What do you think someone could get for it?' asks Abe Rosen, speculatively.

'You think it might turn into a multiple-bidding situation?' asks Phil Steinerman.

Instinctively, the Pisk pulls the piece of paper toward his chest.

Nadler rolls his eyes. 'Once again, withholding evidence.'

Now the Pisk crumples the paper into a tight ball.

'I'd really love you to reconsider,' says Professor Liston.

He does. Because after a moment of looking at the crumpled sheet, he puts it in his mouth. A moment later, manages to swallow it.

The class silently watches the Pisk eat the poem. Shy, small, scholarly Jonathan Levy, sitting next to him, clenches his face, imagining the taste.

'Destroying evidence,' says Nadler with a shrug. 'Tampering with evidence, and then destroying it.'

'Not the first time you've had to eat your words,' says Steinerman.

'Your testimony once again will turn to shit,' says Rosen.

'A man who swallowed his own tale,' says Adler.

In response, the Pisk leans back, crosses his arms.

But as it happens, Nadler, Adler, and Rosen are all thinking the same thing: That the Pisk, in his short time here, has already learned something. Has already changed.

He's learned not to leave evidence lying around.

Professor Liston sighs. 'OK, then, who's next?'

Nadler's new requisition form, when he shares a scribbled prototype with the minyan, includes a place for the new warden's signature. Nadler is able to find the signature fairly easily, because the new warden, whom they haven't met but whose name they have managed to learn from Macy's and Porno, was in the private sector previously. It's where the current administration almost always recruits from – a deep bench of big donors and ambitious businessmen – and the new warden's signature is on all kinds of documents online. Nadler only needs a few minutes on the library computer to find it, and has already mastered the signature, which he shows them along with his requisition-form prototype.

While Nadler's mastery of the signature is seamless, the discovery of the new warden's name does prompt some anxious discussion.

'Jack Armstrong? Come on. That's a made-up name.

Someone's pulling our leg,' says Rosen.

'No,' says Nadler, 'I'm telling you, that's the guy's name.'

'Can't be.'

'It is!'

'Armstrong. To strong-arm us,' says Sorcher.

'Hey, thousands of Americans have that name,' points out Adler. 'Mr and Mrs. Armstrong liked the name Jack. Simple as that.'

'All-American-boy. All-American warden,' says Steinerman.

'Just the man to get all these Jews in line,' says Rosen.

Seeing the new warden's signature on the forms will, they theorize, be a little extra frisson, a little turbocharge of officialdom, and don't-even-question-it and what-I-say-goes, for the terrified chain of command at Otisville, already feeling a little tentative and off-balance and shaken up by the summary transfer of Warden Edwards after thirty-five years, so they are not about to bring a new requisition form to a new warden they don't know and say, *'Sir, did you really sign this?'* – of *course* he signed it, you idiot, so put the requisitions through.

Including, in line items, the necessary ingredients for rugelach.

And blintzes.

And some other initial tests of the new requisition system that Nadler has inserted. To stress-test it. Help it settle in. Become accepted, unquestioned, *systematic*, for the guards and administrators.

'It's a great plan in theory, but I still don't understand,' Abe Rosen whispers anxiously to a few of the others. 'How are we going to *produce* these new requisition forms?'

'On the big Hewlett Packard printer in the admin office,'

Adler explains. And adds, smiling, 'So big, they keep it in the closet.'

Conveniently out of sight, Abe realizes. He's starting to see it.

'It's networked to the admin office, of course,' Nadler says. 'But here's the thing, Abe. Would it surprise you in the least to learn that when the federal government first installed computer systems in its prisons, every prison got a single hardwired network?'

'What are you saying?'

Nadler smiles. 'The library computer is still networked to that big printer. No one before me ever bothered to check, I guess, or saw a reason to.'

'Or knew how to,' says Steinerman, nodding to Nadler.

'And Abe,' smiles Adler, 'what else do they keep in that closet, do you think?'

'No!' says Abe.

'Oh yes,' Adler says. 'In a neat stack.'

Abe Rosen is incredulous. 'Requisition forms?'

'Makes sense,' Steinerman shrugs. 'Where else would they keep them?'

'Too bad we can't just print the new ones, spin a hundred eighty degrees, and replace the old ones right there on the shelf,' says Adler.

'Why not?' asks Abe Rosen.

'Because Warden Armstrong here has to sign them,' Adler says, gesturing to Nadler. 'So it's a little more involved.'

'You check the printer model number for me?' says Nadler.

'HP Series 3000 S,' says Adler.

'Year?'

'2010.'

'I can work with that. We just need to get me a little time in there,' says Nadler.

'The secretaries head into town Tuesdays and Thursdays for the lunch special at Tony's,' says Adler. 'No one in admin then.' The trigamistic Marty Adler. Obviously working his mysterious yet confident male charm in chatting up the secretaries – and looking around the closet at the same time, apparently.

'Minimum security. You gotta love it,' says Steinerman.

'But won't it be obvious that you just printed them in there?' asks Rosen.

Simon Nadler smiles. 'Abe, I don't know much in this world. But I know how to create phoney documents. Documents that fooled banks and brokerages for over a decade. We are dealing with my life's work here. With my one actual skill. Show me pretty much any computer terminal and any printer, and I'll make your typographical fantasies come true. It'll never even occur to them they came from that HP.'

And for once, Simon Nadler proves as good as his word.

VENGEANCE

THE MORNING 'MINYAN' IS DOWN to eight.

(Lots were drawn. Warshaw and Seavey pulled the short straws. Warshaw: Miraculous penile enhancement supplements that were less than miraculous. Five years. Seavey: Affordable-housing tax abatements on a dozen luxury buildings, undiscovered for two decades. Three years.)

After the minyan service, the eight of them remain in their circle of folding metal chairs. The new restrictions are still on everyone's minds. All have a pretty good sense, the same working theory, about where they originate. How high up.

'Vengeance,' says Sorcher. 'Everything with that guy is about vengeance. Getting even.'

'I know you're not going to like this idea,' says Steinerman, 'but what's wrong with vengeance?'

'OK, Phil,' says Rabbi Meyerson, 'You've got our attention.'

'I mean, vengeance is balancing the scales, right? And balance equals fairness. You want vengeance only when something is out of balance, right? Vengeance, getting even, puts everything back in equilibrium. I mean, just the expression, getting even. That means literally even-ing out the balance.'

'But vengeance brings out all this anger, fury, hostility…' says Rosen.

'Yes. Anger, fury at some injustice. An injustice done to you personally. So your anger is just a motivating emotion to right the wrong. It's useful, adaptive anger. Anger with a purpose, a direction. To restore the balance. I mean, a prosecuting attorney, OK, trying to convict a criminal. He's just looking for vengeance, right? Vengeance on behalf of the people, on behalf of justice, but vengeance nonetheless. Same emotion. We've all faced them, those prosecutors. That look in their eyes. That's their thirst for vengeance. Disguised in heroism, disguised in society's needs. But it's pure vengeance. You can see it. Don the Con's thirst for vengeance? He's just very human.'

'Very human?' says Nadler. 'You're calling the Destroyer-in-Chief very human?'

Steinerman presses on. 'All our crimes – I'd say they were all about vengeance, but we just didn't realize it. They were about getting even with a world we thought had slighted us in some way – whether we were seeing it clearly or not. Our thirst for vengeance took a sneaky form, that's all. It was quiet, behind the back, behind the scenes, but it was vengeance. What do you think, Rabbi?'

Meyerson is dumbstruck.

'Vengeance is just standing up for your rights,' Steinerman continues. 'Not wanting to be taken advantage of. It's primordial. It's clubbing to death the Neanderthal enemy who came into the cave and took your woman. You wouldn't be going after him if he didn't take something. If he didn't violate you in some way. It's the law of the jungle. But what does that phrase mean? It means that in the context of the jungle, it's *lawful*. Hey, it's good the jungle has a law!'

'So you're saying this vengefulness is justified?' says Rosen.

'I'm saying it's understandable,' says Steinerman. 'The fact that the guy operates by vengeance. It's just his primitive, authentic self. It's his instinct, his deep-down, amygdala-driven, maybe unconscious thirst and quest for fairness.'

'I'm gonna be sick,' says Rosen.

'Why are you saying this, Phil? To ruin everybody's day?' asks Adler.

'I'm saying it because I think it's true,' says Steinerman. 'But OK, even if you don't agree with it at all, I'm saying it for a more useful reason. I'm saying it to point out that BLOTUS is not going to stop with his vengeance. It's hardwired in him. It's his very nature. It's who he is. So it's not going to stop. If anything, it's going to accelerate.'

'So we need to be ready to accelerate our response,' says Nadler.

'Thanks for the insight, Steinerman.'

'Don't mention it.'

AGAIN WITH
THE BLINTZES

IN A COUPLE OF WEEKS, they're eating blintzes again.

Chewing on chocolate and raspberry rugelach.

Given what they've surreptitiously accomplished over the past two weeks (flawlessly executed and universally unobserved admin office access; Nadler's computer and printer wizardry; new Otisville requisition forms and orders freshly signed by the new warden, delivered in official BOP interoffice envelopes (also from the closet) to the admin's physical in-box, and dutifully routed by admin staff to the relevant prison areas and functions, foremost the cafeteria and deli) they expected the blintzes to prove irresistibly delicious, to be dripping with the sweet taste of success – and the rugelach to be richer and more satisfying than ever. Which they would have been, if the new chef had any idea what he was doing.

'Boy are these terrible.'

'Blech. Is blech a word?'

'Blech is the *only* word,' says Steinerman.

'This new chef, he's trying his best with the rugelach and blintzes, but let's face it, they just don't taste the same.'

'And they're never going to, no matter how hard he tries.'

'Like we said – Dmitri was a genius.'

'Better than that, *our* genius.'

They chew in silence. Rosen pushes aside his blintzes in disappointment.

Nadler used to pocket pieces of rugelach for late-afternoon snacks. Nobody's pocketing any now.

'Help me out here for a second,' says Nadler. 'Dmitri was transferred out before we heard about this new warden, right?'

'True.'

'And we know it wasn't Johnny Two Screens' idea to dump Dmitri, right?'

'No way. Not his style. Dmitri's transfer out *had* to be under the new regime coming in.'

'So it makes sense that Armstrong ordered Dmitri's transfer,' Nadler continues, 'probably as a cost-cutting measure as he got ready to close the deli.'

'Seems reasonable to assume, sure.'

'So it's also pretty reasonable to assume he never actually *met* Dmitri, right? I mean, *we* haven't seen this Armstrong yet. So he probably never actually saw Dmitri.'

'Whether he ordered the transfer, or it was someone else in the Bureau of Prisons bureaucracy, he has almost certainly never met Dmitri,' says Rosen, sitting up straight, catching on quickly. 'So no, Armstrong doesn't know what he looks like.'

No one sitting at the table knows exactly where Nadler is going with this. But they all know he's going somewhere.

'This new requisition system is working pretty well,' Nadler says quietly to the rest of the minyan, hunched over their disappointing breakfast trays. 'But I wonder if it actually makes the new system *more* secure, entrenches it more, if the *personnel transfer* forms and transfer procedures are also part of the new system.' He looks at the others.

Everyone understands the stakes – and the risks – immediately. *Upping the ante.* There is a moment of silence, of held breath, while each absorbs the idea, assessing its precise degree of craziness.

'Well, it helps streamline the system,' Lerner points out reasonably. 'Good internal management.'

'Makes bureaucratic sense,' says Sorcher.

'Boy, I don't know,' says Rosen, nervously. 'Rugelach ingredients is one thing. But requisitioning a chef, that's another.'

'Listen,' says Nadler, 'if there's one thing I've learned listening to the TVs blaring at us for the last year: If you think big enough, unpredictably enough, wildly enough, nobody even thinks to question it.'

'Bernie Madoff,' says Lerner.

'Enron. AIG.'

'The president's bank loans,' says Rabbi Meyerson.

'The president, period,' says Phil Steinerman.

'Thing is, I see how personnel transfers can be in the form of just another requisition,' says Nadler. 'Just part of the new requisition system that Armstrong seems to be instituting, right? Dmitri is now cooking somewhere in the

B.O.P. system. We're just requisitioning back – with the necessary paperwork and signatures – the highly talented and deserving Dmitri.'

Abe Rosen unconsciously licks his lips. 'We can actually have our kosher deli back?'

'So long as it's not billed as a kosher deli,' warns Nadler.

'As long as Dmitri acts like an old *bubelah*, stays in the kitchen, happily making the food that makes the family happy,' cautions Adler.

'The new warden's never been here. He's never gonna even know.'

'I don't know,' says Rosen, still nervous. 'The whole requisition system that we've got in place could be discovered. The whole thing could blow up.'

'Think big, Abe,' says Nadler. 'Outrageous, unexpected, disruptive. The lesson from our highest office, trickling right down to our prison system. To our little micro-culture here in backwater, bumfuck, upstate New York.'

THE ART OF DISCOVERY, BY ABE ROSEN

I think that I shall never see
A poem as lovely as a fee.
The fee I earned on every sale
Of every canvas without fail.
But the best fee, the real fee-feast
The biggest prize, the art-world beast
Was a newly discovered masterpiece.
Which would fetch seven figures at the least
Which was all mine till that life ceased.
I think that I shall never see
The excitement of such discovery.

ROSEN – ART FORGER, MASTERPIECE mastermind – looks up at Professor Liston with a modest smile.

'Well I certainly like the little opening twist on Joyce

Kilmer,' says Professor Liston. 'But I *really* like the last couplet. Because that's where you reveal yourself, Abe. You say that's what you really miss, the joy of discovery.' She frowns a little. 'Although I'm a little puzzled. How was it the joy of discovery, if you knew it was all staged?'

'Well, yes, I knew it was staged, but the buyers didn't. They got the thrill of discovery, and I got to share it vicariously, through them. I felt the moment of their discovery.'

'Even though you know it was a scam,' says Nadler.

'Yes, but they didn't. For them, it was exciting. Exhilarating. It was always a wonderful moment, the thrill of discovering this masterpiece, and I got to be part of it.' Abe Rosen smiles wistfully. 'I staged the excitement. I staged the joy. I staged the moment of wonder. So that others could experience it! Could revel in it!'

'Very generous and selfless of you, Abe,' says Nadler, rolling his eyes, turning away.

They say revenge tastes sweet.

In this case literally, thinks Nadler.

'Mmmmm,' he says, shoveling in a perfect piece of raspberry rugelach.

'Mm, mm, mm, mm' says Rosen, rhythmic punctuations of gustatory pleasure, savoring his apple blintz with sour cream.

It's the only suitable response to Dmitri's handiwork.

Dmitri is delighted to be back. Delighted to remain largely unseen in the kitchen. Delighted to have new life as a second Dmitri, an entirely new Dmitri, thanks to the accompanying filings and handiwork of Nadler, Adler, et al. It's like he has emigrated again, he tells them. Like he is starting again as a younger man. As a consequence, he feels energized, rejuvenated. Wonderful new dishes come their way. A miraculous *bouillabaisse* that is practically a stunt, a magic trick, given that Otisville is a hundred miles inland from any coastline.

He is perfectly happy to stay behind the scenes, in the kitchen. A prison chef typically never leaves the kitchen anyway, and the trade-off of having his old job back is well worth it. Occasionally, he gives a quick wave, with a broad toothy smile, from the kitchen door.

'The new personnel transfer system – it worked,' Nadler says quietly to Adler, Rosen, Sorcher, Steinerman, Lerner, and Rabbi Meyerson, all of them gathered now in the bright sun-soaked prison yard after lunch. Nadler's pockets bulge with rugelach.

'It's fully integrated,' says Lerner.

'The transfer paperwork worked great,' Rosen admits.

'Hey, just a thought. Just floating this,' says Nadler. 'We've now stress-tested the transfer paperwork, right?' says Nadler.

'Kind of…' says Adler, cautiously.

'I'm afraid, Nadler,' says Rosen. 'I'm afraid already of what you're thinking…'

'Well what about it?' says Nadler, without even having to say it. 'What about a *warden* transfer? Getting this guy Armstrong reassigned. Hell, even getting Johnny Two Screens back in here. We could do it.'

Abe Rosen starts giggling nervously. 'Jumping the shark, Simon.'

'You can't reassign the new warden!' says Rabbi Meyerson

with alarm. 'That's a lot bigger than some paperwork! That's a lot bigger than a chef! First off, it requires an opening somewhere in the prison system, which you don't know anything about. A warden reassignment? *That* gets noticed. *That* gets covered. That is *mishegas!'*

Nadler considers this. 'All right, OK, maybe we can't reassign the new warden,' he says in sober agreement. He narrows his eyes, leans forward a little. 'But,' he says, 'what if we transfer in another warden *over* him? In a newly created position. Leaving Armstrong in his current position so there's no change there. And no paperwork routed to him for him to notice or approve. So everything stays the same for Warden Armstrong.'

'Except he has a new boss,' says Steinerman, understanding immediately. 'Who he hasn't met. The administration is famously disorganized – something Armstrong probably knows better than we do, being inside it. It could easily seem like some kind of administration screw-up, which Armstrong would probably be reluctant to point out, since it would only put his own new assignment at risk.'

'A screw-up, he knows, that's useless for him to point out, because the administration doesn't admit to screw-ups.'

'And after all, *he* might be the mistake, and if he says something, *he* might be the one out of a job.' Rosen is beaming.

'Plus,' says Adler, 'any questions Armstrong might have about his new responsibilities and the bureaucratic structure, he'd theoretically have to take them through the Bureau of Prisons chain of command, right? Meaning going to his new boss. Which, if he's really worried that their jobs overlap, he won't want to do. He won't want to take that risk.'

'His new boss who, like Armstrong, would never be on-site?'

'A new warden who would be, um, always available off-site to sign paperwork, approve requisitions, but would never actually show up.'

'There's precedent, after all. Armstrong himself. Who won't make himself available to the prisoners at all.'

'Well, this new warden above him won't make himself available either,' Nadler assures them, and smiles.

'Are you really discussing this? Are you really weighing this?' asks Rabbi Meyerson.

'Thinking big, Rabbi.'

'This new boss above Armstrong, he likes to work remotely, but…don't you think he'd want to maintain an office somewhere on-site?' asks Abe Rosen hopefully.

Everyone lights up. Nods affirmatively.

'Of course.' 'Absolutely.'

'He'd insist on it.'

'I'd be curious to see his new office,' says Adler. 'I bet it'll have a nice computer or two requisitioned for it.'

'Nice fast internet connection.'

'He probably keeps it generally locked, right?'

'Oh, absolutely.'

'But it'll be ready for him, whenever he shows up.'

'Oh, my God,' says Rabbi Meyerson, shaking his head.

'What's the name of the new warden?'

'Where's he from?'

'I don't know. Let's get started on all that and see,' says Nadler.

A SPIRITUAL CRISIS

'Have we learned anything?'

Rabbi Meyerson wears a stricken look at the minyan the next morning.

He looks around the circle of folding chairs – at Simon Nadler, Marty Adler, Matt Sorcher, Abe Rosen, Greg Lerner, Saul Solomon, Phil Steinerman – the already diminishing 'minyan'. Straws must be drawn at the end of the meeting, further reducing it from eight to six. But Rabbi Meyerson appears genuinely distraught about something beyond minyan-size. 'Have we learned anything? I'm serious. Have we?'

He stares out the window for a moment. Stares at his hands for a moment, as if they are suddenly unrecognizable, or suddenly revealed as utterly useless appendages.

He continues quietly. 'I know I usually begin our

discussions with some Talmudic question or other about faith or God for our contemplation, but today I have only one question.' He pauses. 'A question I am asking myself as much as each of you…and I fear that it all comes down to this one question, for each of us, for all of us, and I have grave concerns about the answer.' His eyes circle the minyan deliberately, looking for a moment at each member, as if to share his apprehension perfectly equally among them. 'By being here, part of this minyan whose existence is now threatened and may indeed be coming to an end, have you…have we…learned anything?'

His face scrunches up suddenly, as if with physical discomfort, physical revulsion. 'I mean, before you came here, when you began to do what would ultimately land you here, you realized at some point that you might get caught, and indeed you *did* get caught. But it was also just as possible that you would *not* get caught; in fact it seemed more likely you would not get caught, which is why you did it. Which is why we all did it. So…would you do it again? And the answer is – the only honest, complete answer to that question is…you might.

'See, we don't really know if we'd do it again or not until we're out of here, so while we're *in* here, we really can't say whether we'd do it again or not, so we can't really say with any certainty that we have learned anything until we're out. But there are clues here on the inside, clues provided to us lately' – he narrows his eyes at the rest of the minyan – *clues like updated requisition forms, the transfer of personnel, the restoration of cooking ingredients, that I can't mention specifically because Big Willie is over there pretending not to listen* – 'which may be a harbinger of where we are headed when we're back on the outside.'

Rabbi Meyerson seems almost to struggle to catch his breath at that thought, at that line of reasoning. He looks smaller, grimmer, folding in on himself.

'As far as the Torah lessons and Talmudic lessons we've had here together, well, yes, you can probably parrot back to me the teachings, the points of law, but the whole *point* of learning any of this is not to fill you with facts and history and points of knowledge, but rather to give you the tools to be a better person in the world, and while we're within the constraints of incarceration, we don't have the inherent freedom and choice required to demonstrate whether we're truly learning, truly becoming better people. At best we can only *pretend* to be better people, play at being better people, while we are in this artificial "as-if" environment, which has little to do with the free world of free men.'

'And yet, even in this "as-if" environment, where we might suddenly, let us say, be facing a challenge that is not merely "as-if"'– again, avoiding the specifics with Big Willie so close by – 'are we – as if inevitably – destined to revert to our old ways? Or is this environment so artificial, so "as-if", that the jury is still out and we can't say yet whether any of us has truly learned?'

The minyan watches Rabbi Meyerson continue to deflate before their eyes. To go limp; to go hollow; to become a husk before them.

'It's making me ask: Has this minyan been just a waste of time? Is this all just a holding pattern? A suspension of time, a ticking clock? Are we all fated to simply become more of who we are as we grow older? To grow into ourselves more, but not necessarily to understand ourselves any better?

Maybe we can't ever really understand ourselves any better.'

At which point, he is silent.

Their spiritual leader. Their guide. The light has gone out.

'Whoa there,' says Nadler. 'Going awfully Talmudic this morning, aren't you Rabbi?'

'Geez, Rabbi, I think you're being awfully hard on yourself,' says Adler.

'And on all of us. Your students!' exclaims Rosen.

'Sounds like you're having a crisis of faith,' says Steinerman.

'That's what people of faith do,' offers Saul Solomon, almost soothingly. 'Have a crisis of faith every now and then.'

'Comes with the territory, Rabbi.'

'So just to be clear,' says Nadler. 'Your issue seems to be twofold, Rabbi. One, can people really change? And two, while we're in here, how do we really know if we can truly change?'

'And even if we do show some changes in here, it's an artificial environment, so we don't know if those are temporary, circumstantial changes or truly authentic changes. That kind of sums it up?' Steinerman asks.

'Can anyone really learn anything? Is that what you're really asking? Can anyone really learn? Learn to be different?' says Rosen.

'And you seem to be implying that you don't think so,' says Steinerman.

'But Rabbi, the good news is… Just as the answer is contaminated by our current artificial environment, the *question* is equally contaminated by our current artificial environment,' Nadler points out brightly, cheerfully.

'The good news is, it's not a matter of not being able to answer. You can't even really pose the question in here!' says Rosen, enthusiastically.

'That's right!' Steinerman piles on.

'You can't even really ask, *Have they changed? Have I changed?* while you're in here. You have to wait to even ask *Have I changed?* until you're out there.'

'In here, the question has no meaning at all. And the Torah, I'm sure, frowns on meaningless questions,' says Nadler.

'A truly meaningless question must not be asked,' says Steinerman sternly.

'A meaningless question is the equivalent of nonsense, and nonsense has no place in the study of law and morality,' adds Adler somberly. Brow furrowed with import.

The rabbi looks around the minyan. He is moved by this sensitive logic. By this Talmudic subtlety. By this show of support.

Of course. They are right. This is not just a place where there is no answer. This is a place where you can't even truly ask the question. It is so simple, in a way. It is such a relief.

He feels buoyed again by them.

As he listens to their arguments to him, he can't help but come to the conclusion: They have certainly learned *something*. What, he's not exactly sure. But something certainly. Something powerful.

He knows of course, that they have learned to twist the language to their own devices and to their own needs. And if they knew it before, they have clearly become more masterful with it in their minyan studies.

They have learned to manipulate one truth with another. To layer truths, to layer meaning.

Of course, he knows the real meaning behind their subtle, curving arguments.

They don't want him to abandon the minyan. They don't want the classes to stop.

Although he sees clearly that they are propping him up with their subtle, crazy arguments, wanting to make him feel better, wanting to restore his confidence, wanting to be supportive, he knows it is not about their rabbi at all.

It is about their own fear. Their own fear of his abandoning the minyan. Their own fear of the minyan stopping.

Why don't they want it to stop? Is it the simple camaraderie? The antidote against loneliness? The primal feeling of belonging? They don't believe a word of it, they haven't learned a thing, so why do they like the minyan? That's the only real question for Rabbi Meyerson. He knows *that's* the only real question.

He unwraps the napkin he saved from last time, with the eight clear soft-drink straws rubber-banded together inside it. He removes two of the straws, leaving six. 'Now,' Meyerson says morosely, 'it's time to draw again.'

SHALOM
SULEIMAN

THE NEW WARDEN IS SULEIMAN SINGH.

Bachelor of Science, John Jay College of Criminal Justice.

Honors in Incarcerative Sciences.

Honors in Rehabilitation Sciences.

Distinction in the Major in Data Analytics.

He comes from a medium-security assignment in Fort Collins, Colorado. Fifteen years there.

Hasn't moved around the prison system much, so not much of a paper trail.

Has given heavily to the Republican Party, which explains his selection for promotion. Explains it enough to Warden Armstrong, anyway.

The minyan likes everything about this Suleiman Singh.

Especially since they've created everything about him. The plan was briefly jeopardized when they couldn't agree on his heritage. Half of them wanted him to be Jewish. 'Come on. A Jewish warden. Marshall Liebowitz. What could make more sense than assigning a Jewish warden here? This is our chance to have one! One who'll understand and empathize!'

'This is a fictional, temporary warden, right? Everybody still knows that, right?'

'All the more reason to choose a Jewish one!'

But the others argued it was too obvious. Too on-point. Too suspicious. They hadn't had one before…maybe there was some reason the minyan wasn't aware of. Maybe, for instance, there *were* none.

'He'll come aboard in another two months. His start date will be in mid-October. The fact that he's coming, but not actually in place yet, can work for us,' says Nadler. 'Warden Singh is a presence, he's a factor that the current staff has to deal with, but it's natural that since he's not on duty yet, they don't know anything about him.'

'But we do. We know everything about him.'

'Like the fact that he's gonna be a great warden.'

In outfitting Warden Singh's new office in preparation for his 'arrival', they are able to requisition, under the new requisition system, most of what Warden Singh is asking for.

Specifically, a brand new PC with a very fast processor, and a high-end printer, providing Nadler much more flexibility and privacy in creating credible new paperwork.

They print a convincing quantity of the new requisition forms. They destroy all the old ones so that there's no question from guards or anyone about new versus old – these are the requisition forms; there are no others. Simple as that; case closed. Disappearing the forms. Creating a warden. If they have to live in a Kafka world, they'll at least try to out-Kafka the other side.

'What would Kafka say? Would he be horrified or impressed?' they ask Rabbi Meyerson quietly. But not in the minyan. Not where Big Willie can overhear.

They quickly come to a realization that simplifies things. It occurs to them that the actual new warden, Armstrong, doesn't actually need to know anything about the high-ranking official they're creating. As long as the guards and the Otisville staff know about and believe in the pending arrival of Warden Singh, his orders will supercede those of the actual new warden, Armstrong, who, after all, is still off-site. The guards, the entire Otisville staff, have an inherent, unquestioning respect for the chain of command.

Minimum-security prison, thinks Nadler. Despite the privileges being slowly stripped away from them, there is still a lot of freedom. The minimum-security system works well with its light sentences and easy conditions; prisoners are motivated to follow the rules rather than risk extending their sentences. But the minimum-security environment also works well for the prisoners – and against the system – when those same prisoners gather around an inside mission. Because they have largely unfettered access to the prison's tools and technologies to accomplish that mission – which they'd have nowhere else.

There's just one thing they don't factor in. Something that, in hindsight, they probably should have anticipated. The fact that Warden Armstrong – the actual warden – actually decides to show up.

STRANGE CHANGE

THERE'S A LOT OF CHANGE GOING ON right now, Big Willie sees, and some of it makes sense, and some of it's pretty weird.

There's new requisition forms, a whole new requisition system, which he guesses makes sense with the new guy coming in – people bring their own new systems, their own new people – but there was really no problem with the old system, and he's not sure why Armstrong changed it without even seeing how the old system works.

Dmitri their chef was gone – transferred out; no idea why – and now Dmitri is transferred back; again, no idea why. Big Willie assumes it was to cover some temporary vacancy, but it sure just seems like some bureaucratic fuck-up, crossed paperwork or something, and no one even knows who to ask about it, but Dmitri is way better than the guy who replaced him anyway, so Big Willie is sure the prisoners are glad he's back. Big Willie sure is.

Yeah, there's a lot of change going on right now, and a lot of it feels mysterious and unexplained, he's sure, because it's coming from the very top, – from way over their heads; he gets that. Some of it maybe has to do with the arrival of their celebrity prisoner, and as a result more high-up people are paying more attention to Otisville. Polishing procedures up around the edges, bringing systems more in line with other places, he'd bet. But he can't shake the feeling that some of the change is coming from within. He knows that's impossible, but he just gets that funny sense. The sense that his guys here – that they're up to something, these guys.

The new warden, Armstrong, was brought over from the for-profit world. Has an MBA. Was on the corporate team that oversaw some Midwest prison system. Said he served as controller and then chief operating officer, and that the prisons were just one of their 'portfolio companies'. He spoke to all the guards in a video conference call. Big Willie figured the call was to set expectations, smooth the way for his arrival at Otisville. But no, it turns out he was in his office in New York City. The office from where he'd be overseeing Otisville. He still hasn't been up here. Just seventy-five miles away. Word is he doesn't like to be inside prisons. They make him nervous. That sounds made-up, though.

Big Willie thinks it's simpler than that. And kind of the opposite. Otisville is minimum security. Everyone's best interest here is in quietly serving out their sentences and getting out, not making trouble. This guy Armstrong is a for-profit guy. He knows he doesn't have to physically be here. There's no advantage to being on-site. There's basically never any trouble. He can be hands off; it can run itself; he can turn his attention to tougher, trickier, bigger prisons where it's needed. Part of his not being here must be that he's overseeing other prisons at the same time.

But knowing all that – that he can leave Otisville to run itself – Big Willie has got to say, the new warden is doing the wrong thing.

There's a bunch of new restrictions. From a guy who's not even here. Which makes Big Willie wonder if he's being *told* to put these new restrictions in. Maybe they're not actually coming from him.

For the guards, these new restrictions cut two ways. On the one hand, making new rules reminds the prisoners who's in charge. Reminds them of their status as prisoners, reminds them of the chain-of-command, and Big Willie's minyan guys in particular sometimes need some reminding. Restrictions make them more docile, more controllable. He's been here twenty years; he's seen that for sure.

On the other hand, privileges and advantages – and especially the *perception* of those things – make the prisoners happier and more relaxed. And happier more relaxed prisoners mean happier more relaxed guards. That's one reason he's trying not to worry too much about the old chef Dmitri suddenly being back. Because good food is good food, for prisoners and guards.

He sees the pattern on the privileges being removed, on the rules being tightened. He sees how it's being done slowly. Little by little. He figures that's on purpose. Tactical. He figures it's because they don't want any kind of formal, organized protest from the prisoners. They don't want any complaints going beyond the prison walls. These prisoners don't want that either. A lot of them have serious gag orders against speaking to the press for the duration of their sentence, so even a single complaint could jeopardize a sentencing agreement. They won't risk a longer sentence for the sake of a few small restrictions.

Truth is, he feels two ways about the new restrictions. It makes him feel kinda good that these felons, with their easy sentences and their laughing and their kosher deli, are finally getting a taste – ha-ha – of a real prison. He feels like there is a little justice in the world. Because punishment is part of justice. But the other side of it is, well, truth is, he likes some of these guys. He doesn't like how his high school pals Andy and Tommy *accused* him of liking them – someone accuses you, you defend yourself. But truth is, Andy was picking up on something. He's gotten to know these minyan guys, they've gotten to know him; it's totally natural that in this environment, guards and felons get friendly. And you don't like to see your friends get mistreated.

Everyone says it has to do with the 'Pisk' being here. That the new restrictions are because of the Pisk. That it's just little dog-nips of revenge, a little hissy fit from the top. But that seems so petty. It's pretty hard to believe that the leader of the free world would be worrying about anything like that, would turn his attention to that with all he has to do. That seems pretty nuts to Big Willie. Some of the guards say that the unseen higher-ups *want* the prisoners to feel like it's the Pisk. They want some of the prisoners to be mad at him because he brought this on them, and they want other prisoners to defend him because how can it be his fault? They say the higher-ups want the division. Divide the prisoners. Divide the guards. Dividing people in a prison, even a minimum-security prison; that's pretty stupid, if you ask Big Willie.

But nobody's asking him. So he keeps it to himself. He does his job. Drinks a few brews and has a few pizzas with his high school pals. And kinda hopes the stupid restrictions stop somewhere. And stop soon.

SUCH A DEAL

Oy. ALL THE RIDICULOUS ETHICAL discussions Saul Solomon has sat through in the minyan.

Suddenly relevant. Suddenly real.

Holding his breath, basically, until he can get out of here, undiscovered.

Suddenly useless. Wasted.

Because suddenly Macy's, that completely un-blimp-like bag of bones, is at his door. 'You're wanted in the warden's office.' A shrug from Macy's, to answer the question before Saul even gets to ask it: *no I have no fuckin' idea why*.

He enters the warden's office.

Four years here; never been in it before.

Pretty nice. Fancy furniture, mahogany bookshelves, matching leather chairs, big executive desk, nice coffee machine, a little oasis within the run-down crumminess of Otisville.

Three men in business suits are here. One motions him to sit.

'Is the warden here?'

'No, he's not here. But he said we could use his office to talk to you,' says the dark-haired one. Somehow featureless. G-man type.

Saul is already getting a bad vibration.

One of the other men shuts the office door behind him.

All three look silently at him. Giving him little choice but to look back silently at them. He's got no idea why he's here. And they know he has no idea. So there's no point in saying anything that could just get him in trouble somehow. Silence is always the best strategy.

The three men let the silence hang a little more. Watch him a little more. He can tell they're purposely letting the silence hang.

Then they fire. There's no other way to put it.

'We know what you've done,' says one of the men. The blond one sitting at one end.

'All three murders,' says the dark-haired featureless one standing beside him.

'James Landon. A waiter,' says the blond one.

'Felicia Lopez. A hotel maid,' says the dark-haired one.

'Lisa Payne. An accounting temp,' says the blond one.

Utterly unrelated in time and place and circumstance. United only in finding the receiving end of Saul's self-protective rage.

He never even knew the names of the first two. These people have clearly done their homework.

'What are you even *talking* about?' says Saul. As if incredulous. Offended. Utterly mystified.

'Same DNA found at both Landon and Lopez,' says the blond one, calmly. 'Yours, Saul.'

'A fingerprint match from Lopez and Payne, run through the Bureau of Prisons database,' says the dark-haired one. 'You again, Saul.'

'Matching clothing fibers from Lopez and Payne. A camel's hair coat.'

Hmm. He was wearing it for both of those. He looks good in that coat. 'I don't *own* a camel's hair coat!' insists Saul.

'It's no longer in your closet, Saul. We have it.'

Saul feels a pulsing in his temples. A telltale sign of his usual impulse to violence – which is not an option here. 'I've been at Otisville four years now,' he says irritably, annoyed at this intrusion on his peaceful prison sentence. 'Insurance fraud. There's obviously some mistake.'

'Oh we agree, Saul. It's a mistake all right. A miscarriage of justice. And now we've got the evidence to set it right.'

Fingerprints? DNA? Clothing fiber? From four years ago?

'You're bluffing,' says Saul. Which he knows, upon saying it, is a bit of an admission on his part.

'No, *you're* bluffing,' says the blond one, smiling. 'You've been bluffing for four years, and we're calling your bluff.'

Saul is definitely not dealing with run-of-the-mill state investigators here. These guys are something different. Something a lot more serious. He doesn't know exactly what yet. And he gets the feeling, he'll never know exactly.

Fingerprints. DNA. Clothing fiber from his camel's hair

coat. They've been busy, haven't they? He feels a shortness of breath.

'All three murders,' the dark haired one repeats. Like an incantation. Like a minyan prayer.

His temples are pounding now. He feels his fists clench. He struggles to unclench them.

Shit. It's over. It's done.

'All three murders.'

Hearing anyone say it aloud like that – that alone is strange. He didn't expect it, and didn't expect it to have such an effect on him. He's surprised to feel suddenly, literally dizzy, so he grabs a corner of the desk for balance. He feels an instant wave of nausea. He feels this shift inside his body. Like…well…like death descending on him.

But then the third man, the older one sitting in the center, a thinner guy with white hair, smiles a little at him. Which is pretty fucking surprising. The smile seems to come out of nowhere. 'Bring us a couple of coffees, if you don't mind,' the older one says to one of the younger guys, gesturing to the warden's coffee pot.

The younger guy brings over coffee for everyone. He sets down a cup in front of the white-haired guy and a cup in front of Saul. White-hair picks up the coffee cup, gestures a little toast to Saul. Sets down his cup. Looks at Saul.

'We'll bury the evidence forever, if you'll do something for us.'

It's like Saul suddenly hears something, senses something, from way far off. Like seeing a flickering light in the darkness. He has to shake off the fog of a moment ago. He's having trouble understanding what he just heard. But he definitely heard it. *Bury the evidence forever.*

Even through the fog he understands: There's definitely a deal being offered here, and he wants to get to it as quickly as possible, before it floats away. 'Do something for you?'

'Kill him.'

'Kill who?'

'Who do you think?'

The Pisk. Obviously, the Pisk. Three mysterious G-man types, the door to the warden's office closed for security and privacy; obviously they mean the Pisk.

'Who's asking?' Saul says. The blond man can't suppress a smile of disbelief. 'We're asking you to kill someone, and you're really asking who's asking?'

'Never mind who's asking,' says the dark-haired featureless one next to him. 'That's the deal we're offering. Yes or no?'

'But…if I do it, won't everyone know it was me?'

'No one will know it was you.' White-hair says it definitively. Clearly, they have thought this through. Clearly, they have some way to do it.

'How do I know you'll follow through on your promise? That the evidence you have will disappear?'

'Hasn't come out yet, has it?'

'No.'

'But clearly we've got it. Because clearly we know, right?'

'Yes.'

'So if it hasn't come out yet, then we obviously have the ability to keep it from coming out.'

Who exactly are you guys? He wants to ask, but he already knows it will be met with only grim smiles and no response.

'Yes or no?' asks the older white-haired guy. As if the younger guy had never said anything. As if it's just Saul and him in there, and the younger guys are both just incidental, accessories.

'I'll think about it.'

'No,' says the white-haired man. 'This is a good deal. We're offering you a good deal. Take it or leave it.'

'And if I don't take the deal, the murder evidence will come out?'

'Right.'

'So I kind of have to take the deal, right?'

'Right.'

'Then what are we even discussing?' Saul tells him. 'I have to do it. It's a no-brainer.'

'We just didn't know how you'd feel about committing another murder,' says the white-haired guy.

Saul shrugs. Kind of casually. Because the truth is, he doesn't really know how he'll feel.

He won't know unless he actually does it, he guesses.

The older white-haired guy sees Saul's casual shrug, and nods. 'That's what we thought. That's why we're here.'

All three of the G-man types stand up.

'Details to follow,' says the dark-haired, featureless one.

SAUL SEARCHING

HE SITS ON HIS BUNK. Replaying the meeting. Imagining who these guys might be and understanding at the same time that they probably have been specifically selected so that he can't figure out, will never know, exactly who they are.

He's weighing the deal, but at the same time knows he has no choice. They're giving him no choice. This actually would be a sentence lifted. He'd be free. The three murders will stop hanging over him. The smart choice is obvious. In a way, there's no real choice.

On the other hand, he does technically have a choice. He can choose not to commit another murder. Yes, to much of America – and certainly to his fellow criminals – the fucking Pisk is seen as a scumbag, a despicable jerk. A guy who turned on his employer. Who turned against the life he had chosen, against the people he had chosen, people who had made him rich. A guy who chose this path, the Otisville path, because it became the path of least resistance. The path that would get him back to his family fastest. Saul could kill the guy, no qualms about it. But it's wrong to kill. Simple as that. Even he knows that.

What would the rabbi say?

What would the minyan say?

So guys, hey, something I never mentioned, I murdered three people, and no one ever figured that out, so I was just biding my time here on a lesser charge, but now some guys let me know they know about the murders, and they'll make them known unless I kill the Pisk for them, and then they'll wipe the slate clean. Rabbi, what should I do? Guys, what do you think? Worth it?

He wishes he could bring it up.

But then again, he can hear the discussion.

Nadler: No brainer, go for it dude. You'll go from four murders to none. Clean slate. Start over. You can start to be good *then*, if you really want.

Rabbi: You know what to do. You don't need me to tell you. You know what's right here, and I know you'll do it.

Adler: A get-out-of-jail-free card! You'll be an unsung hero to half of America.

Rabbi: It's not starting over, Saul. It's admitting instead that you'll never start over.

Etcetera. Ad nauseam. Round and round in his head, sitting here, lying here on his bunk.

✡

'Saul, you're being moved,' says Big Willie from Saul's cell door the next day, appearing there suddenly alongside Porno. 'Put your personal effects into this carton. We'll handle the bedding and the rest of it for you,' says Porno, gesturing around Saul's cell. 'They're moving you in with the Pisk.'

WHAT A PILL

'Up off the bunk, Sorcher. You're being moved,' says Big Willie.

That's all the notice they give him. After a year in his bunk.

'Why me?' he asks.

'Why not you?' Big Willie responds. But with a smile. He's been listening to the minyan, and he knows he's echoing Rabbi Akiba. Although Matt also knows it's Big Willie's way of saying, *Why? Who the hell knows? Because the form says so, that's why.*

'Let me see that,' he says skeptically to Big Willie, gesturing to the requisition form.

Big Willie turns it toward him. Matt checks the form. Ironically, the requisition form that Nadler created, that has proliferated, has been accepted – and now has been turned against him.

He looks at Mighty Mouth, who is staring at them all with his world-famous, internationally recognized hangdog expression from his bunk – the hangdog expression Matt recognized from Camp Wikiwandi, a hangdog expression he thinks Mighty Mouth should be able to patent, to keep it his, to make sure it doesn't go into the public domain where anyone can use it to represent dumbness, blankness, before it becomes an emoji.

'Throw your stuff into these cartons. We'll be back in a few.' Big Willie and Porno stroll away – leaving Mighty Mouth and Matt.

'Guess they're moving you from the Navajo to the Sioux,' he says. 'Or something.' The hangdog expression adds in a sad smile.

'They probably want you to have your own cell,' says Matt.

Mighty Mouth shrugs. 'I didn't ask for it. Maybe they think it'll be safer for me, or something.'

'Safe from me?'

Mighty Mouth smiles again.

'I wonder if they ever figured out the camp connection,' Matt says.

'I never said a word,' says Mighty Mouth. And after a pause, acknowledging the end of their rooming arrangement: 'No more night-time jujubes.'

Which is only half a joke. He has started taking some extra desserts at dinner, some of the crazy-good rugelach the chef makes, and stowing them in the cell, and surprising Matt with them after lights-out. Food in the bunks is prohibited. So he's risking breaking the rule, and sharing food after lights-out, just for old times' sake.

They never talked politics. They didn't talk scams, or families, or finances, which Matt could tell was weighing on Mighty Mouth a lot. They both had purposefully kept it light. Kept it about the past. Their more innocent past.

'Great to, uh, get to know you,' Matt says cautiously, when Porno and Big Willie circle back, and look through Matt's two cartons before moving them.

'Same. See you round camp,' Mighty Mouth says.

'Yeah. See you round camp.'

Big Willie leads Saul into the cell with the Pisk.

Makes a kind of half-introduction, wanting to say something. 'You two are now bunkmates,' states Big Willie with a shrug. 'Don't ask me why – I don't know why, and my supervisor doesn't know why either. You're welcome to talk to each other all day and night and try to figure it out. You know each other, right?'

'From poetry class,' says Saul Solomon.

Macy's and Porno turn over Saul's new mattress, inspect his side of the cell, and while they're at it, they give the Pisk's side the once-over too. They unpack his box of personal items for him, looking at each one. All standard protocol.

'We'll leave you to it,' says Big Willie, and the three guards exit the cell, leaving the door open – the doors are kept open during the day at Otisville.

As Saul begins to arrange his few items – his little radio, his handful of books, his plastic photo frames (they don't allow glass, for obvious reasons), the Pisk asks him, 'What do you think this is about? This switch?'

Saul just shrugs.

The Pisk is looking at him quizzically.

'I didn't do or say anything to be put in with you, far as I know,' Saul volunteers, answering questions that are so obvious the Pisk doesn't even have to ask them aloud. 'Way more likely this is all about you,' Saul tells him.

'Meaning what?'

Saul shrugs again. 'Wanting to keep rotating roommates so you don't get too close to anyone. So no one gets too close to you. A way to keep you isolated without having you literally isolated, which would be seen as special treatment. You know, he's-treated-like-everyone-else kind of thing.'

The Pisk shrugs. 'Makes sense I guess. Although they don't do these switches regularly. So that's not regular treatment.'

'No, it's not,' Saul agrees.

'You think it has anything to do with you specifically?' he asks Saul.

With putting me in a position to kill you? Saul shrugs again. 'I don't see how.'

'So Matt's transfer out, your transfer in – we just have to accept the mystery of it for the time being,' says the Pisk. 'But the mystery puts me on edge a little, you know?'

'Sure.'

'Doesn't it put you on edge too?'

'Sure. A little.' What else is he gonna say? And plus, it's true.

'Well, welcome to 104A,' says the Pisk, with a hangdog smile. 'Wish I had more of a welcome planned.'

'No worries,' Saul tells him, smiling back.

Saul Solomon lies back on his bunk – the little white capsule now hidden beneath him.

✡

Break it open, they instructed him, pour the pink powder down his throat while he sleeps (best if he's on his back, but still effective however the contents get into his mouth and stay there.)

He'll stop breathing within a half hour. No struggle. Just a cessation. It'll be your decision whether to call the guards then – *Hey, something's wrong with my bunkmate* – or wait until morning, and call the guards when your bunkmate doesn't seem to be getting up for breakfast, not even stirring, and, hey, I'm not even sure he's breathing.

A slightly pink powder. Odorless. Tasteless. Untraceable. A forensic pathologist's worst nightmare. A forensic dead end – so to speak.

Terrifying, and no surprise at all. The latest result of the silent biochemical weapons cold war between labs in Russia and the U.S., the dark-haired featureless one told Saul proudly, setting it in his palm carefully. He was suddenly animated, Saul noticed. Face suddenly expressive, elastic. The guy suddenly had features.

For god's sake, don't lick your fingers afterward, the guy said, eyes wide, eyebrows raised. Wash your hands in the morning, just to be sure.

Making it so simple for Saul.

A tiny, powerful little pill.

Powerful enough to erase the prosecutions of three

murders.

Powerful enough to let him walk out free, done, at the end of his term here.

A life, in the palm of his hand.

Two lives, actually. The end of one – the famous guy across the cell from him. And the beginning, the guarantee of another – Saul's.

But here's the thing: 'A *descendant of cyanide*,' the dark-haired featureless one said. Saul didn't ask. The featureless, suddenly-animated one volunteered that. Probably shouldn't have.

Which of course, summons up Saul's ancestors. His cousins lost in the Holocaust – to cyanide showers. The original cyanide. The original, granddaddy formulation.

And even that might not have previously bothered Saul. But amid these new restrictions around here – 'the pogroms'; the 'edicts' as Matt and Simon and Abe are calling them – this little pill in his palm is echoing with those times. A little toxin that is a direct descendant of the concentration camp chemical. And he's going to continue that tradition? He's going to administer it?

He doesn't want any part of that echo.

Handing it to him like they know he'll do it. Like if it's in his self-interest, if it's the easy way out for him, they know he'll do it. Is that how they see him – as a guy who'll reliably take the easy way out? A guy who'll reliably kill his bunkmate, if he can save himself? Turn on his fellow prisoner? Turn on his fellow Jew? Because that's what we do? Because that's who we are? Saul doesn't like that. Doesn't like that at all. And is it who he is? Is it really who he is?

He's presuming that, like they assured him, it can't be

traced to him. Of course, he doesn't really know that. That could just be something the G-man spooks are telling him. He's sure there'll be some kind of investigation, staged or not. He'll be interrogated. But even if the substance is traceable, even if it is discovered and identified in the Pisk's system, presumably Saul Solomon wouldn't have access to some cutting-edge government bio-weapon, so it won't be blamed on him. Unless they *are* going to release the evidence, to make this look like a fourth murder, have the last laugh, make the joke on Saul. But he'd have no motive for this murder, and with such a clear motive for the other three, would anyone buy that he did this alone, unassisted?

And if it's just a little pill, if it's that simple, why wouldn't they administer it some other way?

Because from their point of view, he's proved that he'll actually do it. He's proved it three times.

Just a little pill.

Making it so easy for Saul.

Which is what makes it so hard for him.

His whole future, in the palm of his hand. His prison-free future.

But his past, too. That's the problem. He's holding his Jewish past in the palm of his hand.

Which probably never occurred to them.

Which, with the new restrictions and old echoes, suddenly means something.

And Saul is more than a little surprised by what else now drifts into his thinking as he lies there weighing a murder.

A poem.

A poem from class.

Watching My Ferrari Burn, by Saul Solomon.

In class, they never return to any of their poems after they've read them aloud once. Too many others to get to, he figures.

But of course, each of them can return to any poem on their own. He wonders if Professor Liston knows they'll do that. That they'll think about their poems. That it's part of the exercise. Part of their usefulness. Part of the therapy of them.

He wonders if she knew he'd return to *Watching My Ferrari Burn*. Think more about the metaphors of its sleek sexy shape. Comparing it to a beautiful woman.

Of course, nobody knows that it isn't just a metaphor. That he was actually watching the burning of the sexy, shapely Lisa Payne, whose body he had put into the trunk of the Ferrari.

The primary reason for the insurance fire.

The primary reason, too, for the chemical accelerant he used for it, that the pros he consulted advised him to use, to make sure no human trace was left. Prosecutors simply assumed he was doing a thorough, professional, overzealous job on the insurance fraud. They figured he wanted to make sure nothing was salvageable, that the loss was total.

But he wasn't just watching his beloved Ferrari burn – along with two Lambos, don't forget, to make the disaster look general and not specific.

Poems have hidden meanings, of course, and his was no exception.

A meaning hidden from everyone but him.

But it turns out that his poem, his own poem, is hiding more meaning than he thought. Hiding a meaning that's new to him.

Because writing the poem, putting the words on the page, brings the events back alive in a way, and, well, for the first time, he's lying here on his bunk thinking about Lisa Payne. Payne is right. Payne in the neck, Payne in the ass, but in truth, just in the wrong place at the wrong time. He didn't want to have to kill her – and that's important, OK? He *didn't want to*. He did *have to* – he couldn't see any way out of it – but he would have avoided it if there was a reasonable way.

Yet now, here, lying on a prison bunk, picturing it again because of that poem, he's feeling, well, *something* about it. He doesn't know if it's in the category of what's called guilt, or remorse; he's not sick to his stomach, or getting headaches, or grieving, or anything. He *was* sick to his stomach when those three suits told him they knew about the murders, but that passed once they proposed their deal.

And while it's not exactly what he'd call obsessing, here he is thinking about it, focusing on it, seeing it again. So is this what guilt feels like? Because to him, it feels more like annoyance. Annoyed that he's been made to think about this again. Annoyed that he had to write the fucking poem in the first place, and annoyed that this was the poem he wrote. Part of him wants to take a blunt instrument to Professor Liston and get all this thinking and feeling out of the way. But of course, it's the poem *he* chose to write. It's the poem *he* put the hidden meaning into. So he has no one to blame but himself.

Is this some part of himself, some small previously unknown part of himself, speaking up in him finally? Is it the result of the minyan, of the discussions, of getting to know his fellow inmates? It's also, obviously, the result of his closed-door meeting with those three shadowy guys. It's all working in him, swirling around in him all of a sudden.

Just when he's been moved to the Pisk's cell.

SHALOM, JACK ARMSTRONG

BIG WILLIE IS CALLED INTO A morning meeting, he and the other guards.

They're finally going to meet the new warden.

They last heard from the new warden on the conference call where he explained why they wouldn't be seeing him on-campus, that he oversaw several prisons, with bigger issues, more serious offenders, and he was perfectly happy with the record Otisville had established and maintained. Praising them for their record was clearly his way of saying he wasn't going to bother getting too personally involved or making an appearance.

But something has clearly changed, and Armstrong arrived unannounced a week ago, according to the prison grapevine, went straight into the warden's office and has been holed up in there, largely unseen, behind closed doors, getting up to speed presumably, on staff, procedures, who knows what else. The admin secretaries have been seen going in and out, but no one else.

And here he is at last, in the front of the meeting room.

James Jack Armstrong. Small, trim, standing stock-still up there, no extra movement, an efficiency expert who's actually efficient-looking. Crew cut, white shirt, dark slacks, tailored, expensive-looking. Clothes that scream private sector, and don't you ever think otherwise.

The other thing that's pretty clear: He's not happy to be here. He looks irritable. He looks pissed.

No *good to meet you*, no *welcome*. He just looks silently around the room at the guards, regarding each of them – all of them – as if assessing, sizing them up and not looking too happy with what he sees. It's soon clear why.

'I said I wasn't planning to be on-site, as you remember,' he says – looking in their eyes, lingering individually on Officer Stevenson, Officer DeBenedetto, and Officer Robbins, as if to see if they do in fact remember, to see if there's any light on inside them. (Stevenson, DeBenedetto, and Robbins – Porno, Chatty Chas, and Lightning Larry to the prisoners, and to their fellow guards, who long ago recognized and accepted the casual genius of those nicknames; nicknames now in use for years, the guards using and responding to them without a second thought, as Big Willie has accepted and responds to his own. Big Willie knows, however, that in a sea of incompetence, Porno, Chatty Chas, and Lightning Larry are probably the standouts.) It's instantly clear to Big Willie that Jack Armstrong doesn't think too highly of the entire Otisville guard staff. He soon hears why.

'So you've got to figure, it would be something significant, somewhat important, for me to come address you personally, right? To break with the agreement we had to leave you alone.' Some agreement, thinks Big Willie. They had no say in it.

Armstrong takes a breath. 'I was very interested to learn that here at the prison, to coincide with my new management, you streamlined the requisition process and introduced a new simplified form.'

Big Willie feels the warden's edge already. Picking up on it before anyone else.

'That showed clear initiative, I must say, and a demonstration of intelligence. Unfortunately, it showed the initiative and intelligence of the inmate population. I never authorized any such thing. Those new forms are totally fraudulent and created right under your noses.'

Armstrong's irritation ramps up fast. Big Willie can see he is struggling to maintain self-control.

'But the new forms are proving useful to me. They are demonstrating to me *your* intelligence level, too. They are proving to me the degree of competency that I have in my Otisville guards and administrative staff. A competency that is letting the inmates run circles around you, and not only that, but you didn't even have the slightest idea. You didn't even catch on.'

He looks over each of the guards again. His fury flowing fully now. 'Beautifully conceived requisition forms. Totally sensible. And totally fraudulent. With *my signature*, for Christsake. My signature on there, as if to stick it to me all the way, to taunt me personally, to show me who's really in charge.'

'Those forms are a fraud. The requisition system is a

fraud. Gee, anyone around here know anything about fraud? Anyone in here expert in fraud? Anyone in here among America's foremost practitioners of fraud? Gee, you think maybe you should have been on the lookout for fraud? Since that's what half these guys are in for?'

He angrily grabs the stack of papers off his desk, shoves it at the guards at the front to pass out. 'This is the new requisition form. The real one. Take one, and keep it in your pocket, so you know what a real one looks like.' Pretty insulting, Big Willie is thinking. 'It's printed in a way that no printers here can duplicate.'

He looks at the guards. 'There are going to be further changes around here. I'm going to have to be hands-on. For all I know, based on this, your prisoners are pretty much running things, and you don't even know. I mean, what else are they running? Well, I can't have prisoners running things. So I'm gonna have to be here for a while.'

'I still have no intention of meeting inmates. The famous, the infamous. I'm not fascinated by their fame – some of them – or their clever crimes or their colorful stories or their religion.'

The word 'religion' kind of comes out of left field. Big Willie can hear Armstrong's disgust when he says it. He can kind of hear so much in how Armstrong says it. *Religion – if you want to call it that. Their weird customs. Their strange beliefs.*

'I don't want to meet them, I don't want to even look at them.' The warden's expression scrunches up defensively, eyes and mouth firmly closed, as if instinctively protecting himself from some insect swarm or plague. 'I know Warden Edwards maintained an open door. Believed in dialogue.

Well, Warden Edwards, you'll notice, is gone.'

Is Armstrong maintaining his distance to keep the prisoners from becoming real people? To keep them from becoming human? Maybe Armstrong realizes that about himself, maybe he doesn't.

Big Willie knows the type. They like their power, but they like *faceless* power, because faceless power means more power, it's the unlimited power of the system. It's the power you can't see, the kind of power that the powerless can't get their hands around, the kind of power the powerless can only vaguely picture. Power that's unclear where it's even coming from exactly, so it's the greatest kind of power.

Twenty years as a prison guard, maybe Big Willie doesn't know much about the world, maybe he's pretty limited by these concrete walls, but one thing you do get to know: you see all different versions of authority, all different styles of power.

Warden Armstrong dismisses the meeting with an irritated wave of his hand, and then says, 'Richardson.'

Nobody here has called him Richardson in years. The other guards, even Warden Edwards, have adopted the prisoners' 'Big Willie.'

Nice to hear his actual name for once.

Kind of a fresh start.

'Yes, sir.'

'Stay here, I want to talk to you.'

✡

Warden Armstrong gestures him to the chair in front of the big wooden warden's desk, and pulls a chair up close next to him.

Since Big Willie is the guard who mainly watches the minyan, he's starting to think Armstrong is about to lay into him. Tell him he's an idiot in a special category of one. Instead, Armstrong does the opposite.

'Richardson, even though I haven't physically been here very long, I've been going over personnel files and incident reports, learning a lot about Otisville and what's what here, so I know you're a lot smarter than most of the guards on the floor here, and before you go all noble and modest on me and tell me you're just like everyone else – cause I know that's part of your M.O. too – let me stop you by telling you, you're smarter and you know you are. So spare me the false modesty.'

Well, he *is* a lot smarter. Macy's, Porno, Shaky Jake, Chatty Chas, Lightning Larry – the minyan's nicknames aside, they're nice, hardworking guys, but yeah, they're pretty much idiots. So Big Willie stays quiet.

'Good,' says Armstrong. 'Glad we agree on that.'

He takes a deep breath. As if trying to let go of his earlier anger. To relax, be himself, connect with Big Willie. 'So I know you're smart enough to know these people are crafty,' he says.

Assuming Big Willie knows who he's talking about.

But of course, he assumes right. Big Willie does.

'They're crafty, and you know they're crafty, Richardson, you've seen them close up for years, so you and I don't even need to discuss it, you know exactly what I'm talking about.'

And although Big Willie knows how low, how mean-spirited, how small-minded that thinking is, he *does* know what Armstrong's talking about. Because, well, they *are* crafty. Smart, quick, funny, and not straight-ahead or simple. Crafty.

'I know you know what I'm talking about, because I know your duty includes watching over them, observing them during their morning services. Where they're supposed to have at least ten of them together. What do they call that?'

'The minyan.'

'The minyan,' he repeats.

'Yessir. But I thought…I heard…that you're going to be eliminating the minyan?'

'Oh, I am. And I could eliminate the whole thing right now, this second, if I wanted to. But see, I thought it would be more interesting to reduce the number I'll allow, but just little by little. See how they handle it. I know less than ten is against their religion. They're all upset about it already. And see, I won't even tell them when the next reduction is, or how many. They won't even know when or if it's happening again. I'm going to play god here a little, to see how they respond. Because, mark my words, even though it's against their law to meet with less than ten people, you watch. No matter how much I reduce it, they'll still meet. Because they don't really listen to their God's law. It's just an excuse for them. If just a couple of them are allowed to meet, they will. Because it makes those two people special. And seeing themselves as special is part of who they are. And even if their minyan pals are made 'unspecial' by my policy, the 'special' ones will still meet, because they love being special. They'll ignore their god; no problem. You watch. Think I'm right?'

Big Willie is silent. Because once again, he's sure Armstrong is right.

And it's becoming clear to Big Willie that Warden Armstrong has thought about *Them* quite a bit.

'I want to see how they handle it, don't you? Their group getting smaller and smaller? Let's see who's in, who's out, who has the power, who doesn't.' He looks at Big Willie. 'Here's the other reason I'm letting them keep it where it is for now and reducing it only slowly over the weeks. Because I want you to keep your minyan duties. Keep your eye on them, making sure they have their freedom of worship – and listening in for what they're saying. I hear they trust you, Richardson. So you're in a great position to know what they're thinking, what they're up to. I want to know what they're discussing. I want you to report back to me, whatever it is.'

'Sir…' Big Willie gulps hard before he says it – considering, weighing. He honestly isn't sure how to handle this. But Armstrong, for whatever reason, does seem to recognize Big Willie – Bill Richardson – for his true self, for his true value and intelligence, so he takes the risk of pointing it out. 'Warden Armstrong, sir, I was told by the previous warden that their discussions are private, that a private religious ceremony is privileged, and that I'm not allowed to discuss what I hear there.'

'That's correct,' says Armstrong. 'That's absolutely correct, Richardson,' he says. 'It is private and privileged. And that's why they'll never think twice about your being there. That's why they've gotten used to your being there. Because you've clearly respected that privacy. They'll assume those rules are still in place. That's what makes you such a valuable observer. That's why I'm continuing the practice. Not to put too much pressure on you. But their privacy and privilege and your trustworthiness is the value of the whole idea, Richardson. Do you see that?'

Well, yes, he does see that. 'Yessir.'

'Look at it this way, Richardson. They're going to be bending the rules of their minyan – just you watch – so we're going to bend the rules of their minyan as well.' He smiles.

'That's it for now, Richardson.' He gets up. Gestures that the meeting is over – *we're all done here, we're OK, you and me; we understand each other* – by putting his fingers together in an 'OK' sign. It's normally just a quick informal gesture of agreement and dismissal. But Big Willie can't help but notice – and feels like Armstrong *wants* him to notice – when Armstrong, oddly, points his whole OK sign sideways.

SINGH'S
LAST SONG

THE WORD GOES AROUND THE dayroom fairly quickly.

If anything in the meeting with the guards was supposed to remain confidential, it doesn't for very long. It's a small, close prison community. And some of the guards, as Armstrong said, are not the swiftest. Or very tight-lipped.

By the next day, pretty much everyone is aware of the essentials:

Warden Armstrong is here.

He knows the requisition forms were forged.

He doesn't want to meet any prisoners.

And as if in proof of his new on-site presence, his new focus and attention, his more hands-on approach to making changes…

Chef Dmitri is gone again.

'What do you mean, gone?'

'Gone,' says Ezra Kleinman.

'Reassigned?' asks Rosen. 'Collecting his NY State pension? Dead in a ditch somewhere? Which kind of gone are we talking?'

'Don't know,' Kleinman shrugs. 'Just, gone.'

Kleinman, the messenger, bearer of bad news, shambles away.

In his wake, a long contemplative pause hangs between the rest of them. A silence amid the droning stations, FOX and MSNBC.

They all know which kind of gone. The Armstrong strong-armed kind of gone.

'I can't go back to that other rugelach,' says Adler, his face tightening in disgust.

Which they all understand to mean more than rugelach. The kosher food gradually eliminated. The minyan being systematically reduced. And now the facilitator of all of it – here. What would be next? Something. Where would it stop? Nowhere.

'What are we going to do?' says Rosen, lugubriously.

'What are we going to do?' Nadler repeats back to Rosen rhetorically. 'We are, once more, going to up our game,' he says defiantly.

'With the guy sitting right upstairs?'

'Abe, that's where the expression *right under their noses* comes from.'

'Well, we can't do anything with printed forms. Printing is out. Immediately suspect.'

They are silent for a moment.

'I wonder what Warden Singh has to say about this?' says Steinerman.

'Not much,' says Adler, ruefully. 'Not much at all.'

'Yeah, he was just getting adjusted to his new post. Just settling in. With Armstrong here, Warden Singh may not have as much authority as we hoped,' says Matt Sorcher.

'When Armstrong gets wind of Singh's spanking-new office, I guess Singh's illustrious corrections career will be over,' says Rosen.

'Over before it started.'

'Nothing in there but a desk, a computer, a modem, and a really nice printer. Just looks like an unoccupied office,' says Lerner. 'But even an idiot would eventually figure it out.'

'Warden Singh, RIP.'

They all understand the problem. Warden Singh can only communicate from the computer in 'his' office. Which will certainly now be guarded tightly, locked up, where access had been looser, the guards less attentive, before Armstrong got here. They've had only a few minutes at a time to set things up, to use their duplicate key in the few minutes when the guard shifts change in this section of the prison. Intense bursts of 'office' activity. To print the new requisition forms. To create an email address for Singh at the Bureau of Prisons, using Porno's Bureau of Prisons email address and making an alias that Porno knows nothing about (they're pretty sure Porno doesn't even know he has an automatically assigned B.O.P. email address) – all that in intervals of a few minutes at most. It's been a challenge, but one Nadler has the perfect skills for. He's never had to work his paperwork frauds against the clock like this, but he's enjoyed the extra adventure of it. It's gotten his heart rate up, his blood going, it's probably good for his overall cardiovascular health.

The computer equipment, the furniture, has all been ordered on the new requisition forms. But that's OK, because by this time, *everything* has been ordered on the new universal forms. That alone doesn't point to the illegitimacy of the order.

But even if the office somehow remains legitimate, set-up, how will they get into that office now? Under closer, stricter observation by the guards, more limited movement within the prison, which is already being instituted by Armstrong.

'He was a good man, Warden Singh,' says Adler. 'Would have been a good advocate for us, if he'd had the chance. But as an advocate I guess he had two big disadvantages. He wasn't real. And he wasn't here.'

'Now hang on,' says Nadler. 'You're writing him off way too fast. Not being here, not being real – those are still his pluses.' He lowers his voice. 'OK, Armstrong caught us creating new requisition forms. But I don't think he'll catch us creating a new warden. I don't think it would ever occur to him. It's too weird. It's too big.'

Steinerman angles his head hopefully. 'Maybe Singh can still get some prison reform done before his, uh, part-time status gets discovered.'

'If Warden Singh can think of something, quick,' says Adler. 'If we can think of something reasonable, believable, for him to do. To at least try. See if he's still got any clout.'

'Believable? Reasonable?' says Nadler. 'I don't think we should get too hung up on that. He doesn't exist. And to the degree he does now exist, he won't exist for very long. So why make him reasonable or believable for his tragically short lifespan?'

'Plus,' says Rosen, 'while it's true Armstrong has discovered the new requisition forms, he might be embarrassed by the screw-up. It happened on his watch. So maybe he's too embarrassed to even mention it to this Warden Singh, who he's still confused about, and still afraid might be his superior.'

'True,' says Adler, 'better for Armstrong to just take care of it, and not risk jeopardizing his career by revealing the screw-up.'

'Armstrong's coming from the private sector; Singh is entirely a public-sector guy, right?' says Rosen. 'Armstrong still assumes one of them is in the job by bureaucratic screw-up, and there's a fifty percent chance it's him, and he might figure it's better to just not say anything and let things be, right?'

'Is he the authoritarian type who respects the chain of command no matter what?' says Nadler. 'We just don't know.'

'Singh lives!' says Rosen.

'Maybe,' says Nadler, 'maybe for one final dying act.'

'Maybe one quick, useful act from Warden Singh, before he disappears forever into the internet,' says Steinerman.

'A way for him to finally get real,' says Nadler.

QUESTIONS
FOR THE RABBI

IT'S A DILEMMA. AN ETHICAL DILEMMA. The kind of thing the minyan gets to discuss with Rabbi Meyerson, and Big Willie doesn't. They get to float and bounce hypothetical situations back and forth with the rabbi and with each other. Whereas Big Willie now has a *real* dilemma, but has to stand in the corner silently, listening to their random philosophizing – *what if*, *what about*, *what then* – and has no one to talk to about it.

What if he could, though? He knows so well by now how they discuss these things – the pace and pattern of their questions, the rhythm of the answers – like every question is a puzzle, and you spin each piece around in the light, examine it from every angle. He knows by now the very sound of it, he can hear it in his head.

Rabbi, what do I do? Warden Armstrong has asked me to listen in on the minyan's conversations, and report back to him, even if you're not saying anything conspiratorial or illegal or threatening.

And yet I know, Rabbi, not only is this private time that you have with your minyan, and not only is it religious freedom and free speech both protected by the Constitution, which was all explained to us by the last warden, but it's also therapeutic for the inmates – it's a safe space to talk; that's the spirit of the minyan, so for me to spy on you and the minyan is wrong on three levels at once. Wrong in every possible way.

But if I refuse, I could lose my job, and be unable to feed my family. Should I meet him halfway, Rabbi? Is that the reasonable tack to take, a middle ground, give him something, so that I am respecting both you and him and myself in equal measure? Is that a path open to me, Rabbi? Or is that actually the worst path? Simply short-changing and cheating all three parties – you, the warden, and myself.

How would Rabbi Meyerson respond?

A man must be able to feed his family, Big Willie. But he must also be able to live with himself. Your integrity, your conscience – those are a part of your 'family' too. Your impulse to give every party a little of what they want is admirable. It shows your desire to solve the problem to everyone's satisfaction.

Unfortunately, as you're already pointing out, this is unfair and unjust to everyone – including yourself. As I see it, William, you must confront the new warden, refuse to do it – and perhaps he will admire your forthrightness, your brave bold ethical stance, and keep you on.

Fat chance, Rabbi.

I agree, William. I have experienced just enough of the new warden to agree with you fully – yes, fat chance.

Big Willie feels the tension, the tightness in his throat

and chest.

Here's the other thing, Rabbi. My other dilemma. Maybe even bigger, believe it or not. This guy Armstrong. He gets me. He likes me. The last warden, Warden Edwards, he was a nice guy, but he was very into equality – no favorites; everyone must be treated the same. This guy Armstrong, he's already indicated that he finds me special. We seem to kind of click. My twenty years of knowledge, my ability to understand and connect with the inmates might finally be helpful, useful, and valued. And after twenty years of paying dues, maybe my career would finally start moving along too.

Now I wasn't born yesterday. I know Armstrong might just be saying what he sees in me to puff me up, keep me loyal. I know it might just be a tactic on his part. Wanting me to feel good, to prep me for more bad stuff he's going to ask me to do.

I can feel already that he's a bad guy. But he sees something, admires something in me. Which of course doesn't mean I'm bad too – not in the same way – but it does make me wonder about it. And my ability and my potential – that's something I agree with him about. And ability and potential – those are good, right?

My average size, my average life – that's what's made me invisible, and I've had to live as invisible. That's why I always kind of liked the nickname Big Willie. It shows they see me – not just average, not just invisible.

But average, invisible, is also what's let me fit in. Why they accept me watching the minyan, forget about me. And why Armstrong is now selecting me as a spy. He's going to finally lift me out of average. So do I go along with him? It's kind of my only choice.

A whirl of rabbinical questions. And no one to answer them but himself.

ONWARD, CHRISTIAN SOLDIERS

'STEVENSON, CAN I HAVE A WORD with you?'

'Yes, sir.'

Officer Stevenson (aka Porno) heads obediently into Armstrong's office. Armstrong closes the office door behind them. 'Have a seat,' says Warden Armstrong.

'Yes, sir.'

'I know what the prisoners call you in here, and I'm not calling you that,' says Armstrong sternly.

Stevenson shifts a little, turns bright red, ashamed the name Porno has made its way to the new warden already. He certainly won't mention that the nickname is so powerful, so long-standing, so amusingly contrary to his Christian values, apparently, that not just the prisoners, but his fellow officers, have been calling him Porno for years too. How in the prison corridors, and even in dreams at night, he responds to the name Porno.

'No reason to feel ashamed, Stevenson, it's not your fault at all. I know which inmates gave you the nickname,' he says. 'In fact, I understand you're pretty much the opposite of that name.'

'I am, sir,' Stevenson blurts out loudly, still embarrassed, trying to correct things. 'Or I always try to be.'

'You're in fact, a follower of the Lord?' says Armstrong.

'I'm a Christian,' affirms Officer Stevenson. *I'm not Porno. I'm Officer Stevenson.* He feels his former identity bubbling up, resurfacing in the warden's office.

'Which makes me doubly impressed that you are serving in this prison,' says Armstrong with a smile. 'Daniel in the lion's den,' he says. 'That can't be easy.'

In here with all these Jews. Armstrong doesn't say it. But Stevenson understands that is what he means.

'No sir.'

'And I understand you and your wife attend the Church of the Resurrection?'

'Yes sir.'

'Now that I'll be up here more, we're looking for a church, me and the missus.'

Stevenson lights up. 'We'd be glad to introduce you.'

'But it's way out in Binderville. Kind of far to go every Sunday, isn't it?'

'Yes, sir.'

'But I guess nowadays, there's no place to build a church any closer.' Armstrong smiles.

Officer Stevenson knows what he means. How the black hats, the Hasidic Jews, have bought up almost all the property. Own the whole town of Otis. And pretty much all the surrounding acreage. They're not about to sell some to an evangelical congregation.

The conversation weaves around a little – how Stevenson came here originally, because his wife's family has been up here for hundreds of years and had this nice piece of land for them to build a house on and start a family – ten acres free and clear. So with steady jobs, even if they don't pay a lot, they still end up way ahead.

'Guess it's changed up here, hasn't it?' Armstrong says, with a sad smile.

Stevenson nods.

'Not the place it was when your wife's family bought that land, eh?'

'No, sir.'

And they talk some more, and Officer Stevenson is impressed with Warden Armstrong's feel for the region, and understanding and sympathy for Stevenson and his family, and even his command of scripture and the Bible.

'Well, I sympathize, Stevenson. I sympathize. That's all for now.' Armstrong raising his palm, pressing thumb and forefinger together, to give Stevenson a quick 'OK' sign. *We're OK, we're done here.*

Then holding the 'OK' sign, but turning his hand so it points sideways.

Stevenson blinks on seeing it. He knows the meaning. He knows it's an unspoken signal of like-thinking people about restoring the proper order to America. He's surprised at first to see that silent, subversive signal come from a high-ranking federal official – but in the next moment, he's not surprised at all.

Coming from Warden Armstrong, Stevenson realizes, the

signal might have actual power.

It might mean, *we're just beginning.*

Stevenson nods, backs out of the office.

Smiling.

✡

'*Stevenson, can I have a word with you?*'

Big Willie overheard Armstrong say it to Porno, before they disappeared into Armstrong's office behind his closed door.

The same invitation, the same tactic Armstrong used with Big Willie.

Being singled out. Invited to a private chat behind closed doors.

What Big Willie thought of as 'special' treatment obviously wasn't at all.

Is Porno special too? But he isn't. He's an idiot. Big Willie knows it, and Armstrong certainly knows it.

What Big Willie is, he realizes with annoyance, is a fool.

An average fool. Special briefly in his own mind before Porno got called in, and now totally-average Big Willie again.

MORE QUESTIONS

'I'M SUPPOSED TO GO HELP you with the minyan.'

'What?'

Porno shows Big Willie the assignment sheet the next morning. Holding it up as if already knowing Big Willie will question it. Pointing to Armstrong's signature. Original. In pen. As if Armstrong is saying personally, *no requisition-form or signature monkey-business from now on.* But Armstrong hasn't bothered to explain to Big Willie why Porno is suddenly accompanying him.

So Big Willie has no choice but to lead Porno to the minyan. Silently. Thinking. Porno has never had minyan duty. It's never been part of his rotation. Why suddenly now?

Richardson, stay here, I want to talk to you.

Stevenson, can I have a word with you?

The same tactic from Armstrong, used on both of them.

Big Willie is still stewing about that. Is he so simple he fell for it? Fell for the same thing that Porno did? Maybe he isn't as smart as he thinks.

They take their place in the corner of the room as the minyan assembles. Big Willie can see that the minyan notes Porno's presence. They're probably wondering exactly what Big Willie is: What is Porno doing here? He's never had this duty before.

Yis-ga-dahl, v'yis-ga-dash, shmae rabo…

'What are they saying, anyway?' Porno whispers irritably. But Big Willie also hears an edge of fear in Porno's voice. He seems a little freaked out by the chanting.

'Just some prayers,' says Big Willie quietly.

'So why don't they do it in English?'

'It's their traditional language.'

'But they could be talking about us. They could be planning something right in front of us.' Porno crosses his arms. 'They should be forced to pray in English so we know what they're saying.'

Technically of course, Porno is right. They *could* be communicating with each other, planning more stunts and disruptions like the new requisition forms that had returned their food and their chef without prison approval. Stunts that made all the guards look bad for not having a clue.

But Big Willie knows by now that most of them don't even know the Hebrew language – they just recite by memory the prayers they learned as kids, with no idea what they mean.

And then – maybe because he's already whispering – Porno whispers one more thing: 'He don't like 'em…' Porno says under his breath. '…and I don't neither.'

There it is. Porno dumb enough, simpleton enough, to

just say it plainly like that.

But it still leaves Big Willie the question of why Porno's here.

'So I guess, what, you're supposed to just watch the minyan with me?' *Like I need help? Like after all these years without incident I can't do it myself?*

'No, he told me you'd still be the one watching the minyan.'

No, he told me you'd still be the one watching the minyan.

Poor dumb, straight-ahead Porno, doesn't realize what he's just revealed.

Because if Big Willie's assignment is to watch the minyan, then Porno's new assignment here is suddenly clear as day, by process of elimination: To watch Big Willie.

Why? Because Willie wasn't respectful enough to Armstrong? Didn't click his heels together fast enough? Maybe when he mentioned the minyan rights, that rubbed Armstrong the wrong way?

Maybe when Armstrong started probing about the black hats, Big Willie didn't say enough. Maybe Porno spilled more about his black-hat thoughts. Which maybe made Porno seem more reliable, more loyal, more controllable. Porno's nickname comes from being a straight-arrow Christian fundamentalist. But the minyan doesn't know, like Big Willie does, that he's only a Christian fundamentalist because his wife's family insisted on it. He just went along with it. Did what he was told. Maybe Armstrong picked up on the fact that he does what he's told. Hell, Porno got ten acres out of it. The benefits of being dumb, Big Willie thinks.

Maybe the problem *is* that Big Willie is smart. Armstrong commented on it so directly. *You're smart, Richardson. And don't go all humble on me and pretend you're not.* But it only occurs to him now: maybe Armstrong sees that as a *bad* thing.

So being smarter than Porno makes him *worse* than Porno. Porno is here because Armstrong trusts Porno. But doesn't trust Big Willie?

Is this a first indication of Porno moving up? Soon to be formally promoted, as Armstrong starts to build a more rigid chain of command? The previous warden, John Edwards – 'Johnny Two Screens' – prided himself on his 'flat', horizontal management style. Equity among the guards. No playing favorites. Would Officer Stevenson – dumbass Porno – soon be Big Willie's boss?

Or maybe it's just a new culture of everyone watching everyone else. Big Willie can feel that too.

Big Willie notices that he's irritated to have Porno here with him. He's surprised that he's so irritated. But the minyan is his responsibility. Always has been. They're his to watch, to be with. A part of his day. It feels like Porno is intruding.

Big Willie realizes. Shit. Maybe Armstrong is right. Maybe he *is* too close to them. Maybe he's right to send Porno. Dumb, loyal Porno, to keep an eye on Big Willie. Because what will Porno see and report back on? Big Willie's relaxed friendship, his easy relationships, his familiar banter with the minyan? It would all be true.

The other thing that bothers Big Willie. He notices how Porno is, well, a version of Big Willie. An *earlier* version of him. Porno's suspicious, narrow, closed-off nature. *He don't like 'em…and I don't neither.* Big Willie can only see it now, he realizes, because something in him has shifted in his years of watching them, spending time with them, and, well, he's not that earlier version anymore.

It's like Armstrong is swinging Big Willie over, in a funny way, from guard to prisoner. He's now being watched. Being judged. Not trusted. It's not what he expected after twenty years' service.

Rabbi, they're questioning my loyalty. But they don't realize, it's making _me_ question my loyalty too. I was trying to come up with some way to keep Armstrong happy, to report back to him, but not ruin things for the minyan. Some middle path, to give everyone a little of what they want. Maybe let the minyan give me fake information that I can feed Armstrong. And then I'd throw in some real information with it. To stay in the middle. But trying to come up with some way to stay in the middle – it's not just about keeping my job, Rabbi. It's really about trying to decide…being unable to decide…where my loyalties are. Having to decide who I am. What I am. The fact that I want to talk it all over with you. It shows how much it's bothering me. How much it's on my mind.

More that he can't discuss with Meyerson. That he has to answer for himself.

A CLOSE READING

THE HIGHLY ACCOMPLISHED con men of the minyan agree: Professor Deborah Liston is the furthest thing from a con artist, but is nevertheless an extremely deceptive and misleading figure.

While she comes across as – indeed *is* – a diminutive, unprepossessing and ethereal poetess, she's also, they're starting to see, iron-willed, streetwise, and good at getting what she wants. As Poetry 101 continues to meet, Nadler, Adler, Rosen and the others gradually realize what it must take to push a program like this – a poetry program for white-collar criminals – through her university, then through state approvals, then through donors and funders big and small. How many reluctant parties she needed to convince. They could tell by now that she did it with her cordial smile, her unrufflable manner – and a backbone of steely conviction.

Amid experts in the art of deception, Professor Liston proves arguably the most deceptive of all. They respect her. They like her. As scam artists, their M.O. is generally to over-promise and under-deliver. It occurs to them that she does exactly the opposite: Under-promise and over-deliver. Making her, oddly, the literal opposite of a fraudster. Utterly forthright and honest and direct. They each did what they did (and landed in here) by working around the system, playing in the margins, going wide – so wide they're off the field, outside the rules, sneaking along the sidelines to step back onto the field next to the goal line. She got it done by never deviating. By insisting. By saying it again and again, unvaryingly. By plowing up the middle, an unexpectedly diminutive fullback who you never see coming, whose highly effectively blockers are one's own prejudices and preconceptions.

When Deborah Liston herself has thought about it, she's realized, with some surprise, there might not have been *any* occasion where she hasn't gotten what she wanted. She is well aware that her modest stature, tranquil demeanor, and demure personal style serve her well by continually providing her iron will with the element of surprise. She's taken martial arts classes for years, but has never been called on to use her skills, and with her customarily long blouses and loose skirts she knows that no one suspects all the taut muscle lurking beneath. But perhaps, she speculates, all the confidence of that training has seeped into her life more broadly. She doesn't cultivate her outward appearance – it's just her. But she recognizes how it operates. And how well.

She's aware of being a kind of uber-do-gooder – bringing poetry to inmates, after all – amid all these uber do-no-gooders, scammers, con-men, and cheats. But she knows that isn't the full flavor and nuance of reality. She isn't all purely good, and they aren't all purely bad. They're all closer to each other than one might think, in their thoughts at least, if not their actions.

'Hey, Saul Solomon,' she says after class one day, as everyone is exiting.

'Yeah?'

'Could I, uh, chat with you for a couple of minutes?'

'Uh-oh, Solomon has to stay after class!' Nadler taunts, channeling a ten-year-old.

'Uh-oh, Solomon's in trouble,' Adler joins in, teasing.

Saul Solomon squints confused for a moment, then shrugs in response to Professor Liston. 'Sure.'

✡

'So, Saul,' she says, as they sit down together.

'What's up, Professor Liston?'

'You know, Saul, I've been teaching poetry for a long time. Many years now.'

'I'm sure.'

'And over the years, I've gotten pretty good at interpreting students' poems.'

'I'm sure.'

'As you know, poetry can have hidden meanings – hidden from the reader, of course, there waiting to be discovered, but sometimes even hidden from the author too.' She settles her skirt a little. 'There's a tradition in American poetry called the confessional mode – have you heard that term? John Berryman and Elizabeth Bishop are two of our greatest practitioners. It's a particularly American poetic mode that began, arguably, with Emily Dickinson. It's where a reader is invited deep, very deep, into the poet's interior thoughts. Your poem made me think of that mode. Sometimes dispensing with form, to go into, concentrate on, the deepest recesses of meaning and double meaning and triple meaning.'

Saul Solomon is silent. Staring at her.

'Saul, you're kind of unfortunate, I'm afraid, but I'd say fortunate too, that I've been doing workshops like this, studying student poetry like this, for so long. You could easily have gotten a teacher with less experience, who would not have asked you to stay a few minutes after class for this chat.'

Saul is listening silently.

'I promise you, no one in the class noticed what I'm about to point out about your poem. But I just want you to know that *somebody* understood your poem. Understood it deeply and thoroughly. Because I understood, Saul, that the hot body you refer to was not merely the Ferrari itself. I understood that the hot body was *in* the Ferrari. That the 'accelerant' you referred to was the fire's accelerant that you used to hide the crime. I understood that you killed a young woman – a hot, sexy young woman – and got rid of her body in the insurance fire.'

He doesn't say a word.

'Believe me, I'm not interested in telling anyone this. A poem isn't proof of anything anyway. But I just want you to know, I understood your poem.' She looks at him. 'I think it's important for a poet to know that he or she is understood. What do you think?'

'I think I should never have taken this poetry seminar,' says Saul.

'You don't have to say any more than that, Saul. You don't have to ever tell me if I'm right. But it is, as I said, in the tradition of confessional poetry, and I really just wanted you to know that I heard you. That it was communicated. That it was shared. That in that way, your poem worked. And in that way, your poem was excellent.'

She cocks her head at him, narrows her eyes. 'I also know enough about human nature and about felons to know that woman in the Ferrari might not be – probably isn't – the first person you ever killed,' Professor Liston says. 'But I imagine the poem is written as it is, and written now, because you intend it to be the last person you ever kill.'

Professor Liston gives a quick, sad smile, and gets up.

'But see, they want me to kill someone else…' says Saul Solomon.

Deborah Liston sits back down, looks at him. 'What?'

He shakes his head. 'They want me to kill the Pisk.'

'Who does?'

'I don't know. Some people from the government. They moved me into his cell.'

'So I heard.'

'Well, that's why. They gave me a way to do it that they say can't be traced. It'll look like a heart attack or stress or a suicide. They want me to…you know…Epstein him.'

Epstein him? She's about to ask, but she quickly realizes who and what Saul means. 'I'm assuming you're telling me this because, well, you're not sure you want to do it.'

'Exactly.'

Deborah Liston studies him for a moment. 'You realize,

Saul, this is kind of a confession *before* you commit the crime. That's certainly a sign of progress, I guess. To be telling me about it is a pretty strong sign you're not going to do it. That you've already decided. Am I right? Again, you don't have to tell me.'

'You were right, Professor. I have killed others before, and the government is going to let me off the hook on those if I do this. It's a pretty good deal.'

She is momentarily silent, absorbing the unexpectedness – the bizarreness – of what he's saying. But she jumps right back in: 'Committing a murder, to be officially excused for the others you've done,' she says speculatively. 'Interesting. That's got to be fairly unique.' She looks at him. 'I know you know it doesn't usually work that way. And from the perspective of one's soul, it doesn't sound like a good deal to me.'

'I know. I can't tell if it's the minyan, or the poetry class, that has me rethinking everything.'

'Probably both.'

Well, one thing Saul Solomon has got to admit: Professor Liston is a pretty good reader. Pretty insightful. Paying attention.

He also noticed she wasn't telling him what to do. She was saying she wouldn't do it, she didn't think it was a fair deal, metaphysically speaking, but she wasn't telling him whether to do it or not.

She didn't say that she would report what he told her, but she didn't say that she wouldn't. The fact that it's just a poem, as she said, means it doesn't really rise to the level of evidence under the law, but her reporting it – and, more importantly, reporting their conversation about it – could cause the authorities to re-open the investigation, which might lead to his other murders. He doesn't think she's going to do that, but he doesn't know.

And she's right – he's thinking about whether he's going to take the deal. Whether he trusts the deal or has too much to lose by chancing it.

The other thing he's thinking about, is this little pill. Hidden in here for now with him and the Pisk.

The Pisk, the pill, and Saul. A tight little three-pointed puzzle to solve.

Fact is, he doesn't really know much about this pill, beyond the fact that it's powerful, effective, and undetectable. Yes, a descendant, a distant relation, of cyanide. Get it into the Pisk's pisk when he sleeps, and it will do the rest. But they never said how it works exactly.

Which is a little frustrating, because being who he is, Saul Solomon is thinking not just about not using the pill on the Pisk, but, if he decides *not* to use it on the Pisk, what else could he do with it? Where else could he deploy it? Who else could he use it on?

He doesn't know whether, say, putting it on someone's food in the lunchroom will kill them quickly, undetectably, painlessly – a new undetectable poison. He has a feeling it doesn't work like that, or they would have just had someone poison the Pisk's food. But maybe that would have been too obvious. And maybe *they* haven't actually killed anyone, those government types, and Saul has, so they figure Saul is a safer bet. He's pre-tested. Experienced.

Or will spreading it, say, across the hot lasagna tray, just make everybody sick? Or actually kill some of them? Is it that powerful? Saul doesn't know. He doesn't know if it would do nothing or kill them all – and there's a little piece of him that's curious to find out.

He does know that if he gives it or sells it to someone, anyone else here, they can presumably use it on their cellmate for the same quick, deadly, undetectable result. That might have value to several people here. That's an option.

Another safe option is just to use it on himself.

Not as crazy an option as it sounds. It's actually one of the options he's weighing. Because it gets him out of all the stress of being discovered for three murders and standing trial and going to jail for the rest of his life. And out of the stress of being forced to commit another one. And out of the stress of not knowing if he'll be discovered committing that fourth murder.

And if he refuses to cooperate with them, and the evidence of his previous murders comes out, he'll spend the rest of his life in prison (New York has no death penalty). Is it worth staying alive for that?

He's of course gone to great lengths for self-preservation so far – much farther than most – killing three people for self-preservation, after all. But Saul's honestly not sure now that it was worth the effort. The option of using the pill on himself is something he's weighing as rationally as he can. Or as rationally as a serial killer can, he supposes. One who may have changed his ways. Or maybe not.

Like the others in the minyan, he doesn't like the clampdown – these vaguely and not-so-vaguely anti-Semitic actions they're starting to see. Unlike the others though, he has something he can do about it. A small thing – in the palm of his hand. But potentially a helpfully disruptive thing. That, deployed correctly, could help create some real chaos. Could help wage their battle for fairness. Could the palm of his hand, with this little pill, serve as a bigger hand of fate? Not a hand of fate for the Pisk, but for something more meaningful, more in all their interests?

What to do? He can't be consulting Meyerson on this.

What to do?

SURE AS SHIT

'SHIT,' SAYS ARMSTRONG BITTERLY. 'Another email from Warden Singh.'

Who? Big Willie wants to ask. But he's very aware now of trying not to look too smart. Just toe the line. Just be who the warden wants him to be.

He knows why he's been called into the warden's office. It's his chance to update the warden. Give him a progress report. He doesn't have much to tell yet – he still doesn't know how he'll handle it – so he's just as glad that the warden is suddenly distracted by what's on the computer.

'What a fucking name,' mutters Armstrong with disgust. 'Suleiman Singh. Sometimes a name tells you pretty much everything you need to know about someone, doesn't it? Suleiman Singh.' He looks up. 'You heard of this guy?'

'No, sir.'

'Well, he's somewhere in the Bureau of Prisons bureaucracy, and he generally leaves me alone, except when he doesn't.'

Armstrong narrows his eyes, looks at the screen, looks at Big Willie, and suddenly spins the computer screen.

'Take a look at something for me, would you Richardson?'

Oh, so now you think I'm smart again. Or you only want my smarts when you need them. Smarts on demand. Smarts only as needed, Big Willie thinks.

Big Willie looks at the email addresses, from this Warden Singh to Warden Armstrong. Both with their Bureau of Prisons email addresses.

He reads the email's subject line:

Jack Armstrong – Eyes Only

And then Singh's short email: *Just looking at several of the line items from last month's TMUs and BOSs. Hey, Jack, since we're now saving on the C45s and C46s, I think we should reinstate them. OK by you? Nice job on those structural costs, btw.*

'Whoever this guy Singh is, obviously he's looking at our monthly receipts; he's obviously in the loop.'

'Yes, sir.'

'Richardson,' Armstrong says. 'I've got a question for you, Richardson, and it's a confidential question, OK?'

'Yes sir.'

'What are TMUs and BOSs? Do you know?'

Big Willie knows exactly what they are. 'Sir, those are some cafeteria food staples that are sourced from two different suppliers.'

'Yeah, I thought so,' says Armstrong,

No, you didn't, thinks Big Willie.

'Thanks for confirming,' says Armstrong confidently.

Big Willie watches Armstrong type in: *Totally agree on TMU and BOS reinstatement*, and hit reply.

'Whoever this Singh is, he doesn't ask for much. That should hold him. That's how bureaucracy works, Richardson. You scratch my back, I'll scratch yours.'

'Yes sir,' says Big Willie. Who can see what Armstrong is doing. Maintaining the current arrangement, the current power balance, between the two wardens. He can tell Armstrong wants all the power, doesn't want to share it with this Warden Singh, whoever he is, wherever he is in the chain of command. He gets the sense that Armstrong isn't really sure in fact who outranks who. And he obviously doesn't want to rock the boat. So he's agreeing. Playing nice in the sandbox. This Warden Singh, Big Willie can tell from the email, is working remotely, but that's what Armstrong had been doing too, so it's not so unusual these days, Big Willie assumes.

Big Willie finds it such an interesting lesson in power dynamics. He learned a lot about the B.O.P. bureaucracy in that little email exchange. More than he ever expected. More than he could ever imagine.

I am smart, he thinks. *Smarter than you, Warden Armstrong*.

He knows about TMUs and BOSs and the Warden doesn't. He knows exactly what they are.

TMUs and BOSs are totally made-up, official-sounding item identifications from the minyan, for some food items they sorely miss.

TMU, in fact, stands for Totally Made Up. BOS stands for Bullshit Ordering System.

He heard the minyan discussing these order codes, as if

discussing them made them real.

But he sees by this email that, well, they *are* real.

Truth is, he was surprised the minyan let him overhear that discussion. He thought it might be some kind of test of him. He'd gotten the strong impression that they were discussing other things too, that they were not letting him hear.

What they weren't letting him hear, apparently, was about Suleiman Singh.

When Armstrong asked him about those codes, it was obvious to Big Willie that the minyan was fooling with Armstrong again. Pulling a fast one on him. Again. And he doesn't yet know it.

But to say now to Warden Armstrong – '*Oh, that's the minyan making fun of you, pulling a fast one on you again.*' No fucking way. He's keeping his mouth shut. When Armstrong discovered it the first time, the guards all looked like idiots. Now he's going to be the one to tell Armstrong that this time Armstrong's the idiot? No fucking way.

And besides, if the minyan has somehow pulled this off? Good for them. Completely impressive.

Because the more he's thought about it, the more it's all been rubbing him wrong: Warden Armstrong sending Big Willie to spy on them. Using him. Pretending they're friends. Conveying how much he values him, trusts Big Willie. Then sending Porno to keep an eye on him. Because he *doesn't* trust Big Willie. Because he doesn't trust his intelligence? Because he wants someone stupider, simpler, to do the job of keeping an eye on the minyan? How insulting is that?

The other thing about Warden Armstrong he sees. Something that's obvious to Big Willie, maybe only obvious from the combination of his twenty years guarding prisons and his living up here alongside the blackhats in this little section of upstate New York.

He don't like 'em and I don't neither.

So it's something Armstrong didn't feel comfortable revealing to Big Willie, but did feel comfortable saying to Porno.

Armstrong's a Jew-hater. Straight up. Sure as shit. Anti-Semite is the technical term, but Big Willie is cutting to the chase: *Jew-hater.*

Not like his high-school pals, whose slurs are just something to say, just parroting what they've heard, who say it just because they know they shouldn't, who have no real belief or knowledge behind anything they say.

This is someone who, Big Willie senses, has beliefs behind what he says. Someone who has thought about it. On Armstrong's desk, he'd noticed a magazine called *American Guard.* He'd figured it was some prison-industry monthly and was surprised he'd never heard of it before. But that night, looking it up online to maybe subscribe, he saw that *American Guard* was actually a white nationalist publication. *We are patriots. Committed to guarding America against domestic threats, and to preserving our way of life.* It didn't take much reading to see where Jews figured into their point of view.

And realizing what *American Guard* is, he now re-pictures the weird OK-sign dismissal Armstrong gave him to end their conversation, and sees now that it's the white-supremacy sign. If he worked in any medium- or maximum-security federal prison, he'd have recognized it right away. But here at Otisville, it was so out of context – Big Willie just found it weird. But Porno? Maybe Porno sent the sideways OK sign right back to Armstrong.

Armstrong: Jew-hater. He knows one when he sees one because he's been at least a little bit of a Jew-hater himself. Maybe a little bit still. Their strangeness. Their arrogance. Their clubbiness. The high-school pals he grew up with – he's still one of them.

But as opposed to his stupid-ass high-school pals, this is a Jew-hater with a lot of power.

A Jew-hater in charge of a prison full of Jews.

Big Willie is kind of stunned by the simple fact of it. His prison guard instincts are calling out loud and clear, how that simple fact could be sending them all somewhere ugly.

TMUs and BOSs.

Big Willie is totally impressed with the minyan. Not just idle talk. If he's reading this right, holy fuck. They've made up a fucking warden!

And while there's a part of him that knows this is headed somewhere ugly, another part of him can't wait to see what happens.

Bedminster Food Supply receives a food order code list as an attachment in an email from an S. Singh at a Bureau of Prisons email address. The email explains how the new coding is to streamline the ordering process, as part of an efficiency initiative by Warden Armstrong.

Bedminster Food Supply has never heard of this S. Singh. But Singh clearly anticipates that Bedminster Food Supply won't know who he is, because he's also forwarded the approval of several items – specifically some TMUs and BOSs from the new coding list – in an attached email from Warden Armstrong. *Totally agree on TMU and BOS reinstatement*, Armstrong's forwarded email approval says.

Bedminster Food Supply packs the next shipment according to the new code list.

The code list from this S. Singh and the approval from Warden Armstrong.

The latest five-minute handiwork of Simon Nadler.

In a few days, the kosher food is back. Once again.

The rugelach. The blintzes.

Now there's even challah too.

'Nadler, you're a genius. A criminal genius, but a genius.'

One of those five-minute bursts in Singh's office was all Nadler needed to send the email to Armstrong, and once he had a response, to forward it to Bedminster Food Supply. He'd written it out in his head beforehand.

'You're the real thing, Nadler,' says Rosen. 'Why, with your criminal skills, you could be President of the United States!'

'Why, thank you,' says Nadler.

'You're such a criminal mastermind, I think you deserve a longer sentence,' posits Steinerman.

'That's very flattering,' says Nadler. 'I'm honored, and I hope to do you proud. I'd be proud to be your next president, and I promise to throw the power structure into chaos.'

They want to air-toast him, but they need to play it close to the vest. Keep it secret from Big Willie and everyone else.

'It's just like you said,' says Adler. 'Armstrong can picture the requisition form scam. But he can't picture a new warden being a scam too. It's too big, too unimaginable an idea.'

'The Bureau of Prisons is probably in the same chaos as every other government bureaucracy. Nobody knows who's really in charge, who's in, who's out. Therefore,' Rosen smiles, 'Warden Singh lives.'

'For now.'

'Great. I love that guy.'

'Might not be around much longer,' warns Steinerman, somberly.

'His firing will be ugly,' acknowledges Adler.

'Well, he did a good job while he was here.'

'That's true.'

'Maybe Singh's got time for one last order?'

'More ingredients?'

'Only if it's the ingredients for something big,' says Nadler.

'One last order from Warden Singh.'

'It needs to be big.'

'So what's the order?'

In the dayroom, the minyan leans back, goes silent, pondering it together. *Yeah. What's the order?*

FOXES AND
MUSENBACKS

BY NOW THE GENERAL SPECULATION among the minyan is that the new restrictions and directives likely originate at the Very Top.

'As in, Carrot-Top,' says Nadler.

'Don the Con,' says Adler.

'The Thief in Chief.'

'The Orange-n-Tan Orangutan.'

'El Hefte.'

It's only speculation, and will remain only speculation, because there will never be proof, they know, and even if there *is* proof, if proof somehow emerges, it will be contested, challenged, denied, leaving everyone confused and doubtful and suspecting conspiracies, because that's the M.O. at the Very Top.

Vengeance against the Pisk. Making life difficult for the

Pisk. Flowing from the Very Top, streaming down through the Office of the Attorney General and his Department of Justice, trickling down to his freshly re-appointed Director of the Federal Bureau of Prisons (BOP), who in turn oversees the national portfolio of wardens within the system, each operating their respective prisons with relative autonomy. It's presumably the BOP that has shifted Warden James 'Jack' Armstrong to his posting at Otisville. It's unclear to the minyan whether the actual placement of Armstrong in Otisville – and Armstrong's new regulations and directives – are in direct response to the Very Top, or simply self-starter initiatives to please the boss.

It's a speculative flow of cause and effect that not just the minyan but almost all the Otisville felons seem to accept, though not all have the same irate response to it.

Hence the Two-TV solution in the dayroom.

With folding chairs in a semi-circle around each one.

Two camps. Two teams.

Team Fox. Referred to in the dayroom as simply The Foxes. 'Sly, crafty, snatching away the truth in their jaws and making off with it in the night,' Nadler has said to Big Willie.

And Team MSNBC. Referred to in the dayroom as The Musenbacks. 'It's just a somewhat pronounceable version of the network's abbreviation,' Nadler's explained to Big Willie. 'They're the Foxes, so we wanted a team name too.'

'The Musenbacks. Like the name of some midwestern college football team,' Adler observed approvingly.

'Musenback? Sounds like just another Jewish name to me,' Rosen shrugged.

The Musenbacks, gathered around their TV screen over

the past months, have become increasingly alarmed by the behavior going on outside of Otisville – nationalistic rallies, voter suppression, gerrymandering, a deep fluency in prevarication, cronyism throughout the government, the increasing exercise and abuse of absolute power. But now they are witnessing mirroring parallels *inside* Otisville— suspension of privileges, senseless new rules and random repressions, new intimidations that more than faintly echo their Jewish history.

The Foxes have observed all those parallels too, both outside and inside Otisville, and don't deny any of them. But some of the Foxes see a different way, an alternative, time-tested response, for dealing with this alarming rise of absolute, unchecked power. A response that also, arguably, echoes their Jewish history.

They are Foxes, after all.

And the chatterbox, busybody Ezra Kleinman – (insurance fraud, five years; selling phoney policies to overseas military families for years, policies which simply replicated existing coverage the government already provided, so they were already insured, unbeknownst to them, and he pocketed the premiums) – Ezra Kleinman is a Fox.

FUCKIN'
KLEINMAN

'LET'S HAVE IT,' says ARMSTRONG, annoyed, suspicious, impatient. 'What have you got to tell me? I haven't got all day.'

'Oh, I think you have got all day,' says Kleinman, smiling. 'Because you'll be spending all day thinking about what I'm about to tell you.'

'Which is what?' says Armstrong, exasperated. He's been extremely reluctant to accept this meeting to begin with – *I don't want to deal directly with any of them* – but Ezra Kleinman conveyed to Porno that he has something to tell the warden which he'll be *very* interested in hearing.

And now, this Kleinman's smug self-importance. His self-satisfied smile. His slouching in the chair like they're old friends. It's already confirming everything Armstrong feels about these people. He's ready to throw Kleinman out of his office.

'Something very helpful to you. Something interesting about your co-warden Suleiman Singh.'

Armstrong sits up, alertly. Is this Jew Kleinman somehow onto the mistake? Aware of the BOP's bureaucratic fuck-up? Aware that two wardens are actually doing one job? 'Yeah, well I don't find anything remotely interesting about Suleiman Singh, so we're not discussing him.'

'How about the fact that Suleiman Singh doesn't exist?' says Kleinman.

Which provides exactly the reaction in Armstrong that Kleinman was hoping for.

Silence. Stony, cold, frozen silence.

'He was concocted by several of the inmates,' says Kleinman, studying Armstrong, but he can't resist dropping the other shoe. He doesn't have the patience to wait, is too eager to see what happens. 'He's got an office here in the prison, you know.'

'What?'

'Downstairs, end of the second hallway.'

'That's ridiculous. He's never even been here!'

'No, he hasn't. But it's a very nice office. Nicely equipped. Set up for him by the prisoners themselves.'

Armstrong sits rigid. Immobilized. Trying to absorb what this Kleinman is saying.

Kleinman leans back, smiles, satisfied.

He's a treasure trove of information. The rewards will certainly be substantial and forthcoming. The rest of his stay here will be enveloped in privilege. Knowledge is power, and he has shared the knowledge, so the power will now be shared as well.

But if Ezra Kleinman thought this would curry favor, imagining it would put him in good up the line – Bureau of Prisons, Department of Justice, maybe all the way to the Very Top, maybe even make them reconsider his prison term or even a pardon, Kleinman is sadly mistaken. Armstrong's rage supercedes everything, is the only occupant in the room.

'Get out!' screams Armstrong. 'Get out right now!' He opens the door, screams for Porno and the other guards. 'Get this piece of dirt out of here right now!'

Ezra Kleinman is confused. Does Armstrong not believe him? Is that the problem?

No, Ezra, that's not the problem. The problem is, he *does* believe you. The problem is, he knows it's true. And his need for revenge is filling the Warden's office so repletely, so magnificently, there's really no room for you in there anymore.

YOU MUST
BE HIGH

THE DELI FOOD DISAPPEARS AGAIN.

Shabbat services are entirely eliminated.

The minyan is eliminated. Completely. Immediately.

The truth doesn't take long to surface.

'Kleinman told. Told everything.'

'Oy, Kleinman.'

'Judenrat.'

'As if that'll work. What an idiot.'

Warden Singh's office gets emptied out and permanently locked. 'First it gets set up, then it gets closed down, and Warden Singh never even used it,' Porno says to Nadler. 'I don't get it.'

'Hey. Bureaucracy,' says Nadler, realizing Warden Armstrong hasn't told any of his staff that Warden Suleiman Singh never existed. Obviously, it's too embarrassing for him to admit it.

The river of retribution is swift and deep. The subtly shifting, mysterious currents from before are now an unrestrained flood. Now that there is no co-Warden Singh, Armstrong's autonomy seems total. And as Nadler encouraged the minyan to 'think big', to be boldly imaginative in their resistance – in their creation of a new requisition system, in their wholesale concoction of Warden Singh – Warden Armstrong shares with them, it turns out, his own penchant for thinking big.

A few mornings later, the prisoners are ordered into the dayroom, to discover four folding chairs lined up, and four white-smocked barbers holding electric razors standing behind the chairs.

And – for the first time – Warden James Jack Armstrong, appearing personally, in front of the Otisville prisoners.

'It's time to standardize the Otisville personal hygiene code with that of the rest of the Federal Prison System,' Armstrong announces, his chest thrust out, his voice projecting to the back of the dayroom. 'Shaved heads; no facial hair; no exceptions; period.'

Big Willie is standing close enough to Armstrong to catch the vague hint of a smile. At first, Big Willie figures the smile is because Armstrong's only kidding. He quickly realizes, though, that the little smile is because Armstrong's not kidding at all.

'But the religious exemption…' mumbles Rabbi Meyerson in the first row, timidly, voice wavering and cracking.

'NO exceptions. The religious exemption is a thing of the past. This is the directive.'

'The directive from who?' someone asks from the back. Big Willie can't tell who it is.

'The directive,' Armstrong announces again. 'Line up. Let's go.'

The directive. There it is, thinks Big Willie. The style of faceless power he predicted.

Porno, Macy's, Shaky Jake, Lightning Larry and the other guards hand-select the first few customers and push them toward the barber chairs.

Is there a reason they select Rabbi Meyerson and Rabbi Samuelson to be first with the barbers? Because it will make the most dramatic statement? Because the transformation will be most stark? Is that, too, a directive from Armstrong?

Their copious beards, their wild locks, are soon in dark gray piles on the floor.

Joined shortly by Nadler's wild crazy curls. His grey goatee.

Adler's proudly bushy mustache.

Lerner's goofy monk's cut.

Saul Solomon's 1970s sideburns. Thick, defiantly anachronistic, the look of an old-time pornographer.

Even the Pisk's thick black mop, going slightly salty… now gone entirely.

All of it on the floor within an hour.

At the same time, other prisoners are directed to stacks of wrinkled dark gray uniforms on folding tables, and instructed to change out of their federally-issued matching green shirts and drawstring pants (what the minyan affectionately calls their 'surgical scrubs') into the gray ones. The guards select small, medium, or large for each prisoner to put on, right there in the yard.

In less than an hour, they all look like one another.

They all look *at* one another.

With their shaved heads and dark gray outfits, it doesn't simply look more like other prisons in the federal system. It doesn't look like a super-max lock-up in Texas or Colorado.

It looks, instead, like the archival photos they've all seen. Buchenwald. Bergen-Belsen. Treblinka. Auschwitz.

The identical thought spreads through the dayroom.

We look like concentration camp inmates.

Shorn. Dehumanized.

Rabbi Meyerson takes in – attempts to take in – the scene around him. He is instantly, almost supernaturally, alert to the contradictions, the opposing forces at work here: a pastiche, a lampooning, play-acting, and yet a wholesale reigniting of the darkest of mankind's history. It is a moment of utter novelty, yet also filled with repetition and echo. He clenches in an instinct of horror, yet feels an open fascination and curiosity – and even within the moment, even aware of these oppositions, he knows he will never experience this again. On the one hand, it's merely a morning of haircuts and new uniforms, some reinstated regulations of the federal penal system; on the other hand, it is a moment stretched across history and steeped in mockery, humiliation, derangement; a jostling of time and a jumbling of memory. He understands the otherwise mysterious change from green uniforms to wrinkled gray: Enhanced historical accuracy.

What happens now? Rabbi Meyerson wonders vaguely,

dizzy, mute.

But at the same time, he notices something more. Something unexpected.

Yes, they are dehumanized, made to look the same, indistinguishable. And yet, in looking the same, in the attempt to dehumanize them, it brings out, paradoxically, their connection. Their deep brotherhood. Their humanity.

We look like concentration camp inmates.

But we also look like brothers.

Meyerson fully, intuitively, understands the warden's intent. To demonstrate absolute power and control. To show no regard for consequences, no fear of protest or repercussions. To commit a violation so outrageous that it screams out, *You are in a new place now. My place. Inside my walls. Where there is only me.* Rabbi Meyerson is sure the reverberation with the Jewish past is intentional. It is no merely accidental echo. But this demeaning pantomime, this cruel act of reverberation – will it actually backfire?

Although there are no mirrors here in the dayroom, Meyerson knows how radically different he looks by how radically different all the prisoners suddenly look.

Nadler comes over to him. Meyerson doesn't recognize him at first. Nadler's head has a bulbous, off-kilter shape Meyerson would never have suspected. Little skin folds along the edge of his skull.

But the rabbi soon realizes it's Nadler, and he realizes how he knows it: by Nadler's eyes, and Nadler's smile.

That's how they'll know each other now, thinks Meyerson, with a little swell of feeling that surprises him. That's how they'll now identify one another. By their smiles, by their eyes. So is there some good in this? wonders Meyerson, with a little buzz of shock and doubt and belief, rolling around together in his brain. He starts to ponder something he hasn't thought about seriously since he was sixteen.

Is there some other force at work here, creating deeper connection and communion? Is it possible there is a God?

'So there you are,' says Nadler to Meyerson, eyes swimming with delight, grinning with unmediated, childlike joy as he beholds Meyerson unadorned, stripped down, bared of any hirsute artifice or layered identity.

'And there you are as well,' says Meyerson – polite and diffident and somewhat formal as always, but feeling more connection, feeling something warmer toward Nadler. Toward all of them. The hair, the beards will grow back, he knows. Technically speaking, they have started to grow back already, this very instant. Rabbi Meyerson knows this. He knows that Warden Armstrong knows it. The warden got his perverted moment. His perverted wish. The twisted, perverted moment for which Armstrong has some dark fathomless need.

But Meyerson sees there is something bigger going on here.

Unsaid – and clear as daylight – *I'm glad to see you like this, this clearly, this close, this new, with nothing between us somehow, nothing in the way.*

They mill around one another a little more – looking one another in the eyes. Looking one another in the mouth. Looking at one another in the smile. Identifying each other by their familiar voices. Regarding each other anew.

Yes, it's shocking. It's demeaning.

But there's an utterly surprising, counter-intuitive feeling and perception of brotherhood and camaraderie amid this debasement – likely produced and considerably amplified by Rabbi Meyerson's earlier ingestion of pot rugelach. Courtesy of Warden Suleiman Singh.

Singh's last song.

A dreamlike, surreal quality hovers over the morning. Considerably more dreamlike and surreal for some than for others. Because of Warden Singh's final act, via Nadler. *Only if it's the ingredients for something big.* Well, yes. Exactly.

Since Warden Singh had previously, via his earlier emails, established his role as a part of the supply chain, he was able to secure tetrahydrocannabinol (THC), approved by the state of New York for medical use. On top of that, he even managed to obtain a small sample of psilocybin, for compassionate use by an Otisville prisoner undergoing late-stage cancer treatments, as part of the controlled psilocybin drug studies then being conducted, as was standard protocol, on selected prisoner populations throughout the country. Both controlled substances were to be delivered to the Otisville infirmary at the request of Dr Helbrocken, MD, the Otisville physician. Warden Singh was helped especially in his request – counterintuitively, surprisingly – by the fact that there is no Otisville infirmary or Dr Helbrocken. (Medical issues were normally referred to the much larger sister BOP medium-security facility.) Having no actual infirmary or doctor at Otisville considerably streamlined the process. The packages were delivered, unassumingly, with the regular weekly shipment to food services.

So Dmitri could bake the ingredients into the rugelach. A

celebration of his cooking skills. A memorable presentation of his incomparable treat.

Pot rugelach. That was the plan. Plus a small platter of psilocybin. Nadler's instructions were clear. The THC was for the raspberry rugelach. The magic mushroom was for the chocolate. This way, you could choose and control the intensity of your celebratory experience. They froze it all, to save for the right occasion.

But then fucking Ezra Kleinman ratted on them, and the minyan realized the rugelach would be Dmitri's final treat.

They agreed the chocolate ones should go – in unnervingly heavy doses – to Team Fox. *Here guys, enjoy. Our deli is being closed again, thanks to you. But you'll really enjoy this chocolate rugelach. Made special, for you.*

It was Nadler's last requisition, they realized wistfully. His final, intense five-minute barrage of email requests and official forms as Warden Singh of the BOP.

So while Nadler, and Rosen, and most of the minyan (including Rabbi Meyerson, an old pothead) enjoyed the expected raspberry rugelach buzz, they observed the otherworldly events occurring around them in a distancing, softening haze. The same familiar and paradoxical intensification and relaxation from their high-school and college days. Just a bite or two to soften the Auschwitz experience a little.

They particularly enjoyed the panicked, abject terror they could see in the faces of Ezra Kleinman and chocolate-loving Team Fox. Mumbling, muttering, stumbling, disoriented, through the whole head-shaving, new-uniform procedure.

Simon Nadler remembered the edible weeds that his father Herman described, growing along the edge of the

Auschwitz fence. A made-up memory, to make a point, yet the parallel strikes Simon as uncanny: This is an edible weed too. Simon Nadler has partaken in the bounty of the pot rugelach along with most of the minyan, and thus his experience of the haircuts and the uniforms is, he knows, both softened and sharpened for his observation.

He can't help but compare it to his father's camp experience. He's reliving it in a weird mirror. A staged version. A joke version. Foisted on well-fed prisoners with two flat-screen televisions who sleep soundly and securely in warm bunks. The brutal, literal experience of his father's imprisonment; the symbolic, echo version of this morning.

The goofy pleasure of their shaved heads, an unexpected re-discovery of each other. *Hey, Rabbi! Hey, Simon!* It was all meant by Armstrong to horrify and humiliate them, he knows, but for Nadler the THC is altering it, modulating it, intellectualizing it. *Pop, you'll never guess what happened at Otisville today.* He's close to laughing aloud. And this all began, Nadler realizes, not with the wrenching disappearance of a beloved, innocent aunt or uncle taken from their Berlin shop or apartment, but with the annoying disappearance of a favorite dessert. Before that same dessert was momentarily restored in high – *very* high – style. All these thoughts and connections rushing at him.

Nadler watches Kleinman retch in the courtyard after his haircut. Staring disconsolately. Weaving dizzily. Clearly he has overindulged on the chocolate. The guards watch Kleinman with pity.

'I can't breathe!' yells Kleinman, hyperventilating. 'I'm telling you, Porno, I can't breathe!'

'Oh come on Kleinman,' says Porno with disgust. 'It's just

a haircut!'

Nadler had brooded over it: Pot raspberry rugelach. Magic-mushroom chocolate. Was it enough of a final act from Warden Singh, before Kleinman got him terminated? It was all Nadler had been able to come up with. He worried that it was a failure of imagination. But the raspberry rugelach had made the morning's transformation into Auschwitz – or into this weird, faux Auschwitz – not only bearable, but even, well, somewhat enjoyable, for the minyan and others who partook of the raspberry. He feels pretty good about that. And watching Kleinman hallucinating in the dayroom and hurrying out into the courtyard to retch, he feels like maybe the chocolate rugelach was also, well, the perfect recipe. Vengeance, as Steinerman has eloquently opined, is just a primal urge to bring the world back into balance, into order. Maybe magic rugelach was just the ticket.

AGAIN WITH THE POETRY

PROFESSOR LISTON IS SHOCKED BY what she sees when Nadler, Adler, Sorcher, Rosen, Solomon, Steinerman and the rest file into class for their poetry workshop.

But Nadler, Adler, Sorcher, Rosen, Solomon, Steinerman and the rest are equally shocked.

Shocked to be meeting at all.

In Ezra Kleinman's stunning revelations to Armstrong, did the existence of a poetry seminar simply get overlooked? Momentarily forgotten? Certainly it would be Kleinman-like to forget all about poetry.

'Well,' Professor Liston says, looking around, trying to seem calm, neutral. Trying at first, among all the shaved heads, to simply ascertain who's who.

But here they are in Poetry 101, as if nothing's happened, and seizing what they all sense must be their last chance with Professor Liston, poetry goes quickly aside.

'They'll start to starve us, just to complete the Holocaust look,' says Rosen.

'Next they'll electrify the fences,' says Steinerman.

'I'm sniffing for the gas,' says Nadler.

Professor Liston looks confused. Rosen jumps in to clarify for her, to catch her up. 'They've been systematically taking things away, Professor Liston. Our kosher foods, our rugelach and blintzes, our favorite chef, our minyan, everything.'

'But not your poetry seminar?' she asks. A poetry workshop – wouldn't that be the first thing to go?

But it *hasn't* gone yet, which leads the inmates all to the same and only possible conclusion: The new warden is simply unaware of it. It was approved with a genial laugh by the previous warden, Edwards, and is probably not officially recorded anywhere, so Warden Armstrong knows nothing about it. Maybe guards and underlings are too embarrassed to even mention it to him, and thus he has issued no order to bar a Professor Liston from entry at the prison gates, or even issued a directive to be watching for her.

So here they are in class as always. Like a little miracle. The lamp of learning burning a little longer. A temporary, flickering miracle, no doubt.

Shaving their beards and skulls, taking away their kosher meals, eliminating their freedom of worship, a broad crackdown on privileges, you'd think a poetry class would be the first thing to go, thinks Professor Liston. But after decades of teaching poetry, she is sure she knows the broader reason they're still sitting here together.

Because *nobody* thinks about poetry. Not just the new warden – nobody. For most of the world, it's completely forgettable. And here at Otisville, they forgot about it too.

The prisoners of course scoffed at the seminar when it began. But now, she can sense, it's the last thing available to sustain them. Now, it had sudden value. They suddenly want to be here. Desperately. Eagerly. A last personal piece of them. Professor Liston can feel it in the room.

'Who's doing all this?' she says, gesturing loosely to the haircuts – but meaning: everything; all the changes.

'Warden Armstrong.'

'White nationalist. Anti-semite. You can feel it from a mile away, Professor.'

'Here lording it over the Jews. A dream job for him. A gem assignment. He's waited all his life for this.'

'His sadism has a home at last.'

'We're his little lab experiment.'

'Only seen him once. Guy won't ever come down onto the main floor.'

'Either thinks we stink, or can't stand looking at us, or is afraid he'll catch something from us.'

'Warden Armstrong?' she asks. She assumed Warden Edwards was still in charge.

'All-American goy.'

'Edwards is gone.'

'Armstrong was hired from some private-sector prison management firm.'

'Typical administration appointment. Find the meanest, ugliest candidate to disrupt the system to the greatest extent possible.'

'Because of the Pisk, we figure. The administration is trying to exact revenge on the Pisk.'

'Because Don the Con can't just let it go,' says Steinerman.

'All the power in the free world, and he can't just let it go.'

'All the power in the free world, and he's got to exercise it in the smallest meanest ways possible,' says Adler. ''Cause a prison sentence isn't enough.'

Professor Liston listens and nods.

The chair in the back has been empty for a while. After the Pisk ate his first poem, then stuffed his second poem down his pants, he lost interest and stopped coming to the poetry seminar altogether. For all his comedic flourish there in the back row, like a bad third grader, nobody knew whether he'd actually written anything at all. But his empty chair now provides a powerful symbol for them. A rallying cry. His absence is far more useful than his presence. They all get it – he is better, more impressive, more meaningful, when he keeps his mouth shut and doesn't say anything at all. That's when the Pisk is at his most poetic.

Professor Liston knows that the administration has proved endlessly deft and brutally efficient at upending, dissolving, disrupting, anything and everything and everyone in its way.

But they have not dealt with Deborah Liston, she finds herself thinking.

They are not prepared for Deborah Liston.

No one ever is.

She even feels a little sorry for them.

And she senses it already, somewhere between a message and a vision: Lives, the future, sanity, madness, chaos, order, morality, good and evil themselves – are about to spin on the fulcrum of poetry.

✡

Something else, too, is thrumming in her, further animating the shock of the moment, and it becomes clearer to her in the next few minutes, further undergirding her feeling of resolve. Looking around at the suddenly shorn heads and beards, Professor Liston senses she has stepped into history. Yes, Jewish history, the history of oppression, the history of persecution, but much more than that, history in the making.

History unfolding before her, in which, she strongly senses, she will be not merely an observer or witness but a participant, a central player. She is not clear yet on how. But is quite clear on who, and what, and where.

Her. Now. Here.

It's clear to her that the new warden, for the moment, has no idea this workshop exists. Logic says it would be the first thing eliminated if he knew. So its secret, overlooked existence is a perhaps temporary advantage that she does not want to jeopardize.

On the other hand, she'd love to give this warden a piece of her mind. To meet him face to face, see who he is, see what he's about, to devise a strategy to bring justice, or at the very least some balance, to what's happening here.

The inmates are powerless. None of them would dare leak any of this to the press. If they're discovered as the source, it probably violates some element of their strict sentencing agreements, which could then be reopened, nullified, and their sentences extended. Not worth the risk. But more than that, they're probably smart enough to know doing so would be useless anyway. What they've enjoyed at Otisville, what they've taken for granted, are *privileges*, not rights. Haircuts, uniforms, standardized prison food. The B.O.P. was probably well within its own rights and guidelines to institute all of those, and this Warden Armstrong probably knew it. So maybe on the issue of freedom of worship? But the ACLU, if it even took the case, would have a long arduous road ahead of it. A lot of the inmates' sentences would be completed by the time the case wound its way through the courts and the inevitable appeals, so there might not be any plaintiffs left. Plus, for the ACLU, there was the matter of the optics: These were not immigrants, the poor, the dispossessed. These were well-educated, privileged, overly-ambitious, rich white guys – and, if only middle class, then striving mightily to be rich. Jewish white guys, yes, but white guys nonetheless. In a word, unsympathetic. No one would be mounting protests, lifting bullhorns and chaining themselves to the prison gates for these guys. Not over haircuts and uniforms and the loss of traditional Jewish delicacies.

It's all clearly a way of getting even with the Pisk, as they call him. Making the other prisoners blame him, hate him for ruining their relative penal paradise. Inciting violence toward him – the implication being that if he suddenly isn't around, things will go back to the way they were.

The administration probably knows there are plenty of right-wing supporters in Otisville, and enough convicts who consider a stool pigeon the lowest of the low and worthy of a shiv, even in this white-collar setting. So the clock may be ticking. Liston is no admirer of the Pisk – or of any of them, as far as their criminality goes – but he is paying his debt to society, and that does not include added physical injury or death.

So what if *she* goes to the press, tries to bring attention to what's happening at Otisville, raise awareness and hopefully some kind of a storm, be a voice of moral outrage? Then the poetry seminar is instantly revealed to the warden, who instantly shuts it down, and she loses her access; she is cut off, finished, and can't help any of them any further.

To say nothing of violating her own strict confidentiality agreement not to publicize the program or the poems themselves in any way. Plus the publicity would put her whole university career in jeopardy. Although maybe it's the morally right thing. A worthy sacrifice.

She really wants to get in to see this Warden Armstrong. To see what she's dealing with.

The warden doesn't yet know about the poetry class?

She smiles. So don't reveal the poetry class. Tell the warden you'd like to *start* a poetry class.

Of course he'll say no. He'll think it's ridiculous. It's a non-starter.

If not poetry, then what? What new program can she propose to the Otisville warden to get a meeting with him?

If he's really what the inmates are saying, then some glittering trinket that confirms, that glorifies his point of view, that justifies and rationalizes his changes at Otisville.

The academic studies, the flattering proposals, start to form in her head. *The Rehabilitative Benefits of Discipline in the Minimum Security American Penal System. The Inherent Inferiority of the Criminal Mind. Weaknesses of Leniency in the Criminal Justice System. America's Prison Wardens: Portraits in Courage.* Something that praises and memorializes the Warden and his techniques. Something that can feature your reforms, Warden Armstrong, that gives you the recognition you deserve. How far should she go? Maybe nothing is too far.

Whatever can get her in to see this new warden.

✡

Her mind keeps spinning, assaulted by what she has seen, on the drive home in her tiny yellow Fiat. No cellphones are allowed in the prison, you have to check them in lockers before entering, so she couldn't snap a picture of her startling classroom. But the shaved heads and dark gray uniforms are as vivid in her mind as a photograph.

Thinking about the image more, she understands how, on the one hand, it was only the shock of the change. In any maximum-security prison in the U.S. it was probably all shaved heads and uniforms. The standardization of prison life. If she asked, the authorities would no doubt point to statutes and regulations lapsed and ignored and now fiercely resurrected. So what's your problem, Professor Liston?

On the other hand, it was almost all Jews. She couldn't escape the reverberations. And Warden Armstrong, who ordered this, clearly understood it too. Warden Armstrong understood that he could hide this directive, this bit of dehumanization, behind the rules and regulations, but he understood very well its echoes, what it was saying to the prisoners, and what it said to his satisfied, darkest self. He shaved their heads because he wanted to. Because he liked it. Because he knew it would feel good to do. To see their reactions. To cow them. To shame them. To demean them. To render them faceless. Take away their identities and individualism.

Exactly the opposite, it occurred to her, of the individuality she sought to bring out in her poetry classroom. To let each of them shine.

✡

In bed that night, Professor Liston turns to her partner Sandra. She likes to keep their home life separate, peaceful, inviolable, and she knows Sandra is anxious about her being at the prison at all, so she's always kept her work there to herself. But this is different. This is bigger.

'There's something going on at the prison,' she says.

'What?'

'Something…well, disgusting.'

Sandra looks at her, waits for more. She knows it must be significant. Deborah never discusses her prison work.

'They shaved their heads, and gave them uniforms, and their religious privileges got taken away,' Deborah tells her flatly, holding her emotions in check.

Sandra frowns. 'It's a prison. Is that so bad?'

Deborah thinks for a moment. Wondering how to condense everything, sum it up effectively for her partner.

'There's a new warden. An anti-Semite, a white nationalist, running a prison of Jewish prisoners.'

Sandra takes this in.

'I'm afraid of what's going to happen.' Deborah stares into the darkness outside their bedroom window. 'Because he won't stop with haircuts and uniforms. That's only whetting his appetite. Only getting his juices flowing,' she says.

Deborah Liston realizes she is everything the warden is not. They are the polar opposites, almost spoofy counterpoints. A lesbian poetry professor. A white nationalist prison warden.

'He's planning more,' she tells Sandra. 'I don't know what more means, but I need to do what I can to stop it.'

She doesn't convey this next thought to Sandra, doesn't want to rattle her, but she senses it: this is what her life has been leading up to. This is why she's here. This is what she's meant for. There is a confrontation building. A battle royal. A showdown. She doesn't yet know the form it will take, but she feels it.

For Professor Liston, one of the lessons of the Holocaust is how it defies the imagination. How its horrors go beyond comprehension. She's a poetry professor. She does not want to be guilty of too little imagination. She senses that if she can harness adequate imagination, she can rise to the challenge, rein him in, head him off, defeat him. If she fails, it will be a failure of imagination only. It's a realm in which she can compete.

These white nationalists. Despite their typically thuggish looks and attitudes, clearly donned to inspire fear, she has always suspected that they're weak, fearful children underneath. If you can just unmask them, unman them, they'll quickly enough reveal their weakness and fear. Well, here is her chance to test her hypothesis, see if she's right. She just needs to devise the right experiment.

First step: confront the oppressor. Let him know she has her eye on him. A lesbian poetry professor. That right there will get under his skin. That right there may have a power to it. She is everything he hates. The perfect reason to set up a meeting with him.

She looks around her. Their cat Archer and dog Rex, curled at opposite ends of the bed. Their 1820 farmhouse. Her yellow Fiat parked outside. She thinks of these things as her life. The life she's made for herself, the happiness she's found, against the odds. The deep peace, the reliable quiet satisfactions. She smiles. She never imagined they could all become a weapon. That her life could be weaponized, wielded. But she would wield it mightily, cleverly against the warden.

'First, I've got to meet with this new warden, Armstrong,' she says. 'See what I'm dealing with.'

'He'll see what *he's* dealing with,' says Sandra, smiling.

But Professor Deborah Liston is already thinking, planning, and doesn't smile back.

THE STORY OF SAMSON

Rabbi Samuelson, the Lubavitcher rabbi, emerges on the next visiting day to see his sixteen children.

A chorus of gasps. The younger children scream and back away.

His shaved head. His clean chin.

So vivid, so unimagined for them. So deeply, so monstrously their father yet not their father.

Shrieking, whimpering, bursting into tears; the end of the world is nigh.

Rabbi Samuelson – shorn smooth but still enormous – silently takes his seat, gesturing for his children to gather around him as always. Slowly, cautiously, terrified but ever obedient, they move cautiously toward him.

'Today,' he says, 'we shall have the story of Samson.'

A quick glance over to Big Willie, on visitors' room duty

again.

Of course, Big Willie thinks. *Samson.*

'OK, *meine kinder*, what do you know about Samson?'

'He was strong!'

'Very strong. He went on a hike and was attacked by a lion, and he tore it apart with his bare hands.'

'So we shouldn't go for walks by ourselves?' says one of the young children, trying to anticipate the lesson, score points.

'There's no lesson yet, *meine kinder*. I'm just telling you how strong he was. Like the time he killed a thousand Philistine soldiers with the jawbone of an ass.'

Jawbone of an ass alright, Big Willie is thinking.

'What are Philistines?'

Rabbi Samuelson shrugs. 'Not Jews.' It's all the explanation he gives. All that is required. *A world of us and them.*

A couple of the younger children sitting on his lap grow brave, reach up and touch his shaved head. They squeal happily at the smooth feel.

'He was such a great warrior that in battle, even the hairs on his head would rise and clash with one another and could be heard from a hundred feet away,' says Samuelson. 'But alas, one day a woman got her hooks into him, and that's when he lost all his strength.' Big Willie sees Samuelson look over to his wife – the bearer of his sixteen children – who bows her head and shakes it in exasperation.

'You see, Samson was beguiled by a woman named Delilah, a very attractive Philistine woman, who wanted to know the source of his strength in order to take it away. At first, Samson told her to tie him up with bowstrings to take away his power – and then to use ropes, and then to tie his hair to a weaving loom – and she tried all those, but he was lying to her, just teasing her. All that tying up… he might have just enjoyed being tied up, who knows?' says Samuelson, with another look over to his wife.

'But then he told Delilah the truth, and that was his mistake, children. He told her how the source of his strength was his long hair, and she cut it while he slept, and he awoke in the morning with no strength at all. But what do we know about hair?'

'It's brown and black.'

'You have to wash it.'

'You can sell your hair, and wear a wig, like Mom.'

'All true. But what happens to hair?'

'It grows back!'

'And when Samson's hair grew back, so did his strength. Now at that time, they had him imprisoned in the Philistine temple as a slave,' Samuelson looks around at the visitor's room, 'thick bricks, ugly old building, very much like this one. And one day, when his hair had grown back and nobody was thinking about it, he leaned against the temple walls, and with his enormous strength, he brought the temple crashing down around him, and killed the enemies of the Israelites.'

'Did he die?'

'I don't remember,' says Samuelson.

Big Willie is startled: does Samuelson want to keep the story simple for the youngest children – or does he really not know?

'So, when my hair grows back,' says the rabbi, looking around at the visitor's room, 'should I lean against these prison walls and bring the whole place crashing down?'

'Yes, Abba!'

'Yes!'

'And free all the Jewish prisoners who are in here?'

'Yes, Abba! Yes!'

'And so now,' turning to the child who tried earlier to gain points by guessing the lesson, 'is there a lesson in today's story of Samson?'

Everyone chimes in: 'Don't get a haircut!'

'Don't talk to girls!'

'Don't let girls play with scissors.'

'Don't tell the truth, or it might take away your strength and you'll be put in prison!'

'Don't stop at just three lies. You need more than that to stay alive.'

The shorn rabbi stands up. Grandly raises all 260 pounds of himself. Some of the little children fall from his lap, as if he is a giant. He looks enormous to the little children.

'You are all excellent students,' he says. 'All very good thinkers. See you next time.' And he nods to each of them. His last nod is to Big Willie. As unreadable, as unknowable as ever.

His thick beard and wild hair gone, it leaves Samuelson's words, his tale, more naked in a way as well, thinks Big Willie. It exposes Samuelson's strangeness even more. Big Willie feels a familiar annoyance rise up in him anew. Sure, it makes perfect sense on the surface, when they see their father's naked scalp, to tell them the Samson tale. But what was his point? Big Willie can't get over how Samuelson lets the children stab around blindly at meaning. Is *that* the lesson of mighty Samson? The lesson that there *is* no lesson? Is it a lesson for Big Willie too? About the nature of the universe? That it's all only questions?

But he does hear a lesson in there, meant just for him. As he endured Samuelson's childish fantasy of power, of toppling the Otisville walls, he did imagine, for a moment, the feeling of pushing against the walls – *all* the walls – that imprison *him*. How it would feel to push against them and have them give way. Find a little power, see a little daylight, a little freedom, a little sense of self.

POETIC JUSTICE

Saul Solomon is summoned to the warden's office suite once again.

He opens the door to find just what he expected. The same three operatives, in those same nondescript suits. Even the cups of the warden's coffee. Including a fourth fresh cup in front of an empty chair, where the older, white-haired guy gestures Saul to sit.

They see Saul's newly shaved head, of course, and the uniform, but they say nothing. They seem utterly unsurprised. Saul wonders if they knew in advance about the new Otisville regulations – how involved and aware they are, or if, as he suspects, they're completely separate from it. Functioning entirely independently – and unknown. Some part of Saul had hoped that, with all these startling internal prison changes, this little project of theirs would be temporarily put aside – a naïve hope dashed when he was called to the warden's offices.

White-hair is smiling, trying to smile, but Saul can see he's none too happy. Saul can see the smile is a big effort. Once again, just like last time, White-hair takes a sip of coffee and sets the cup down before saying anything.

'So what happened, Saul?'

'What do you mean?'

'Saul, you know what I mean. He's still walking around. We gave you the pill over a week ago.'

'Yeah, yeah, I know.'

'We'll bury the evidence, Saul. You'll be free forever.'

'Yeah, but how do I really know that?'

White-hair takes a deep breath. To produce patience. To suppress other emotions. Saul knows that breath. The breath to remain calm. 'We obviously know about the three murders.'

Saul says nothing. But obviously they do.

'So we must have evidence, and yet you haven't been charged. Because we've got control of it. Meaning, Saul,' and White-hair leans forward, 'we can release the evidence where it needs to go, to the appropriate prosecutors' offices, anytime. Or never at all. We've got receipts for the purchase of the accelerants a few days before the fire. Phone records of your conversations with arson experts days before the fire. Video of your entering the hotel room and of the deceased maid servicing that same room. Testimony from the restaurant owners about your interactions with the waiter.' He leans back. 'The clock is ticking. Tick-tock, Saul.'

Saul Solomon feels a tightening in his stomach. He feels antsy. He shifts in the chair a little.

'So what's the delay?' asks the blond-haired younger guy, impatient, almost puzzled.

'Listen,' Saul says. He's uncomfortable. He's stalling for time. 'How do I really know this pill works like you say? I mean, have you really tested it? Is it reliable? Or am I a guinea pig here along with my cellie?'

'Oh, it works,' says the other young guy, the dark-haired featureless one, almost proudly – a mean smile. 'Don't worry so much about testing and reliability. All you gotta know is, it works. Believe me.'

White-hair is still concentrating on Saul. Still bearing in. Still examining him like he's a museum exhibit or something. 'But that's not really it, is it Saul? What is it, Saul? What's the delay?'

Saul looks at the younger two, then back to the white-haired guy. He's pretty surprised at what comes out next. That it's him saying it. 'The delay is, I don't want to.'

'You don't want to?' says White-hair, blinking.

Saul looks away, then back at them. He struggles with what he says next, it makes him so uncomfortable he can only mumble it at first.

'Because, well…it's wrong.'

He feels disoriented. He doesn't really know who's saying it, although he knows it's him.

All three look at him, confused.

'It's wrong?' says the white-haired guy. 'Since when do you care if something is wrong?'

'Since now. Since today. Since being here. Since thinking about it.' Technically, his own words, but they still don't feel like they come from him.

'Oh Christ,' says the blond-haired guy, turning away in

frustration and disgust.

The white-haired guy bears in. 'This guy is a rat, Saul. A rat on a massive scale. You know that. If he ratted you out, you'd have snuffed him without a second thought.' He looks at Saul. 'What's happened to you in here?'

'I guess exactly what's supposed to,' Saul tells him. 'I've been thinking about everything. You know. Crime. Remorse. Being human.'

'But Saul, that doesn't really happen in prison. We both know that's ridiculous.'

Which Saul totally agrees with. He's right. It's ridiculous. Saul doesn't know how to explain it. One possibility occurs to him, though. 'I've been writing poetry.'

'Aw Christ.' The blond guy clutches his arms to his shoulders like he's in physical pain at what Saul just said.

'You're going down, Saul. You'll be pulled out of this country club and find yourself in maximum-security hell in no time flat,' says White-hair.

'Where you'll have *lots* of time to think about humanity and write poetry,' says the blond guy.

'I'm ready to face the consequences of my actions,' Saul says. A totally stock phrase, so he's surprised to discover how much he likes the sound of it.

'No, you're not,' says the white-haired guy. 'You're really not.'

'We'll just get someone else to do it,' says the dark-haired younger guy. 'Look at us. You know we'll just find another way. The guy will die. We'll get it done. So why not get something out of it? Why not benefit?'

'But it won't be me,' Saul tells them. 'That's the point. I'm sure you'll find some other way that I can't stop, but it won't be me.' Which feels liberating, definitive.

'Last chance,' says the white-haired guy, impatiently.

'My last chance,' Saul explains to him, 'is to not do it.'

'So where's the pill?' asks the dark-haired guy who was so proud of it. He looks concerned.

'I flushed it down the toilet.'

'You *what?*' He looks stricken.

Saul smiles at him. 'Oh, you wanted me to return it? Yeah, flushed it.'

The blond guy is furious. Doing his best to keep it under control. Truth is, it's the little bit of confrontation, of antagonism, that Saul Solomon has been looking for. To help make him a little more comfortable with this new, unfamiliar self of his. A little flicker of familiar antagonism. Of conflict. Of his old self.

'I flushed it down, because I knew it would piss you off,' he says.

The blond guy is having trouble containing his anger.

'Go ahead, you can go down my toilet after it,' Saul says. Now he's feeling better. More like himself.

''Cause you were a fucking chicken, afraid to do it,' the blond guy says to him, getting more pissed off.

Just what Saul needed. This is good. It's escalating. He's feeling more at home. 'I wasn't afraid, I'm not afraid of anything. I flushed it 'cause I don't like being muscled.' And he stands up fast, the element of surprise, and leans across all their coffees to push the young blond guy in the chest. Sudden. Hard.

They all get up. 'Hey, hey, whoa, calm down, Saul.'

'You push me around, I'll push you around,' Saul tells them. He's pissed now, too. A hot familiar anger, coursing through him.

'We weren't pushing you around. We were making a deal,' says the white-haired guy. 'A deal you reneged on,' he says, anger rising, clearly rattled by Saul's outburst. 'We're done,' he says, 'and you're done,' waving his arm dismissively. 'And we're keeping our end of the deal. We're turning over the evidence.'

Saul shoves an office chair in punctuation and turns to go.

But he feels good. Like he's definitely done the right thing.

Because the confrontation, the escalating tension, was just the right thing. Just the moment he needed to crush the pill into the white-haired guy's coffee with one hand as he leaned over the coffees to shove the blond guy hard with his other hand, distracting them all with the sudden violence.

They still haven't answered his questions about the pill – how quickly it works in the bloodstream, what it does specifically to which organs, what are the physiological interactions. Treating him like a child who couldn't understand the weapon or the chemistry.

So Saul doesn't really know whether the old guy will die in the warden's office before Saul even gets back to his bunk, or die mysteriously at home in a week complaining of a bellyache, or whether he and the other guys will just toss their half-drunk coffee cups into the trash, disappointed and pissed off at what just happened with totally useless Saul Solomon.

He doesn't know and doesn't much care.

But he does know this is better than flushing it down the toilet.

✡

Has he really changed? Tough to say. Certainly the rage in him hasn't changed. But it's still a useful tool. He'd have distributed the crushed powder to all three of their coffees if he'd had the time. Or shivved them all if he'd seen a quick simple way. Not necessarily indications of any profound change in him.

But he did see their confused expressions when he spoke of right and wrong, and he sympathizes. Because he wonders too: why the change? Is it the minyan? Is it all the Talmudic discussion? Is it the fellowship? Is it reflection and prayer?

Maybe all those things together, as a preamble, as a set-up, but not the main event. Because he feels like he knows what the change really is. One thing, primarily. Primarily, and miraculously. His after-class discussion with Professor Liston.

Because it amounted to a confession, an admission, an acknowledgement. Acknowledgement shared with another person. Sharing the deepest darkest part of himself. If only for a moment. A few minutes. Is that all it took to cause a shift in him? To wiggle something free in him? But Saul thinks it has just as much to do with the professor's reaction. With her taking it all in, hearing it from a fellow human. Someone whose poetry she seems genuinely interested in.

Poetry. Poetry did it. Poetry is changing Saul Solomon.

SHALOM, WARDEN. SHALOM, PROFESSOR

'WARDEN ARMSTRONG?'

'Professor Liston?' He looks momentarily puzzled, off-balance, seeing her standing on the other side of his desk for their scheduled afternoon appointment.

She can tell already her stupid little trick has worked. Signing the proposal D. Liston, PhD, Arnold Professor of Humanities and Social Sciences, and with the seal of the university, he has assumed she's a man. The dumbest little trick. And quick confirmation of what she's dealing with.

She can see the disdain dancing immediately in his eyes. Her short hair, thick glasses, small stocky stature, black clothing, blocky jewelry. It must be screaming lesbian to him loud and clear. He stands with that ramrod-straight, chin thrust, chest out, *don't fuck with me* stance, the stormtrooper barely hidden beneath the suit.

She smiles warmly, reaches out first to shake, so he has little choice. Whereupon she delivers her third surprise – beyond her femaleness, and her lesbianism on flamboyant display just for today.

She grips his hand and squeezes it hard, intensely, and can see the surprise in his face, the rage at her little physical ambush. His rage is enough, and so close to the surface, that he is able to react quickly enough to squeeze hard in return, and even smiles at the chance to respond physically, to defend himself.

They stand there, squeezing, in silent little bloodsport, immobilized in the moment. She half expects, in such a handshake, at such a meeting of opposites, that there will be some kind of ignition or combustion, some contrary electrical charge or lightning flash or small explosion.

She won't release first. She has already decided. And knows, somehow, that he will want to withdraw his hand from hers at some point. He does, and gestures for her to sit. He is already rattled. Good.

'Warden Armstrong, thank you so much for seeing me.'

'Your project sounded interesting,' he says. *Improved Outcomes in Criminal Justice: The Otisville Model*. She senses how thoroughly his original excitement has evaporated already.

She delivers her fourth surprise. Why not? 'Yes, but I've shifted my focus since contacting you. Instead, I'd like to teach an introductory poetry class to the men. How does that sound?'

It takes him a moment to absorb this. It clearly seems nonsensical to him. His eyes and mouth go thin with fury. 'That's not happening,' says Armstrong.

She smiles. *It's been happening for weeks*, she wants to tell him, *and you don't even know*. 'My colleagues have conducted similar poetry programs in several other prisons, with much tougher prison populations, and the success has been enormous. It's a time of reflection, meditation on their crimes. It can be very therapeutic.' All the reasons and rationales that will drive him crazy, she knows. 'You really see them thrive. Come out of themselves. Express themselves.' She's laying it on thick while she can. To get under his skin as deep as she can. While she has a chance.

'Suffice it to say I'm cutting back on those kinds of programs, Professor,' Armstrong says, irritable. He slaps a little pile of papers on his desk to emphasize it, to make it physical somehow.

'Oh, for budgetary reasons?' she asks. 'Because my university can subsidize the program entirely–'

'I don't have to tell you why,' he says, cutting her off. 'I don't have to tell you anything. I didn't even have to see you today.'

'Oh, I'm sure you wouldn't have if you knew I was a woman,' she says. Her big warm smile remains unchanged.

He looks at her. Pausing. She can tell her little ambush was successful, but that he'll never admit it to her, never admit that she fooled him. And she doubts he'll sputter something apologetic or explanatory or try to cover up somehow, which would give her the upper hand.

Suddenly, though, he smiles. 'Professor Liston, your being a woman is not really a problem.' Grinning fully now. 'Because you're *not* really a woman, are you?' he says. Clearly delighted with himself to land that blow.

'I figured something like that would be your next line,'

says Deborah Liston. 'I'm not really a woman?' She looks as if she's puzzling over this. 'Like you're not really a white nationalist?'

This visibly rattles him. She's guessing it's something he has kept quiet, is not 'out' with. She presses ahead before he can recover. 'But you're kind of a soft, fake white nationalist, aren't you? Following the sites, but not really participating…'cause let's face it, you're afraid to. Whereas I'm a real lesbian. With a little yellow Fiat and several cats and a wife and everything. I'm unafraid. As opposed to you, Warden Armstrong.'

He's not sure what to say next. 'I've already decided,' he asserts again. She can tell he wanted something more clever. He wants to match wits with the dyke professor, wants to best her in this and every arena, but he doesn't have the ammo.

'Oh, you've already decided,' she says. 'The Warden has Spoken. The Warden—'

'This meeting is over. Get the fuck out of my sight,' he says. All pretense gone. 'Go back to your university and your theories and your bullshit biases…'

She stands up, reaches out to shake his hand, daring him to take hers again, daring him into a second handshake to the death, when someone comes bursting into the office.

'The fucking door was closed!' Armstrong explodes.

Professor Liston recognizes the guard. The men call him Porno.

'It's an emergency, Warden. There's some guy I've never seen coughing and choking and blood's pouring out of his mouth in the conference room next door—'

'What the fuck?' says Armstrong. He leaps up, scurries

around the desk and runs out the door toward the conference room.

Professor Liston is right behind him.

✡

A man lies gagging on the floor. His skin blue, the veins of his forehead and neck popping, grotesquely elevated, like they're about to burst. Red blood and greenish yellow bile both sliding from his mouth onto the floor beside him, pooling there, the puddle growing steadily.

Another man is kneeling over him with emergency oxygen pulled from somewhere, but there's no chance of even getting the mask on him. He'll only choke on it. The man holds the mask helplessly.

Deborah Liston has stepped into a horror movie in real life.

She can see by the overturned chairs, by the disruption in the room, that there has been a mad scrambling. But the scrambling has now stopped, useless, foiled, and there seems to be a quiet acceptance in the room; silence from all of them except the victim. Older, early sixties, thick white hair, she notices. They are now going to simply stand by and watch the man expire. Die painfully, brutally, and to Liston, very mysteriously.

They watch him struggle, writhe, gurgle. Deborah Liston has never seen someone die. It is all men in the room, bent over, on knees, surrounding the body as it goes quiet, gives up the struggle, shudders a couple of times, and goes slack. It is almost as if she's inadvertently observed some private, secret male ritual.

But the younger man on his knees breaks the silence. A blond, well-built bodybuilder type in a button-down shirt and black slacks. He punches his fist against the floor. 'Fucking Solomon,' she hears him say.

And after a short moment, all of them still looking at the body, Warden Armstrong says to the two men in white shirtsleeves and ties, with manifest irritation and annoyance, 'Slipping in and slipping out, you said. Well, this is not what I'd call slipping in and slipping out. This is your problem, not mine.'

'No one knows we were here,' says the other young guy bent over the body. Surprisingly calm, she notices. 'We'll handle it. This never happened, OK? So don't worry your bureaucratic ass about it.'

At which point the blond bodybuilder-type looks up from the body to Armstrong hovering over him, and only then catches sight of the short, slight, bespectacled woman standing silently in the doorway. His expression freezes.

Armstrong catches the man's frozen expression, turns, and is suddenly aware of Liston there as well.

No one says a word.

But it is apparent to all, Professor Liston included, that she has seen something she shouldn't have. They are no doubt making calculations, assessments, and Deborah Liston has the sense that these men are used to making such lightning calculations and assessments.

Still no one says anything.

Professor Liston takes three steps back from the doorway, turns, and hurries down the hall.

✡

The two men on the floor hustle to their feet.

'Who the fuck was that?'

Armstrong looks at them. 'Professor Deborah Liston,' he says. 'Here proposing some academic project.'

'Yeah, well, now *we* have a project with Professor Liston,' says the blond-haired man.

Armstrong smiles a little at this. 'Well, like you said, no one knows you were here,' he points out. 'She has to be buzzed out the gate.' He looks at the two men meaningfully. 'Should I tell the guards not to buzz her out just yet?'

The men look back at him grimly and nod.

'You said you'd handle it,' says Armstrong. 'Go ahead. Handle it.'

Deborah Liston is moving fast and thinking faster.

She figures she has a finite amount of time. Exactly the amount of time it will take them to do something with the body. A task that will require and occupy the warden and the two younger ones for a few minutes anyway. That will be their priority. Presumably they won't enlist any of the guards to help. They want to keep secret whatever happened in that conference room. That's definitely the sense she got. Maybe the guards don't want to know anyway. The one they call Porno – she noticed that he disappeared. Like he realized he saw something he shouldn't and is hoping they'll forget he was there.

But obviously they are going to turn their attention to her next. She's sure the warden's already told the gate guards not to permit her to leave. Giving the mysterious men in that conference room their chance to deal with her.

So Deborah Liston is stuck in prison. With five to ten minutes at most, she guesses, to figure something out. She's a prisoner at Otisville, she realizes. Like any other prisoner, feeling the anxiety, terror, and oppression of being caught in the American justice system.

But this is not a prison where prisoners are locked in their cells. They're out, milling around. The men from Poetry 101. Her students. She has to find Nadler, or Adler, or Rosen, Steinerman, Sorcher – stumble across one of them. They know the prison. Maybe they'll have an idea. She doesn't want to get them in trouble, but they're her only chance.

She heads down the stairs toward the dayroom.

'Hi Professor,' says Macy's cheerfully.

'Hi there,' she smiles.

'Didn't know it was poetry day,' he says.

'Extra session this week,' she manages to say. 'You should have been informed.'

'Nobody tells me nuthin',' Macy's says with a smile.

Macy's falls in beside her, to escort her to the classroom, as a guard always does. Christ. No running now. With little choice, she is on her way to class.

The classroom is empty of course. 'Guess your class weren't told nuthin' either,' says Macy's. 'Should I go round 'em up?'

Heart pounding. Breath short. But smiling, smiling warmly. 'Yes, please,' she says.

Leaving her suddenly alone in the classroom. Should she duck out the classroom door right now? Try to find some place to hide? Or are her chances better waiting here? It will take the men a few minutes to gather. They'll walk in puzzled, confused by a 'bonus session', not having prepared any work or read their assignment, if they walk in at all.

Suddenly, Nadler is there. Shaved head, prison grays. Looking at her, puzzled. 'I saw Macy's bring you in here.' He tilts his head, regards her. 'We're not scheduled.'

'Simon, I saw a man die in the conference room upstairs just now, and I don't know anything except it's something they didn't want me witnessing.'

Nadler stares at her.

'They're getting rid of the body, then coming after me.'

'Who?'

'I don't know who they are. All-American, scary-looking guys. I've never seen them before. From outside the prison.'

Nadler regards her evenly. Sees that she is drenched in fear. And then he recites an impromptu poem for her. A two-word poem. Maybe his best. Hopefully his best.

'Follow me,' he says.

WHAT'S ONE
MORE JEW?

TWO HUNDRED INMATES, moving around the Otisville facilities and grounds freely, at will.

Two hundred men with shaved heads and identical gray uniforms.

For the prisoners and guards, the shaved heads and gray uniforms are still startling and dissonant. Decades of highly prized and individualized beards, mustaches, mutton-chop sideburns, all gone in a morning. Everyone is still disoriented by it, on edge.

Two hundred men with shaved heads and gray uniforms, moving around the facilities and grounds freely, at will.

Plus one woman. Her shaved head and uniform identical. Hopefully indistinguishable. If only for a little while.

✡

As Nadler rushed her along various corridors, she explained that they probably only had as long as it took those men to take care of the third man's body. Nadler – a contentious chatterbox in class – nodded, listened carefully, moved alertly.

Nadler and Adler and Rosen had acted fast. Nadler grabbing the electric shears from where the guards had stored them. Adler seizing a size S uniform from the shelf of them. It felt good to Nadler to move so fast. Like his five-minute online bursts of productivity before Warden Singh's computer was taken away. Five minutes, and they were done.

'Look at her,' says Nadler to Adler, as he's finishing with the electric shears. His eyes widen, startled. 'Really look at her. What am I thinking?'

'Holy shit,' says Adler, starting to smile. 'I know exactly what you're thinking.'

'Jesus,' says Rosen, coming up behind them, staring.

'What?' says Deborah Liston, terrified.

'Amazing,' says Rosen.

'Dead ringers,' says Nadler.

'Holy shit.'

'What?' she demands, her terror amplifying into a hissing whisper.

'You're Jonathan Levy,' declares Nadler.

Jonathan Levy? The antiquities scholar from the back row of poetry class?

'You look just like him,' Nadler explains.

'With your heads shaved, I don't think I can tell the difference,' remarks Adler.

Nadler plans it fast. Definitive. 'You'll swap bunks with Jonathan Levy,' he says. 'He's only an inch or so taller than you, and we'll put him with Fischler, and we'll move Fischler to Sorcher, who was moved away from the Pisk.'

'It's enough movement that the guards will lose track,' says Adler.

'Most of them will just figure it's an order they missed.'

'This could work,' says Rosen.

'For a little while, we'll just have two Jonathan Levys.'

'We'll keep rotating the two of you. Shifting you around,' says Nadler.

'Will Levy go along?' asks Rosen.

'He's Team Musenback,' says Adler. 'He'll go along.'

She has no idea whether they're all just fooling themselves. Whether this is a wilful shared delusion on their part – wanting to help her, desperate to do something. With shaved heads, do she and Levy really look alike?

'This will never work,' says Deborah Liston.

'Maybe not.'

'I'm terrified.'

'So are we,' says Nadler. 'Face away when guards come through. Stay busy and preoccupied with your head down. We'll grab you a couple of library books so you can pretend you're reading.' He leans toward her, explains with intensity. 'There's two hundred of us in here. That's a lot. Guards have different shifts. Most of them are idiots. I'm not just saying that. Really idiots. And most don't know all two hundred of us anyway. A lot of them try not to know any of us.'

'Plenty of the guards think Jews are all alike,' says Rosen with a smile.

'Anti-Semitism finally workin' for us,' says Adler.

Her mannish looks have always been a source of discomfort for her. Anxiety as a little girl and a teenager. And then, a badge of honor. A part of her identity. A defining feature and experience of her life. And now, maybe, a chance to save her life.

'Just don't talk,' Nadler says to Liston. 'Not a word.'

Her silence starts with a nod of assent.

✡

It will never work, thinks Nadler.

But it might.

The hanging out, milling about, is always purposeless, aimless, to kill time. Now it will have purpose. Now it will be highly choreographed, for at least a key handful of them, over the course of the day. It is something to do, and the minyan welcomes it. Another way to fight. Another opportunity to do stealthy battle, to sabotage, to protest, to derail.

'Look, it's just a little game of chess, keeping Levy and Liston apart. There are no mandatory showers. There's no bunk check or roll call. This could work,' says Nadler. 'At least for a little while, until we think of something else.'

'Maybe long enough to drive Armstrong crazy.'

'It's thinking big. Outside the box. And that's always our best shot,' Nadler reminds them.

And unspoken but unnecessary to say: how much they love the idea of beating Armstrong at his own game, on his own turf.

He shaved their heads and put them in the same gray uniforms, and now they can hide someone in their midst thanks to that. Hats off – hair off – to Warden Armstrong.

Suddenly, cleverly, insanely, and unpredictably, Deborah Liston is a prisoner at Otisville.

Unpredictably. Or so they all hope.

LEVY'S NAP

BIG WILLIE, MACY'S, PORNO, and eight more Otisville guards move together through the prison.

Everyone's pretty amped up, excited, unusually alert, Big Willie can see. Still a sorry collection of out-of-shape, sleepy prison guards, but feeling suddenly like a team of commandos. They've been briefed. They're on a mission. On the hunt. The target will certainly stand out from the environment. A woman. Short-cropped black hair, barely five feet tall, around 140 pounds, black rimmed glasses.

They all knew who it was immediately. They could tell from Armstrong's description. Some of them, of course, suspecting something strange going on here, knew enough to keep their mouths shut during the briefing. But Macy's, trying to impress the boss – and having recently escorted Professor Liston into her regular classroom – made the mistake of saying something.

'Warden Armstrong, sir, that sounds like the poet.'

Armstrong had looked at Macy's, annoyed, confused. 'The poet? How do you know she's a poet?'

'It's, you know, the poet,' says Macy's. 'Who teaches the poetry class here?'

'What poetry class? What are you talking about?'

Big Willie watched Armstrong turning red with rage.

Even the dumbest guards quickly realized Armstrong knew nothing about it. And nobody wanted to tell him now and make him even madder. 'Uh, nothing, sir. Never mind, sir,' says Macy's, with the deception skills of a twelve-year-old.

Armstrong stares at him. Can barely believe the idiocy of this guard they call Macy's. 'What poetry class?' he repeats, more insistent.

'The one that meets in the conference room every Wednesday morning.'

'You mean, she already teaches here?' asks Armstrong. He looks like he's going to punch Macy's, crack him across the inviting target of his big, misshapen head – whatever Macy's answers.

Macy's manages to nod, and ducks his head a little, a dog waiting to be beaten.

'You find her, you hear me?' Armstrong screams at all of them.

Yes, we sure hear you, Warden, thinks Big Willie.

'The gates are locked. So she's somewhere in this prison. You find her and bring her here. Now!'

So they're moving in teams systematically through Otisville. Big silver flashlights for the closets and storage areas, waving them proudly around like weapons. Searching the buildings, the grounds, the outbuildings, cell by cell, closet by closet, motivated mostly by the prospect of *not* finding her, and having to report that result to the warden.

But the search teams have not found her yet, and they grow silently more desperate, more anxious. The commando enthusiasm has already drained out of them.

Big Willie and Porno are assigned together. They're searching Kirschenbaum's cell (diploma-mill lawyer, negligence attorney, who began hiring out-of-work actors, staging mall accidents, and splitting the proceeds with them 80/20 when his ambulance-chasing business slowed down. Fraud; four years). Kirschenbaum has a single because of his loud sleep apnea machine, and he's in the yard at the moment, so his cell is empty, which is probably why Porno chooses that moment to admit quietly, to Big Willie: 'I saw her earlier, in Armstrong's office. I should have kept an eye on her. But I had to get out of there.'

'Why?'

''Cause of what I saw. That I know I shouldn't have.' He takes a breath. 'Some guy dying on the floor.'

'What were you doing up there anyway?'

Silence. Porno looks away from Big Willie. Christ – he's so friggin' obvious. The guy can't hide anything. No wonder Armstrong likes him. *Waiting to see Armstrong, huh? To give him your own report on the minyan? On me? On my easygoing friendship with the minyan?*

It's Big Willie and Porno who end up searching the cell next door to Kirschenbaum's. The cell of Larry Lustig (glossy mail order and online catalogue with five-star reviews but no actual products, mail fraud; 3.5 years) and Jonathan Levy.

Porno – dumb, and totally obedient. Big Willie now figures more strongly than ever that's why he's been teamed up with Porno. So Armstrong can keep an eye on Big Willie, through Porno. Big Willie keeps replaying that first meeting with Armstrong. *I know you're a lot smarter than most of the guards on the floor here.* But Big Willie wasn't smart enough to know – never even imagined – that the warden, apparently, didn't like that one bit.

In Lustig and Levy's cell, they execute a quick visual around its perimeter, under the bunks, in the closet, like they've been trained. That part is second nature to them.

Lustig isn't in the bunk.

But Levy is. Napping. Pillow over his head.

Porno looks, shakes his head, whispers to Big Willie. 'Jesus…napping at four in the afternoon…like he needs the rest from such a busy day of sitting around.'

Porno heads over to wake him, but Big Willie puts out a hand to hold him back. 'I got this,' he tells Porno with a wicked little smile – to let Porno know he's got something in mind – something Porno's gonna like. A little bit of fun to break up the drudgery. And more than that, thinks Big Willie, something to prove his loyalty. Prove it to Porno in dumb Porno terms, who maybe will report it back to Armstrong, and maybe quiet the warden's doubts about Big Willie once and for all.

Big Willie approaches the bunk. Bends down. 'Levy,' he whispers, his voice high and taunting, stretching out the name. Levy doesn't move.

'Levy,' Big Willie says a little louder. Levy remains still, asleep.

Now he's smiling as he turns to Porno – *watch this* – and

turns back to Levy and shouts sharply. 'Levy!'

Poor Levy is startled awake, pulls the pillow off for a moment, stares disoriented at Big Willie for a second, grunts and moans some crazy half-awake protest, turns over and pulls the pillow back over his head.

Big Willie stands up, smiling, shaking his head at the midday nap.

Porno smiles too, and joins in, yelling, 'You're a lazy slob, Levy!'

They check off Levy's name, exit the cell, and continue their search, finishing with Nadler's cell – Nadler lying there reading something, never even looking over at them, like they're the lowest of the low, which is always Nadler's attitude toward guards in general.

'Nothin',' says Big Willie to Porno, when they're done searching. 'I'm startin' to worry.'

'Me too,' says Porno.

'I don't want to be the one to tell Armstrong we can't find her. We gotta find her, Porno. Somehow. Somewhere.'

'I know,' says Porno. 'I know. Somehow.'

It had been such a quick conversation.

A quick conversation that, in a way, his twenty years here had all led up to.

That, in a way, Big Willie's whole life had led up to.

Like Armstrong's whole life had led up to the shaved heads and uniforms in the day room, Big Willie's life had pointed to this.

Just Big Willie and Nadler, and two minutes at most –

and for those two minutes, there was nothing else in the universe.

Nadler had looked at him. Nadler, who's been in here for years now, so they've known each other a long time.

For the rest of his life, he'll never forget it.

'You know us by now,' Nadler said to Big Willie. 'And we know you. You sit in listening. You know who we are.'

Nadler had stared at him. Intensely. But warmly. Like a brother, it had occurred to Big Willie. And then Nadler had just said it flat out: 'She's in Levy's bunk. 'Cause she looks just like him.'

Which, damn, she does.

And then: 'You know who Armstrong really is. What he's really about. And you know who Professor Liston is, too.' He looked at Big Willie. 'You know people. You know what's right and what's wrong. You know the difference, Bill.'

His real name. As if Nadler had saved it for this moment.

'You've always known.' Nadler smiled. 'You never had to learn it, like a lot of us have.' He'd glanced up and down the empty hallway, making sure they were still alone. 'Each of us gets his moment, Bill. We all had ours, and that's why we're here. Well this is yours, Bill. Your moment of right and wrong.'

Nadler had glanced both ways nervously again. 'There's no time to say more right now, but in a way, there's nothing more to say. And while I'm sorry this moment falls on you, Bill, I couldn't be happier about it.' Nadler had smiled and teared up a little too. 'You know how we all feel about you. How *I* feel about you. And that's how I know you're the right person, the *perfect* person, for this to fall on. It makes me feel like maybe there *is* a God. Even though we both know there's not. Even though it's up to us to play God, here and always, and we both know it.'

And with a quick smile he turned away, scurried down the hall, and left Big Willie alone.

A shiver went through Big Willie. A literal shiver. A shiver of recognition.

Nadler was right. Right about everything. Big Willie's always known what's right and wrong, and he knows it here too. It didn't take some long Talmudic discussion between them. It needed only a moment of connection. *You know the difference, Bill. You've always known.*

Big Willie will never know how much it's the indoctrination, standing there guarding them, yeah, but listening too. The daily, unavoidable seeping of their discussions, their teachings, that brought him a connection to these people.

Or is it just something that was always in him that was allowed to come out, to express itself to him as he listened in?

But he's always known how much some of his high-school buddies' attitudes bothered him. And he's noticed how he's gotten more and more impatient and pissed at their narrow-mindedness over the years.

And he's just as bothered, just as pissed, by how Armstrong sees him. Guard jobs are bad enough to begin with. Everyone making assumptions about who you are, what kind of person you are, how limited you are, just by the uniform and the environment. And you're always following orders and routine, so you're always seen as sort of a child. Yet Nadler showed in just two minutes, in just a few words, how he doesn't see Big Willie that way at all. In twenty years at Otisville of being seen as a child, Big Willie suddenly got two minutes of manhood.

And the way Armstrong holds Big Willie's perceptiveness, his intelligence, his abilities against him. Excluding him. Not trusting him. Making him an outsider. Big Willie saw with a nearly physical shock of recognition: that's how Jews feel. Have always been made to feel. Here in the prison hierarchy, made brutally clear by Armstrong – but long existing in Big Willie's interactions with the other guards, and high-school pals, and the world – *he* is the Jew. Different. An outsider. Armstrong has merely confirmed it. Providing Big Willie – oddly, ironically – his best understanding, his closest bond yet, to the prison minyan.

Big Willie understood how big a moment this was with Nadler. How meaningful.

He had the sense he might never get to talk to Nadler about it again.

But those two minutes were enough.

So when Porno and Big Willie hit Levy's cell, and there was 'Levy' presumably napping, Big Willie played a little game of rousing Levy so Porno could get only the quickest look. He shone his flashlight in Levy's eyes to wake Levy, make Levy shift a little, and he was lined up with his back to Porno in that moment, so he could give a big, warm smile to the terrified woman staring back at him.

He knew she wasn't asleep of course. He knew she was lying there, cowering in the bunk, forcing her eyes to remain closed, pretending to sleep, terrified that this was the end. Thinking, sure, this was it.

A smile that calmed her, reassured her, he hoped. Since he couldn't say a word to her, and she obviously couldn't say a word to him.

A smile, a look, an instant, where he tried to say, *don't worry. You'll be OK. Believe it or not, you'll be OK. We're together on this.* And even to somehow convey, *And together, we're making history.*

Like Nadler said, it's a moment when he's playing God. Because the moment requires a god. And he guesses he's the god it requires. Is that what he learned, listening to them talk about God for years? That there is no god, so each of us must be our own? Then what a sham, what a major failure, all their worship is. And right now, what a major success.

'You were fuckin' out like a light,' Porno says to Jonathan Levy at dinner. 'You probably don't even remember that we searched your cell. I never knew what a lazy dumbass you are.'

'Yeah, well,' the normally soft-spoken, scholarly Levy retorts, 'not as much of a dumbass as you.'

MEANWHILE

SANDRA PAULSON-LISTON PACES back and forth in their bedroom, wrings her hands, replaying the ominous, distressing phone call in her mind.

'Otisville Correctional,' a gruff, weary female voice had said. 'How can I help you?'

'My name is Sandra Paulson, and I'm looking for...' she pauses...' a friend of mine, Deborah Liston.'

'This is a men's prison, dear.'

'No, my friend is *Professor* Liston. She teaches a poetry seminar there. She had an appointment with Warden Armstrong yesterday.'

A pause. 'I don't see anything in his calendar. I'm sorry dear.'

'There must be some mistake. She is definitely still at the prison.'

'Why do you say that?'

'Well, her cellphone is there. That's where her cellphone is on my location app. It hasn't moved in twenty-four hours.'

A puzzled silence on the other end. Sandra rushes onward, to make sure the woman keeps listening. 'I'm afraid it's just sitting there on some security shelf, waiting for her to pick it up when she exits. She told me there are no cell phones allowed inside. Can you check for her cell phone at least?'

The female voice is now more cautious – and, it seems, concerned. 'Well, my shift started this morning, dear, so I don't know what happened yesterday. I guess I can check on her phone for you, sure.'

'She was due home here last night, and never made it, and this morning I'm just in a panic…' Trying to appeal to the woman's basic humanity.

'I'll check and get right back to you. Leave me your number, hon.'

That was three hours ago. And her subsequent calls went unanswered. No one picking up.

Sandra wrings her hands some more. She paces. Because Deborah had had a feeling, and mentioned her anxiety about going there, pulling a little stunt to get in to see the warden and not knowing how it would go or what exactly would happen if she was discovered or caught. And now, she hasn't returned. Sandra sat awake all night, and had been dialing the prison since early morning, until finally the staff arrived, and this woman answered.

They've lived together for twenty years. They've built a life. They married as soon as the state sanctioned it. And Deborah is the brave one. Deborah is always fearless. Deborah makes Sandra brave. But after twenty years, you know someone, and Sandra had detected in Deborah an unusual little edge of anxiety about the stunt she was about to try. She wouldn't tell Sandra much about it, because she didn't want to risk Sandra having information someone might use against her. Sandra thought Deborah was being paranoid. Over-imagining the importance of this meeting and what could happen. Now she's afraid that Deborah, so often prescient and right, is prescient and right one more time. One more, last time.

She's had a rich, full life with Deborah. And without her, in truth, it would be no life at all. She'll do anything, whatever she has to, to make sure Deborah is OK.

She's called every half hour. She never gets an answer.

But a short while later, on her own phone's location app, she notices Deborah's phone is finally moving.

The app lets her go in closer on its map.

It looks like the phone is moving *into* the prison.

And then, the signal suddenly stops.

For the signal to be moving and then stop like that – did someone grab it from the locker where Deborah said you had to leave it? Grab it and then…destroy it?

Sandra's heart pounds.

My god, what's going on, Deborah? Where are you?

'You've searched every fucking inch of this prison and you can't find her?' Warden Armstrong shouts. 'How is that possible?'

Porno shrugs uncomfortably.

'You're idiots, that's why. She's here. But you're such low

life-forms you can't find her.' He looks at them with disgust. Shakes his head. 'I guess I need a more intelligent life form to do it. Dogs, I'm thinking. A canine search team. A lot better than you, I'm guessing. What do you think? You think the dogs are better searchers than you? Should we bet your monthly salary Stevenson? Richardson? Who wants to bet?'

Big Willie watches silently as Armstrong picks up the desktop phone and navigates with authority through the maze of the Bureau of Prisons and the Department of Justice, and hangs up, and says with satisfaction, 'The canines are on their way.'

Dogs. Shit.

How's Nadler gonna handle that?

Dogs.

Armstrong dismisses Big Willie and the other guards with a flick of his wrist.

DOGGED PURSUIT

CYNDI REED, OTISVILLE CORRECTIONAL administrative assistant, sits looking at her phone in frustration. The prison is on lockdown, and lockdown procedure for administrative staff means no calls in or out. The last call Cyndi took was from a woman trying to reach a female visitor at the prison. Cyndi told her she'd check into it, she still owes her a call back, but all communication is cut off while the prison is searched. What a dumb rule, thinks Cyndi. She has no idea what it's supposed to accomplish. She desperately wants to let this woman know they're looking for the female visitor she called about. But Cyndi needs this job, she can't risk it, so she doesn't dare go against such a clear directive.

Lockdown. It's just accepted now as a procedure at schools, at offices. A safety measure nobody thinks twice about. Everybody just shrugs and accepts it.

As soon as they find that poor lost woman, Cyndi will call her friend back and let her know.

✡

'Listen up,' Armstrong says to them. 'You've got all the prisoners gathered in the dayroom? Every one? You checked against your master list, Stevenson?'

Porno nods. But Big Willie can tell Porno is a little unsure. Porno shuffles the papers in the clipboard he's holding, as if to indicate that he's just double-checking the list. Armstrong has put Porno in charge of the master list. Choosing him over the other guards, including Big Willie – something he's sure the other guards have taken note of. *Figured Big Willie would have that job. Guess Armstrong doesn't think he's as smart as we thought.*

'Good. Now hold every prisoner in there for the next hour. No exceptions. Everyone kept in the dayroom until I say.'

Big Willie is staring at the six search dogs, circling lazily on leashes, held by two handlers.

Four German shepherds and two Doberman pinschers.

'How come there's two kinds of dogs?' Porno asks.

Big Willie can see Armstrong is annoyed by the question. *Idiot guards.* 'The four shepherds are regular sniffer dogs,' he says. 'In a plane crash or a bombing or an earthquake, they search for survivors by picking up the human scent. That's why we've got all the prisoners in the dayroom, so they can search for a human scent everywhere else.'

'But the whole prison is human scents,' says Macy's, confused – pretty reasonably, Big Willie is thinking.

'They know the difference,' explains one of the trainers. 'They're trained to pick up scents that are hidden or inaccessible. That's why they can work alongside rescue workers.'

'So if that's the shepherds, what are the two Dobermans?' Macy's asks.

Now Armstrong smiles. Looks suddenly gleeful. 'The Dobermans are specially trained to pick up a female scent. The estrogen produced by a women's menstruation gives off a scent that remains detectable to dogs for most of the month.'

Big Willie feels his spine tighten.

'She's here somewhere, and we're gonna find her,' Armstrong says.

'They'll be more efficient if we can unleash them, Warden,' says one of the trainers.

No hesitation. 'Go ahead; unleash them.'

And now there are four unleashed German shepherds and two unleashed Dobermans – six noses to the ground – starting to make their way around Otisville.

THE HAND
OF GOD

STRANGE ENOUGH, THINKS BIG WILLIE, seeing two hundred inmates with identical shaved and gray uniforms wandering the grounds of Otisville.

Stranger still to see them forced together into the dayroom like this. Shoulder to shoulder. Guards at the doors. A handful now armed. A rarity at Otisville.

Big Willie has not been assigned a sidearm.

All two hundred jammed together in here. How will they kill an hour?

Just like always, Big Willie sees. Divided and clustered like any other day. The Foxes and the Musenbacks.

Luckily the Foxes are glued to their screen as closely and obediently as ever. So they're poorly positioned and fully distracted from noticing any irregularity in the Musenback camp.

Meaning, the presence of two Jonathan Levys.

As previously instructed by Nadler, the other Jonathan Levy is keeping her head down, facing away, limiting her contact with others as much as possible. She's trying to stay buried in a copy of *Anna Karenina* from the prison library. Nadler and Rosen have argued about the fact that the real Levy, forbidden from researching antiquities, never reads anything but box scores.

The minyan's careful choreography has so far kept the two Levys successfully far apart. But forced into the dayroom together per the warden's order, they are coerced into risky proximity.

Where finally, inevitably, she and the real Levy pass close to each other. Finally catch a glimpse of each other, glance at each other, curious, appraising, *let's see if it's true.*

Whoa, Deborah Liston thinks, *it's true,* and she sees in that moment on Jonathan Levy's face a mirroring expression of appraisal, and surprise, and even a note of humor amid their shared terror – to indicate he's thinking exactly the same.

Two hundred inmates, with shaved heads and identical uniforms.

To Rabbi Meyerson it was, at first, only a cruel mockery of history. An intentionally evil echo. A repetition of shame and brutality by this warden whom they didn't even know.

But someone had happened to notice that, shorn and

uniformed, Professor Liston and Jonathan Levy looked practically identical. And because of that, the prisoners could protect her.

What was the chance that among just two hundred inmates, one of them would look so much like Deborah Liston?

That they'd look so startlingly alike – with heads shaved clean and identically uniformed – on the capricious order of this same unpredictable warden?

Purely on the odds of it, it felt pretty much miraculous.

Meaning it felt, to Rabbi Meyerson, like God's hand was in it.

Leading him to a wholly unexpected but perhaps inescapable conclusion: Not just that there is a God.

But that He has a knack for fraud.

That He is very much a presence, a brother, a fellow traveler, here at Otisville.

A fraudster who – through the perpetration of a fraud, ironically – is finally proving Himself to be real and present to Rabbi Meyerson.

Who can't help but smile.

(He knows that this could simply be a residual sense of wonder left over from the pot rugelach.)

But Rabbi Meyerson, the minyan's teacher, is also a perpetual student, and while he sees the hand of God, he can't ignore the hand of Nadler. The practical lesson along with a spiritual one. And he absorbs now, finally, the lesson Nadler has conveyed. He sees how clearly, how instinctively, Nadler sees it.

Because the lesson the rabbi has finally absorbed from the various Otisville scams is the same lesson to be learned from the current administration: the more outrageous the scam, the more inconceivable and unbelievable, the better its chance for success. If it defies belief, then many – conveniently and helpfully – will not believe it could possibly be untrue.

A lesson that Armstrong and Nadler seemed to share: one of them shaving prisoners' heads, the other one using those shaved heads as a brilliant disguise.

Outrageousness as inspiration. As a quality of leadership. As a formula for success.

While other guards stand watch at the dayroom exits, keeping an eye on the prisoners, Officers Stevenson, Bergen, and Richardson (Porno, Macy's, and Big Willie) are instructed to fall in behind the warden and the trainers and the sniffer dogs.

Noses to the ground, moving quickly but stealthily, the dogs now weave through the conference rooms. The trainers and Warden Armstrong a few steps behind.

Porno, Macy's and Big Willie a few steps behind the warden. Like useless dogs themselves, thinks Big Willie. Untrained, tagging along.

The dogs go skittering through the empty cells.

Finding nothing, of course. And making no sound, Big Willie notices. Not a bark or whimper from any of them.

No curious stopping, no circling, no doubling back to check something again. Nothing, amid the scents of all these men?

Fully focused. Extremely well trained.

Through the library. The musty-smelling rows of second- and third-hand books. The mold of the carpeting.

Through the cafeteria and the kitchen area. Silent, amid all the kitchen scents – detergent, frying oils, cleaning compounds.

Nothing.

Big Willie can see the growing distress on Warden Armstrong's face as the dogs and the trainers and the warden now head outside, to search the outbuildings, the storage sheds, the fence perimeter.

He's the only guard who knows the search party won't be finding her.

He's the only guard who knows exactly where she is.

He's also the only guard who knows *why* the warden is so frantic to find her. He understands the warden's distress. The pressure on him to find her. The high stakes, the full extent of the pressure.

Because he's the only guard who's talked to Saul Solomon.

Big Willie tells Porno he's heading back to check on the dayroom and the dayroom guards. Which he does. But first, while the dogs and the warden are searching the grounds, and the prisoners and the others guards are all bunched together and occupied by the TVs, he takes a few minutes to slip upstairs to the warden's office and attached conference room to do a little searching of his own.

He's no German shepherd. He's no Doberman. But maybe, just maybe, Big Willie's a golden retriever.

MEANWHILE

'OFFICER NELSON, OTISVILLE POLICE.'

'Hi, my name is Sandra Paulson-Liston. My, um, my wife, Deborah Liston, is a poet and professor at SUNY, and she entered Otisville prison to discuss a new poetry seminar for the prisoners, and I haven't heard from her since. Her cell phone's GPS was sending a signal from inside the prison, but that's now stopped. I keep calling the prison's general number but I get no answer…' Fighting to hold back tears, and not succeeding.

'Calm down…calm down Miss…state your name again, please?'

'Sandra Paulson-Liston.'

'And the person you're reporting about, so I have it?'

'Deborah Liston.'

'She's at the prison?'

'That's where she said she was going.'

'So you don't actually know if she got there, right?'

'Well like I said, her cell phone GPS…'

'Oh I get that her cell phone is there, ma'am, but we don't actually know about *her*, do we? Let's face it, cell phones and their owners get separated all the time. Now has she been gone more than forty-eight hours?'

'Well…not quite.'

'Well we can't file a missing persons until after forty-eight hours. And in this case, even then we can't.'

'Why?'

'Because if she's at the prison, like you say, then she's not actually missing. She's at the prison. And one more time, here, I'm confused, ma'am, what's your relationship to her?

'She's my…wife.'

'Wife? Oh, ah, I see. OK, sorry. Just checking – you mean legally, right?'

'Yes. Yes. Legally. Isn't there anything you can do?'

'Well, not at the moment. Not while the prison is on lockdown.'

'Lockdown?!'

'Yes, we're told they're on lockdown.'

'Because of her! Because something has happened to her!'

'In which case they're probably looking for her, so we don't have to. In which case, they'll find her. She can't get far. It's a prison. So calm down. You'll have her back real soon I'll bet.'

The Otisville Police. A handful of officers in a small town in upstate New York. Cops no doubt friendly with the Otisville guards. Drinking buddies.

Threw me off at first, when she says it's her wife.

Yeah, married lesbians.

Cat fight of some sort.

By the sound of her, I'd be looking for a place to run too.

Who wants another beer?

Sandra Paulson-Liston hangs up the phone.

She shouldn't even have bothered making the call.

A BARK
IS WORSE

BACK AT THE DAYROOM, the prisoners are getting restless, impatient.

The six dogs and the two trainers and Armstrong and Porno and Macy's have just come in from the prison grounds. They're all standing at the door of the dayroom and Armstrong is looking plenty pissed, Big Willie sees.

The dogs are still unleashed.

Maybe Armstrong catches the uncomfortable expressions on Rosen, Nadler, Adler, a number of the others, that Big Willie sees. Standing paralyzed, looking over at the unleashed dogs.

Big Willie knows what shepherds and Dobermans might mean to Jewish prisoners. If Big Willie knows that, Armstrong certainly would.

But something about all those Jewish inmates standing

together, and having German shepherds and Dobermans at his feet, proves irresistible to Armstrong. And not finding the poet. It just all sets him off.

'Let's let the dogs wander around in there,' he says to the trainers, nodding disdainfully to the crowded dayroom.

The first trainer looks confused. 'Why?'

Armstrong stands up ramrod-straight. 'I just want them to. Simple as that.'

'Normally we're vigilant about scent contamination,' explains one of the trainers.

'Yeah, well, they didn't find anything, did they?' says Armstrong, annoyed, 'so what difference does it make now? Look,' he says, 'I hired you, right? I'm paying you. And I want to complete the search, OK?'

The trainers are still puzzled by the directive, but he did hire them. The first trainer shrugs.

The dogs are released into the dayroom. There's nothing Big Willie can do.

Shaved heads. Wrinkled gray uniforms. German shepherds and Dobermans wandering unleashed. It's a moment that's lined itself up for Armstrong. A moment that's letting him forget for the moment about not finding the poet. Big Willie sees Armstrong's face. He looks…electrified. Buzzing. Face flushed. Eyes big. Like he's watching porn.

It's a moment that's delivering big for him.

A moment that's about to deliver more than he knew.

The dogs wander aimlessly, sniffing, still silent. All the inmates watch, shifting around nervously. Stuck here, sealed in here together in the dayroom.

Until one of the Dobermans stops. Starts growling. Then a couple of sharp barks. Professional-sounding, Big Willie has got to say. The first sound he's heard from any of them.

'What is it, Millie?' says the Doberman trainer.

The dog holds its ground. Stares up. Doesn't move.

A group of Musenback inmates back slowly away from the growling dog. Out of its way.

Except the inmate it seems to be staring at. Barking at.

The dog stands silently for another moment.

Then starts barking maniacally. Seemingly uncontrollably. Eyes watering. Rearing up on hind legs, jumping in place.

Right in front of Jonathan Levy.

Or what everyone thought was Jonathan Levy.

'Whoa, Levy, what does she smell?' says Porno jovially as he approaches Levy.

Porno stops short. Narrows his eyes. Stares silently. Realizing this isn't Levy at all.

Professor Liston's startling disguise, its success at hiding her until now, the obvious collaboration of at least some of the prisoners, is clear to everyone, without a word being said, based on her uniform and her shaved head.

The inmates gathered around the Fox channel drift over now, away from the TV screen. The Foxes are not so sly, as it turns out. They had no idea, had been kept completely in the dark, on the very good chance that they'd turn her in to score points with the warden, and maybe even with his bosses.

The Foxes are clearly amazed.

Ezra Kleinman who usually can't shut up. 'Whoa,' is all Kleinman can say.

Millie the Doberman is still barking, her trainer now trying to soothe her into silence. 'Good girl,' he says. 'Good girl.'

He looks up at the warden, who's now standing in front of Deborah Liston, and offers a mild smile. 'Millie, she loves the ladies,' the trainer says proudly.

Armstrong stares – the reality obvious to him, though his expression says he still can't quite believe it.

'Say something, *Levy*.' Wanting to hear Liston's female voice, Big Willie figures. Hear it quiver? Hear the panic in it?

Liston remains silent. Stares back at him. Big Willie immediately sees a toughness in her that he wouldn't have guessed was there.

'Nothing to say?' Armstrong narrows his eyes. 'You bet you'll have nothing to say.'

He points to Porno and Macy's. 'You, you, grab her; follow me,' says Armstrong, and Porno and Macy's grab Liston by the arms and escort her roughly out of the dayroom.

Warden Armstrong turns to the rest of the guards. 'Nobody else follows us. Nobody. All prisoners remain guarded in the dayroom.' And then to Big Willie specifically. 'You keep them here.'

ARMSTRONG AND LISTON: SHALOM AGAIN

WARDEN SINGH'S OFFICE IS EMPTY NOW. No desk anymore, no computer, no printer. It's now just a bare room – empty white walls, bare linoleum floor – with a heavy lock on the door to keep prisoners out. Since there's nothing in the room, the lock is largely symbolic, to make abundantly clear that no more mischief or hi-jinx will be allowed to emanate from it. That no more mischief or hi-jinx will be allowed to emanate from anywhere, in fact.

A bare room – except for Deborah Liston, sitting on the linoleum floor. And Warden Armstrong, standing over her.

And one more thing they're both acutely aware of.

The holstered gun strapped to Armstrong's side. That he had strapped on at his office when the search for Liston began. In her previous visits to Otisville, Professor Liston had noticed only a few of the guards carried sidearms. They had seemed to her surprisingly unobtrusive. Not true, of course, of the one she is staring at now.

'So. Teaching poetry,' says Warden Armstrong. *I didn't know about it before, but I know it now.* 'Well think of this as your final class. Your final exam.' He smiles. 'This is *my* kind of poetry class, Professor.'

He sets his right palm on the black handle of the sidearm, rests it there comfortably. 'What do I do with you? I bet you think that's what I'm asking myself. But I know exactly what to do with you.'

Deborah Liston is terrified, and yet in her terror – either as a direct result of it, or else to subconsciously counteract it – she is outside herself, observing events, and is surprised, even a little gratified, to realize that she is observing these events in the context of poetry.

The raw, simple, oppositional geometry of the room. An empty room, a man, a woman. A man, a woman, a gun. The form is haiku. A kind of physical haiku, it occurs to her. And she thinks of the Japanese death haikus. The distillation of a life into a simple, final, metaphorical observation.

And the overlay onto that simple, physical haiku, of good and evil? Of poetry and aspiration versus crudity and the basest instincts? Of the feminine principle – nurture, support, nourishment of the soul, versus the masculine principle of power, war, competition, winners and losers, zero-sum? She knows what each of them represents in that little white room. A room unadorned in every way.

And how does it look to him? The diminutive poetry professor. From whom he will be expecting a pitiable plea. A raging defense. A female scream, of either rage or terror.

How does it look to him? The hunt finally over, the prey

finally flushed out of hiding, the predator finally capturing the prey, all the power of the locked room, the gun, his white hierarchic authority; this is what he's waited for, and he will bask in the moment, will feel the impulse to extend and amplify it. How can he help it? It's like a drug, a high for him, this moment of domination and total control. Preparing his smug little commentary to his captive audience. His smug victory strut. She senses it all seconds in advance.

What is the ultimate act to upend his expectation? To wrest control? What can this tiny, shaven-headed, prison-garbed, trembling, quaking, terrified, powerless-looking academic do?

It is not only obvious to her. It is inevitable. The only possible course.

She can cut it all off before it begins.

She can do so without a word, with no preamble.

Before he can settle into the pleasure of the power – before he can bask in his dominance of the moment, the irresistible *rightness* and ripeness of the moment for him –

she lunges for the gun.

To seize from him his irresistible, dominant moment.

Literally, at any cost.

BLOODBATH,
BY PHIL STEINERMAN

A, B, AB, and O.
Just four types you have to know.
Those are the four that brought me low.
A, B, AB and O.
The shortest, saddest poem I know.
A, B, AB and O.
Negative? Positive? Yes and no,
I'm positive it's negative, this tale of woe.
A and B and AB and O.
O and A and B and AB.
The letters that took away my M.D.

'PRETTY CLEVER, DOCTOR PHIL,' Nadler said.
   'Great summation of a blood lab scam,' Adler added.
   'To me it was all about testing,' Steinerman explained. 'Or,

well, not testing. It was just a matter of a pinprick. It was cellular; it was abstract. I never really thought about it as actual blood, you know? That's why I like the ironic title, Bloodbath. Just a comment about my own downfall. Not, you know, about actual blood running out of someone onto the floor, pooling there, thickening, sticky, you know, a matter of life and death…'

Initially, it was all about her size.

Deborah Liston's diminutive size that first led her into the self-defense courses which she attended mainly for the exercise, but she had nevertheless absorbed their self-defense aspects, until they were second nature.

Her diminutive size that compelled her to maintain those skills to protect Sandra Paulson when they got married. Someone had to be the defender in the family, and it wasn't ever going to be Sandra's thing, so Deborah upped her game in martial arts as part of her commitment to Sandra. Her diminutive size led her to the complementary strength training, which would substantially increase her defensive capacity and the element of surprise in a troublesome situation.

And part of what she had learned in martial arts, as an outgrowth of her size, was the importance of first-strike capability.

And with strength training, first-strike capability, and years in martial arts until it has become second nature, she has the gun out of Armstrong's holster and in her hands, its muzzle turned on Armstrong in the little locked room, almost before either of them realizes what has happened.

Man, woman, gun, locked room.

The geometry shifts.

✡

The shifting geometry, its wicked little twist, leaves Armstrong blinking. His reaction, unfortunately, is instinctive, unthinking, impulsive. In that way, it's entirely predictable. But for the same reasons, not predictable at all, and a direct mirror of Professor Liston's unpredictability.

He lunges to get the gun back.

The difference in their actions, of course, is that the gun is not in a holster.

The gun is pointed at him.

And when he lunges, the diminutive professor has little choice but to fire.

✡

The sound of the gunshot brings the guards streaming to the locked office.

As well as several of the prisoners. Much of the minyan. Nadler. Adler. Rosen. Solomon. Steinerman. Rabbi Meyerson.

They stop at the door.

All guards and prisoners had been in the dayroom as ordered, so no one knows who exactly is in the locked office. Who exactly, or how many.

The prisoners and guards look inquisitively at one another.

The guards don't want to unlock the door. If it's Armstrong in there, they assume Armstrong doesn't want them barging in on him.

Nadler screams at Porno. 'He shot her. He fuckin' shot her! Open the goddam door!'

Porno looks at the door. Trying to decide what to do. 'Everything OK in there, Warden?'

'No, everything is not OK!' Nadler screams at Porno again. 'Open the fucking door!'

'No,' comes a male voice, a voice in pain, the voice of the warden, repeating what Nadler said exactly, 'No, everything is not OK. Open the fucking door!'

Several guards draw weapons.

Porno opens the door.

Armstrong is on the floor, clutching his bleeding knee, blood running onto the linoleum floor.

Professor Liston is standing over him, holding the gun.

The guard they call Big Willie – *he's OK*, she's heard some of her students say – walks calmly over to her, holds out his open palm. His open palm both a request and a directive.

Deborah Liston hands Big Willie the gun.

WHITE TRASH

WHILE WARDEN ARMSTRONG and Porno and Macy's were with the dogs searching the grounds, and all the other guards and inmates were in the dayroom, it meant no one was in the warden's office or the conference room next to it.

Pretty much no one ever went into either of them except the warden.

Which is probably why the used Styrofoam coffee cups were still in the conference room, sitting in the little trash can with the plastic liner. Nothing else in the trash can.

Big Willie carefully pulled up the plastic liner and tied it tight, all three coffee cups inside, and was careful not to put his hands anywhere near the cups, just like Saul Solomon warned him. He stowed the tied trash liner in his locker, before rejoining the other guards in the dayroom – just before the warden and the trainers and the dogs came back in from the grounds.

✡

The next time Big Willie goes up to Warden Armstrong's office suite, it's filled with New York State troopers who, for the moment, have pretty much taken over the place. The inmates are all back in their bunks, and the Staties are temporarily working alongside the guards, watching the inmates, and – Big Willie can tell – also watching the guards, and that's when Big Willie brings the used coffee cups back to Armstrong's office.

He holds the bag out in front of him, carefully.

'What's this?' says a Statie at the office door – suspiciously, staring at him.

'I don't really know,' Big Willie says. Which is the truth.

'It's trash. You're bringing me trash? You're supposed to take out the trash, not bring it in.' The Statie says this, but he suspects there's a reason. 'Why you givin' it to me?'

'Because apparently it contains evidence of a murder inside the prison.'

That gets his attention. 'What kind of evidence?'

'Some kind of lethal substance whose residue is inside one of the cups.'

'According to?'

'A jailhouse informant.'

'You're protecting his identity?'

'For now. I said I would.' But Big Willie adds, to show he understands how the world works, 'I think he'll want a lawyer and maybe a deal, based on the quality of this evidence.'

The Statie regards Big Willie. He cuts through all the formality – it's man to man, crewcut to crewcut, law enforcer to law enforcer. Same team.

'You believe him?'

Big Willie nods. A nod that says *No question. It's true.*

The Statie nods back. *OK then. No question.*

'Just keep it sealed in the bag,' Big Willie instructs him. 'It's highly, highly toxic.'

'Don't worry,' the Statie says. One more nod, and he turns.

As he does, Big Willie can see through the open office door. Armstrong's office is filled with police, state officials, and Armstrong, in his chair, his bloody knee taped up and elevated on his desk. He is silent – the world moving around him, with him still at its center.

He looks up to see Big Willie, who turns away before their eyes meet.

EAT THE POEM

THE PRISON'S ELECTRIC FRONT GATE opens, and Deborah Liston emerges. Unaccompanied. Holding her cell phone. In her own clothes. Exactly as she entered through the same gate roughly seventy-two hours ago. Except for the buzz cut, of course.

In fact, she's had a full – though highly condensed – American prison experience.

Not just the uniform and haircut and fear, but also the plea deal.

A tense, high-speed plea deal, right there in the warden's office, where she sat, cuffed, surrounded by guards and officials of the State. She had been charged with felony assault of a law officer, grievous injury, criminal possession of a weapon, unlawful discharge of said weapon. The list of charges was long. But those charges would all be dropped if she agreed to never publicly discuss, in oral or written form, what had happened in her last seventy-two hours at Otisville.

Specifically: how a woman had been successfully hidden amid the male prison population. How a woman had disarmed and injured the warden. It would be an embarrassment, an outrage, a news story that would know no bounds. It would make the prison seem out of control. Make it look run by the inmates. To say nothing of its reflection on the entire criminal justice system.

The plea deal grates against everything she has stood for. The liberating effects of self-expression. The power of confession. The necessity of the truth.

'You don't have to do it,' the lawyer for the state said to her. 'You can refuse the deal, reveal what happened here, do a hundred interviews, embarrass the prison system, but you will face various assault charges, and weapons charges, and grievous injury charges, and many courtrooms and judicial delays and maneuvers and interviews, and the case will take over your life, and your private life will be completely gone, and you'll probably never teach again. Just recognize the reality of that.'

The state's lawyer is a bright guy, who likes her, she can tell, and clearly gets her, because he adds a detail that clinches the deal for her. 'And by the way, rest assured, Warden Armstrong is finished here, no matter what you decide.'

Which, as he probably realizes, not only takes away her worries about retribution against the prisoners, but offers an even more tantalizing idea: That with Armstrong gone, she can continue teaching the poetry class.

It can only work if she stays quiet. That's what the lawyer is saying. Quiet enough so there is no story. Quiet enough to return to her old life. Because if she returns, it is a way of saying to the world, *See? Everything is OK at Otisville;, everything is under control; everything is normal.* An impression that the state would very much like to maintain.

She realizes she may ultimately hold more power if she does agree to the deal. Certainly more power over protecting her private life. But also, if she doesn't say anything now, there will always be the threat that she could say something someday. A threat she can continue to hold over them. A power she'll always have. Whereas if she doesn't take the deal, she gives up that power.

She is never asked explicitly about what she witnessed, she notices. She realizes that the state officials may or may not know anything about that. But she understands that it's part of the plea agreement too. The unspoken part.

The would-be assassins will never be caught. She knows that. They'll be protected. Operatives of some sort who are already absorbed back into whatever secret, largely autonomous under-the-radar administrative arm they hail from. Back into the ongoing criminal enterprise, the functional and quickly-ensconced crime syndicate that is the current administration and, not a little ironically, the actual deep state. No sweeping arc of justice. So you have to make do with little victories. For now, in these times, it was all about little victories. And this is certainly one. A big little victory. Or that, at least, is what she is willing to tell herself.

It pains her. But she's going to make like the Pisk, her student sitting in the back.

She's going to eat the poem.

Sitting there, handcuffed, taking in the action around her, hearing snippets of phone conversation, she quickly gathers the other reason – maybe the real reason – for the hastily assembled, attractive deal they've offered her.

Because at the same time, the State was apparently negotiating another deal alongside hers. A bigger deal, which hers is but a shadow of. A deal for the release of the Pisk, in the wake of a failed assassination attempt. She was unsurprised to learn that his team of lawyers had been filing motions incessantly, arguing for his release, since the moment of his conviction, on every imaginable ground – procedural errors, jurisdictional issues, concerns for his personal safety, his precarious health, his medical issues (cardiovascular disease, meaning high cholesterol and high blood pressure on a par with seventy percent of middle-aged American men), compassionate leave to attend to the ailing health of his wife and/or children – everything and anything they could think of. But when his team of lawyers got wind of the poisoning she happened to witness, they quickly recognized the intended target and were up at Otisville in no time. At last they had a winning argument: someone had tried to 'Epstein' their client, they argued, someone presumably powerful and high up, meaning that a subsequent attempt might very well succeed. This was hard to dispute.

The big sticking point for the BOP was the optics of the Pisk's release, and both sides got lucky on that: the national pandemic provided the necessary air cover. Although the Pisk had tested negative for the virus, had no genuine underlying medical issues (in fact he seemed to be thriving physically in prison, was in the best shape of his life, apparently) – he was granted 'compassionate leave' along with a few other inmates in the latter parts of their sentences, so that it would not appear they'd made an exception for the Pisk. As part of the negotiation, of course, the assassination attempt – the attempted 'Epsteining' – was covered up. The BOP made his release look good by quarantining him for fourteen days, but after that, he was gone.

Deborah Liston had to smile on learning that Nadler dubbed the cover-up maneuver the 'Epstein Barr syndrome.' A reference to the Attorney General – supervising the cover-up?

The Pisk's hired pisks had pretty good pisks on them, apparently.

An armed warden disarmed by a poetry professor.

A lesbian poetry professor trained in martial arts.

A warden with ties to alt-right and anti-Semitic websites and conspiracy theories.

Appealing angles to a story that would never make the news.

What exactly happened in that room? No one would ever say. No interviews. No comment. The world would never know.

Warden James Jack Armstrong III was transferred out within days. With no official explanation.

GONE FOR GOOD

'SUMMER'S OVER, SORCHER,' Mighty Mouth says with a wink and a smile as Big Willie and Porno pack Mighty's belongings for him. In the wake of prison visits from Mighty's mighty legal team, Saul Solomon was moved out of Mighty Mouth's cell and Sorcher was moved back in – but mere days later, Mighty Mouth is being escorted out of the cell, into fourteen days in quarantine, then to home confinement in his big fancy apartment with his family and his sweeping views and his pure-bred dogs.

Matt has to smile. All that effort to make it look like Mighty Mouth was getting no special treatment. In the end, his treatment was pretty damn special. Celebrity trumping everything. It makes Sorcher's middle-ness, his criminal non-entity, feel even worse. If that's possible.

As further evidence of his non-entity, there's never any

indication that anyone knew anything about Matt's previous history with Mighty Mouth. His original placement in Matt's cell seems, in the end, to be pure chance. Chance uniquely engineered to torment Matt, to amplify his prison sentence, his personal torture, his penance. The perfect deployment of a cosmic joke.

Which leads Matt Sorcher to briefly consider, lying in the dark one night, whether it *is* a cosmic joke. The one element of his sentence imposed from above the judicial system, above the BOP, above even the highest reaches of the administration. Imposed…well…cosmically. A proof of god. Though an equally convincing proof of no god – no god at all.

He's glad Mighty Mouth is gone. Sure, both mid-Long Island boys and Wikiwandi bunkmates long ago, but they had never connected – then or now. Mighty Mouth's bluster, his blunt, boorish style, his utterly unreflective nature, has always rubbed Sorcher wrong.

It is way worse, however, for Matt Sorcher to realize how much they're the same.

How much of the minyan is the same.

How, for all the cleverness of their various scams, they share what he'd call a total lack of imagination.

Their unimaginative values, for starters. Utterly – ironically – cautious and traditional: A sense of security. Fitting in. Respect in the community. A stable home life (Adler wanted it so badly, he multiplied it times three). Being a contributor. Being proud of their high-achieving kids. Joining a local club or two. That's what most of them want with the money. Bland, conventional success.

Imaginative scams, sure, thinks Sorcher – but no

imagination as people. Imaginative scams *because* they have no imagination as people?

A further irony: it's a *good* life they imagine. A life lived properly, and fully, and worthy of admiration, a life to hold up as a proud example to the neighbors and to the next generation. They can only imagine a *good* life.

Is Matt Sorcher resentful? That his celebrity bunkmate, with a team of highly connected lawyers, got sprung under the convenient guise of 'compassionate release' while Sorcher, another middle-class Long Island felon who grew up with the Pisk, went to summer camp with him, and committed a run-of-the-mill, middle-brow crime, is left in here, in the middle of his middling sentence?

Sure, he's resentful. But he also realizes it doesn't matter much. In here or out there, there's not a lot of difference. That's the weird genius of Otisville Correctional. There's no great liberation, no great relief in release. Your thoughts, your feelings, your interior life doesn't change much on either side of the gate. In here or out there, you're still sentenced to be who you are.

As if to literally prove Matt's philosophical point – the unsuspected fluidity and interconnectedness of *in-here* and *out-there* – Mighty Mouth – the Pisk – is back at Otisville just one month later.

Indicating more strongly than ever how Don the Con is behind it all, jerking the Pisk around like a marionette.

'They couldn't quite Epstein him, but they've definitely Barred him,' says Nadler, revising his earlier Epstein-Barr quip.

'Barred him good,' says Adler. 'Barred him hard.'

'Back behind bars,' says Abe Rosen, 'and Barr is behind it.'

This time the Pisk is kept in solitary, while his lawyers argue for his First Amendment rights, which the BOP is seeking to curtail for the remainder of his sentence.

Solitary. As if he's a political prisoner. An inspiring presence by his absence. Like Mandela. Or Gandhi. Or Martin Luther King. Sorcher almost laughs out loud.

'The administration's getting in one last round of retaliation,' shrugs Nadler. 'Big surprise.'

'But why solitary?' asks Rosen.

'They know they'll have to release him back to home confinement eventually,' Adler speculates. 'Just trying to make him suffer while they can.'

Sure enough – after several more weeks of lawyers, judges, negotiations, media reports – the Pisk is gone again.

'If we never saw him in solitary, was he really even here?' says Phil Steinerman philosophically, smiling wryly.

'His avoidance of the minyan. His empty chair in poetry,' says Adler, expanding the thought. 'Was he *ever* really here?'

'I always figured that was all on the advice of counsel,' says Rosen. 'His lawyers instructing him not to fall in with any groups here, express no opinions, keep to himself, while they made new motions. But no matter. He was always, I don't know, here and not here.'

'Sorcher, you bunked with the guy,' says Nadler. 'Any enlightenment for us? Any pillow-talk to share now that he's gone?'

Matt Sorcher pauses before answering. Weighing for

a moment whether the implicit privacy of their shared whispers in the dark can now be broken. But Mighty Mouth, even in his absence, is making that decision easy. Because Sorcher realizes he has – Jesus – nothing to report. *Not a particularly bad guy*, he is about to say, *but not a very good one*, and he hears both the blandness of that assessment, and its accompanying, distressing profundity.

'Just what you're already thinking,' says Sorcher instead, cutting to the chase. 'What you already know. A black hole. A fucking black hole.'

Nods all around.

'Here and not here,' Rosen ruminates aloud again.

'One of us, but something else entirely,' says Steinerman.

'Isn't that always what it is for a celeb?' asks Nadler. 'You're blessed, or doomed, to be here and not here?'

'Here and not here. Present yet absent. Good fuel for our next minyan discussion,' says Rosen.

Assenting nods all around.

A CUP OF JUSTICE,
BY SAUL SOLOMON

A cup of justice, just a pinch.
Just a sprinkle, just a speck,
Provides the perfect, total wreck.
Just a dusting does all the busting
Sprinkling justice is a cinch.
And when it ends up tossed aside,
Justice will not be denied.
It had no taste, it was mostly waste.
But even justice lightly laced,
Even justice barely traced,
Can still be justice fully faced.
I want a world
That's justice-based.

Saul Solomon finishes reading his new poem, and keeps staring at the paper, like he's waiting for it to say something more.

He doesn't look up at Professor Liston. He doesn't look at Nadler. Nor at anyone else in the class, which is meeting again.

They're all silent. Judging a poem that's about judgment.

Professor Liston begins. Very quietly. 'I think it's interesting, Saul, that you bring yourself into the poem for the first time, and so directly, in just the last stanza. That's the first place you say *you* want justice. You want a world that recognizes and honors and revolves around justice. And you say so in such a sudden, direct, simple way.' She smiles. 'And what is the rest of the poem saying, class?'

'That sometimes there's only a smattering of justice, and sometimes it gets tossed in the trash, but you only need a little in the world. A little justice can go a long way,' says Nadler.

Deborah Liston is pretty sure only she and Saul understand what the sprinkling, the dusting of justice really refers to. That the poem is quite literal as well as metaphoric.

'It's a simple rhyme, on purpose,' she says. 'Because sometimes a simple rhyme, just by its simplicity, signals to us that it means something much bigger, much more important.'

'Like those e.e. cummings poems, right Professor?' says Steinerman.

'Boy, Saul, you really nailed the e.e. cummings thing,'

says Sorcher.

'It's so different from your poem about your burned Ferrari, Saul,' says Rosen.

Professor Liston will not be explicating the text too thoroughly. The poem has already done its job.

She's so happy and gratified to be back here with her students. By now, their hair and beards have grown back – more luxuriously and unkempt than before – and for her it's symbolic, emblematic of her recognizing their individuality again.

She thinks again about the deal. The deal so hastily and urgently proposed in Armstrong's office. She could have said no, taken her story to the press, challenged and embarrassed the state, used the circus of her own trial to stand up on the ringmaster's platform, to keep fighting back, exposing the sliminess and hypocrisy of the system.

But they proposed, instead, a chance to get back into the classroom with her students. They knew her. They knew she'd want to keep teaching. They knew how much she valued it.

She realizes that they took advantage of her humanity. They used her own humanity and open-heartedness and commitment against her. That's what this administration does. Use your humanity against you. And she realizes, that's OK with her. If they recognized and took advantage of the fact of her humanity, she'll accept that as a deal worth taking. A price worth paying.

She looks out at her poetry class. She long ago gave up trying to convince them that their poems don't have to rhyme. Scammers and criminals who broke the rules, they couldn't get past the kindergarten dictate that a poem must rhyme. She'd read them almost nothing but free verse in class – Elizabeth Bishop, T.S. Eliot, Robert Lowell. It had no impact on them. A poem rhymes; period. As if they *needed* rules, *wanted* rules – to be sure of the existence of the rules, before they broke them.

As she focuses once more on Saul Solomon, a little quatrain pops into her head, a little quatrain in the inmates' style (as if giving in to it), a little quatrain that she keeps to herself.

Amazing what a man can learn
Watching his Ferrari burn.
What he can at last discern.
Watching that Ferrari burn.
She can't help but smile.

SHALOM, BIG WILLIE

STANDING IN THE DOORWAY of the poetry classroom, listening in – Big Willie.

Hearing Saul Solomon read his poem, Big Willie realizes something.

Something very satisfying and surprising, he thinks, for a mere high-school graduate in blue-collar upstate New York. He's the only one who really understands the poem.

A cup of justice, just a pinch. Just a sprinkle, just a speck. He knows it's about the crushed powder Saul used to get even with the assassins. To not be manipulated by them.

The little sprinkle, the dusting, that brought down Armstrong and those administration spooks, trying to get even with, to dispense 'justice' to the Pisk. To Epstein him, Russian-style. Sprinkle a little justice on him. What they saw as justice, anyway. Anyone else would call it revenge.

OK, maybe he's not the only one who would understand the poem. Saul does, of course. And probably Professor Liston, who witnessed the murder. By mistake. And almost paid the ultimate price.

Life at Otisville has returned to what it was. Hair, beards, blintzes, rugelach, discussion, laughs, sleep. All the old rhythms of the twenty years that Big Willie has worked here. The patterns and routines restored. Even Chef Dmitri! Summoned back from a grim maximum-security assignment in Kansas. The brooding, shrugging Slav now smiling incessantly.

As for those few strange days of uniforms and shaved heads – well it's not like the prisoners could now all be released or anything. Not like they could be freed in some big moment of liberation – the allied troops freeing the survivors like you see in movies, like he's heard about from his pal Tommy's grandfather, who was there with the U.S. Army in Germany. No, they've got sentences to serve out. Convictions that still stand. It's exactly what Saul's poem says about justice. It's part of the universe. And definitely the universe of a prison guard.

Nadler and Big Willie have never said any more about those two minutes in the hall. But everything got said in those two minutes, and now they just smile at each other. Back to their totally different worlds and cultures. Yet totally connected and in sync. A minyan of two.

Earlier this morning, Big Willie was back at his minyan post. Watching, listening…

Yisgadal, yisgadash, sh'mei rabo…

The Mourner's Kaddish. The minyan back at full force: fifteen of them.

Hu ya'aseh shalom aleinu v'al kol-yisrael v'imru amen.

He still has no idea what the words mean. Neither does most of the minyan.

But he knows exactly what the prayer stands for.

And oddly enough for a prayer of mourning, it seems to be about being alive.

Because the way the minyan uses it here at Otisville, from what he can see anyway, it's not about the departed. It's about those who are still here. Your responsibilities if you're here. The part you play. The presence you express. The noise you make. That seems to be what the chanting is about. Discussing and complaining and laughing. A five-thousand-year tradition of discussing and complaining and laughing.

They're not really mourning.

And neither is Big Willie.

THANKS...

...to Michael Vines, Jeffrey Harper, and Jeffrey Hyman, for your prompt readings, encouragement, and helpful suggestions – to say nothing of your friendship across the years. Thank you also to my Roosevelt Writing Group – Jim, Susan, and Sally. The Roosevelt Hotel is gone, but we persist!

If you have enjoyed *The Prison Minyan*, do please help us spread the word – by posting a review on Amazon (you don't need to have bought the book there) or Goodreads; by posting something on social media; or in the old-fashioned way by simply telling your friends or family about it.

Book publishing is a very competitive business these days, in a saturated market, and small independent publishers such as ourselves are often crowded out by the big houses. Support from readers like you can make all the difference to a book's success.

Many thanks.

Dan Hiscocks
Publisher, Lightning Books